ANYTHING BUT INNOCENT

DAYNA QUINCE

Red Rose Press

PROLOGUE

"Lucille, you are hereby banished from London and the season until I deem you mature enough to behave in a manner befitting of your breeding."

"Father, please. When has breeding ever improved one's behavior?"

"If your great grandmamma were alive, she'd be disgusted." Lucy's mother whimpered.

Lucy wished to roll her eyes but refrained. Not the overused great-grandmamma guilt again.

"What on earth gave you the notion of pushing Lord Whippet into the fountain? In front of the whole of society, for that matter?"

"Would you rather I'd done it in private?" Lucy asked dryly.

She glanced up when silence answered her remark. Her father turned red about the gills. He squinted at her in that insufferable way that meant he found her behavior impossible. She sighed with remorse.

"Go to your room until summoned. Marigold will pack

your belongings, and we will depart for York as hastily as possible."

"That will seem suspicious," Lady Heath interjected.

"She pushed the damn man into the fountain, Augusta. It already *is* suspicious. Is there anything else we need to know?"

Lucy scoffed. The whole situation was absurd. "No."

Her father shook his head and turned his back.

Lucy stared at his reddening neck in angry silence for only a moment before turning on her heel and quitting the room. Her father was furious. She could see that. But banishment? Why was she to blame for one man's foolish behavior?

She stomped petulantly as she climbed the stairs. There had to be more to this exile than a simple shove into a fountain —well, there was. The man had been down on his knees, for Christ sake. Everyone had been staring and laughing while he clung to her skirts and professed his undying love. What was she to do? Surely not agree?

All the blame would fall on *her* shoulders and not the buffoon who sought to trap her into marriage with a public proposal. And she would have to leave her closest friend, Thea, behind. She couldn't ask her to abandon the rest of the season, too.

When Lucy reached her room, Marigold was already there with her trunks.

"I suppose you've heard everything?"

Marigold nodded. "All the staff knows, but we agree with you. That man was inappropriate to demand marriage in that manner."

"I wish my father would see it that way. All he sees is the potential scandal. Pushing a man into a fountain may have been scandalous, but scandal is fodder for the papers, and then

2

it fades. Had I agreed, I'd have to live with that fool for the rest of my life. But does my father care? No. All he cares about is the repercussions to his good name."

Marigold nodded. "Believe me, I understand. It was not long ago that I was in a very similar situation, but my consequences were much more severe."

Lucy paused in her agitated pacing and looked at her lady's maid. She had only been with her for six months, but they had grown close in that time. And Marigold was not the traditional lady's maid. She was exotic. Her skin was a warm brown, and she sometimes had an accent when she talked quickly. But Lucy had never asked where Marigold hailed from. "I'm sorry you went through such a thing."

The maid shrugged. "I am glad to be far away from my homeland and from my father. Women are treated much differently there."

"You must think me a selfish child."

"No." Marigold turned and met Lucy's gaze. "You are lucky, but that doesn't lessen the pain of knowing your life is not your own."

Lucy dropped her gaze. There were shadows in the other woman's eyes that Lucy only now noticed. Wherever Marigold had come from, whomever she had escaped, it was far worse than she could have imagined. Lucy lived in a rosy bubble of privilege. She knew that, but she'd never tried to see past it.

"I should appreciate a stay in the country, then. The season has nothing to offer anyhow."

"You did not like this suitor?"

"No. We danced one time. It is my understanding that he needs a rich wife. A fortune hunter, our society calls the likes of him."

Marigold shook her head in distaste. "And he thought humiliation would woo you?"

"He thought to trick me. 'Tis all it was. Humiliate me into agreeing. Why can't my father see that? I should have bloodied his nose, as well as pushed him into the fountain."

"What will your brother do?"

"I can count on Jonathan to have a word with him to make sure he won't bother me further. I wish my father would care as much."

"Perhaps you will find a husband in the country?" Marigold offered as she closed one trunk and began the next.

"I doubt it," Lucy said, pouting. "There is nothing to do in the country but ride horses, take walks, and read."

"That sounds lovely."

"I know. But Thea won't be with me. She must attend parties with her aunts, and they treat her poorly."

"Can she visit?"

"Father will say no. He will wish to punish me. It will be Thea who will suffer. I will appeal to my mother. She knows of Thea's situation."

"Then all is not lost."

"The rest of the season will be lost. Dancing, intriguing gentlemen whom I have yet to meet. What if I miss the one man who may be somewhat interesting?"

Marigold laughed. "If he is meant to be yours, he will wait for you. I think I have a way to make our stay in the country more enjoyable, but you have to promise me that you will tell no one what we do."

Lucy perked up at the sound of mischief. "I promise."

"It's a style of dancing from my country. It is not done by women of noble birth—not openly, but we all learn a bit."

4

Lucy didn't react to the revelation that her lady's maid was of noble birth in her country. It was part of a mysterious past that Marigold hid.

"Go on."

"I could lose my place here if we're caught."

"I know I don't always behave so, but I can be discreet."

Marigold smiled. "To the country, we will go."

"And great fun will be had." Lucy grinned in anticipation.

CHAPTER 1

Lucy leaned over the balustrade as Thea poured her a cup of tea. She sighed blissfully, enjoying the cool morning air and warm rays of sunlight. She wasn't missing the city after all. Her mother had allowed Thea to keep her company, and Marigold had kept her promise. Lucy didn't have a care about the delights of London. The country was proving to be just as alluring.

She scanned the expanse of lawn, the stables off in the distance, and past there to the rolling hills. She could see it all from the south terrace, a charming picture of country living. Her brother was due back at any moment to fulfill his promise to take them riding.

The only drawback to her exile was the constant chaperone of her brother, Jonathan, which her parents had insisted upon. *As if he had a moral compass more sound than hers.* Lucy flicked a fallen leaf in annoyance.

She saw him striding up the lawn now, waving like a madman. Lucy turned her back to him. She loved that she could still poke his temper by ignoring him.

"I see Jonathan has returned," Thea said from her seat. "Who is his friend?"

Lucy turned back toward the lawn. *Who was that man?* She squinted, shielding her eyes from the glare of the sun. She couldn't make out any identifying features at their present distance.

She shrugged. "I don't recognize him."

Thea went back to the paper she was reading and sipped her tea.

Lucy continued to watch the gentlemen. She lost sight of them below the steps that led to the lower lawn. Soon, they would reemerge at the top of the steps. Two bobbing heads eventually appeared—first her brother, and then a man with dusty blond hair. He'd removed his hat, allowing the sun to shine upon his face.

Lucy sucked in a breath.

She'd never seen him before. She would never forget a face like his. It was beautiful. Masculine but also coyly adorable. He smiled with one side of his mouth, a charming, crooked grin, speaking words she was too far away to hear.

She didn't know why, but she was very aware of her breathing all of a sudden, and her heartbeat accelerated with every step he took toward her. A wave of heat swallowed her.

He glanced away from her brother and toward her.

Their gazes caught.

He walked with a loose saunter, a stride of ease and arrogance. He was taller than her brother by half a head.

An awareness took hold of her as they drew ever closer, and he still held her complete attention. Lucy had an odd sensation of losing her balance, even though she stood perfectly still. Then she panicked, turning and darting toward her empty chair next to Thea. She crashed into her seat, as graceful as a bull, and slid right off the polished wood. She landed on her rear beside Thea's legs.

"Goodness!" Thea cried. "What has come over you?"

Lucy sat in stunned silence as the scuff of footsteps brought her brother and his friend up onto the terrace.

"I slipped off my chair," Lucy grumbled as she pulled herself up and reclaimed her seat.

"You wouldn't have if you—" Thea stopped.

Lucy sent a blessing to the heavens for her friend's good sense.

"Miss Manton, my dear sister."

Jonathan had that strained tone of voice that meant he was trying very hard not to laugh.

Lucy's head snapped in his direction, and she did her very best not to snarl, but instead, employed a practiced smile.

"You've met Lord Winchester before, yes?"

Lucy frowned and turned to Thea. "I don't believe we have."

"We met while riding on the Heath. I had a beard at the time," he answered.

It couldn't be the same man, could it?

"I beg your pardon. I did not recognize you, my lord."

He unnerved her. That happened very rarely. Men were easy creatures to understand, but this one…he was different. She should be heeding the warning her body was giving her, but instead, she remained intrigued.

"What brings you all the way to York, my lord?"

"I'm taking a respite from my travels, Lady Lucy." He cocked his head to the side and squinted at her as if she amused him.

"And his mistress," Jonathan quipped as he took his seat next to his sister. "If you would please, Thea."

"Certainly." Thea poured him a cup of tea.

Lucy smiled behind her teacup as Lord Winchester swallowed uncomfortably and took his seat.

"I didn't think that bit of news appropriate for the present company, Rigsby," he grumbled to Jonathan.

"It's only Lucy and Thea. I've already corrupted Lucy, and she's corrupted Thea. There's no use pretending otherwise."

"Exactly. I'm escaping a mister, and you're escaping a mistress. They are almost the same thing," Lucy said and shrugged.

"I highly doubt it. What reason could you have to escape a man when you have the protection of your brother and father to shield you?"

Lucy stiffened at his condescending tone. "What reason do you have for needing to escape a woman, *feeble as we are*?" She raised a brow in challenge.

"My apologies if I implied—"

She waved away his apology. "Do continue. You won't find delicate ears here."

Lord Winchester gave her brother a look. "Be that as it may…"

"Lucy is banished for tossing Lord Whippet into a pond," Jonathan blurted.

"I did not toss—" Lucy cocked her head to the side. "No, I do believe I *could* toss him if I wished to, but I did not. And it was a fountain, not a pond."

Jonathan chuckled. Thea shook her head and sipped her tea without comment.

Lord Winchester blinked at her. She felt like a strange bug under his magnifying glass.

"I think it best to refrain from topics of mistresses for the moment."

"Congratulations, Jonathan. You've befriended a prude," Lucy smirked.

Jonathan snorted. "Prude? Couldn't be farther from the—"

There was a thump from under the table and Jonathan grimaced. "Very well. Lucy and Thea are on holiday for the season, and so are you, Winchester. May we have some tea and discuss other things now?"

"Will you be staying long?" Lucy tried to sound as bored and unaffected as he did.

"I haven't decided."

Good, Lucy thought. She sipped her tea and gathered her thoughts. She didn't like feeling out of her element, when normally handling men *was* her element. But with him, five minutes in his presence had made her feel young and stupid. She'd already tripped all over herself. Now she needed to find her feet again and converse with him like a normal person with intelligent faculties. How else was she to impress upon him her better qualities?

Did she wish to impress him? Oh, yes. He was the exact sort of man town life lacked. Strong, with edges made hard by the world outside London ballrooms. He wasn't some dandy or a rake who preyed on weak-minded widows and spinster daughters.

He was a *man*.

"Where have you traveled?" Thea asked.

God bless Thea. She could ask all the questions Lucy wanted to know, and she wouldn't be affected like Lucy was.

"I've spent a great deal of time in Asia. India, more specifically, and Egypt."

"How exciting. Have you seen the sphinxes?" Thea asked.

"That I have. A marvel of human ingenuity."

Thea continued to pepper him with questions, and Lucy simply observed. She needed to revise his current impression of her, but she didn't know how. When the volley of conversation stopped, she decided to proceed with her best tactic for drawing a man's attention: ignoring him.

"Jonathan, do you still plan to take us riding?"

"Yes," he answered, eyeing her warily. "Why do you ask?"

"Well, it was clear you came from the stables. I was only wondering. We are able to go by ourselves."

Lucy could feel Lord Winchester's gaze on her.

"No, Father made me swear I would watch over you," he continued. "I will take you riding."

Lucy glanced at Thea. "Are you ready?"

Thea nodded. Lucy stood and smoothed the skirts of her ruby-red riding habit that hugged her waist in a way that made her feel womanly. She ran her hands down the sides of her torso, hoping to draw his attention to her figure. Then she moved to turn away and paused.

"Oh—Lord Winchester, you are welcome to join us if you wish." She smiled benignly.

"Thank you, Lady Lucy, but my horse needs a day of rest, as do I."

"Good day to you then, Lord Winchester," she replied and turned to her brother.

"I'll meet you at the stable, Lucy. Winchester, I'll show you inside and Mrs. Gabe will set you up in a room."

"Good day, Lord Winchester," Thea echoed.

"Good day, Miss Manton, Lady Lucy."

"Please, call me Lucy. I loathe formalities this far from London."

He nodded noncommittally, and she had no other option but to turn away with Thea or look like an even bigger fool.

They descended the steps, both silent until well out of earshot.

"What on earth went on back there?" Thea asked as soon as it was safe.

"I'm not sure, but I think I've fallen in love," Lucy said.

Thea glanced at her. "You don't look very pleased about that."

"It's a very uncomfortable feeling. I've met my match, and he just thinks I'm a spoiled brat."

"He can't think that from what little time you've spent together."

Lucy pulled her friend to a halt. "He is a man who's seen the world, Thea. He can see right through me."

"Then he isn't looking properly."

CHAPTER 2

Dean followed Rigsby into the house, already dreading the time he would spend there. He knew the expression on a young woman's face when she had become smitten with him. He didn't want to see it on the sister of one of his closest friends.

A surge of panic caused his pulse to soar and his chest to tighten.

"Lenora's blood is on your hands, boy. I bet you wish you'd married her now."

Cold sweat beaded over his neck and brow, his father's voice as clear in his head as if he stood at his elbow, whispering the words in his ear. Dean swiped his handkerchief across his brow while Rigsby's back was turned. For four years he'd avoided marriageable young ladies like the plague, preferring seasoned widows and skilled courtesans because their hearts couldn't be broken.

But he couldn't avoid Lady Lucy. He would have to smother those tender emotions of hers quickly, in a way that wouldn't hurt or embarrass her—or destroy his friendship with Rigsby.

That would involve some cold but gentle honesty. Lady Lucy didn't seem to be a wilting English rose, not like Lenora had been. Dean knew the type of woman—nay, the girl—Rigsby's sister was. She held her privileged little world in her hands, using everyone around her like puppets.

She had no experience with men like him. He was a wolf, and she was a helpless little lamb. But this wolf had a conscience and liked his women wicked and equally as untethered as he was. Young ladies were not untethered. They had virginity, dowries, settlements, contracts... Dean wanted none of that. He was an earl, but he hated the ties of being a landed gentleman. Those things had been drilled into him as a boy so aggressively he now loathed anything to do with it. He was his own man now, and he lived as he pleased.

But she... He could see why she'd been banished. Women that beautiful should be betrothed and married off as soon as possible. They caused all sorts of trouble when left untended.

"So what exactly did your sister do to earn banishment to York?" Dean asked as they climbed the stairs to the study.

"Hmm? Oh, poor Lord Whippet thought to propose publicly and trap her into marriage, so she shoved him into a fountain. He's after her dowry, of course. Lucy doesn't suffer fools, and obviously cares not for her reputation."

"She seems to be a handful. I remember the pond incident during the riding party."

"You'd do well to forget that, but yes, she *is* a handful. She isn't dim, but she forgets her place in the world."

"Her place?"

"Being of the fairer sex. She hasn't learned that she can't go about shoving lords into fountains, for example," Rigsby

DAYNA QUINCE

replied. "Or that she shouldn't frolic barefooted in a pond on the Heath. Things of that nature."

"Your parents have been too lenient," Dean said. He saw it often with daughters of wealthy fathers. Pampered and bored and too beautiful to refuse. He never fell for such antics.

"Perhaps. Lucy always finds a way around the rules. Too many people, my parents included, underestimate her."

Dean thought about that. If she were as intelligent as her brother touted, then a simple conversation should stop the sparkle in her eyes when she stared at him.

"What of her friend, Miss Manton? Any relation to the gun maker?"

"Thea? She is, but her family isn't well off. Lucy has taken her under her wing, though. They are the truest of friends. She's as innocent as the day is long, and a good influence on Lucy."

"I won't be using your sister's given name any more than I use yours," Dean warned.

Rigsby shrugged. "Suit yourself."

They arrived at Lord Heath's study. He welcomed Dean and summoned Mrs. Gabe to prepare a room. There was the talk of horses and hunting before Rigsby left to take his sister riding.

Dean found himself in a comfortable room in the guest wing of the house and stretched out on the bed after removing his coat, cravat, and boots. He'd declined the use of a valet offered by Mrs. Gabe, preferring to dress himself as he did on his travels.

Now that he was alone, he found himself thinking of Rigsby's sister yet again. She was trouble, her warm brown gaze assessing and all too eager to engage him. Why wasn't she married? Couldn't her family see how dangerous it was to let her linger in such a way? She needed a firm husband to keep her reined in and children to occupy her.

Now, if she eventually became widowed and seasoned by the passage of time, then she would be the kind of woman he took interest in. Someone no longer tied so tightly to social conventions, and eager for physical companionship to appease her boredom. In that scenario, she would have men begging for her favor, and none would succeed but him.

The thought alone caused his skin to itch with the need to be touched by her. His nerve endings suddenly came alive, blood rushing to his groin with vigor. But it was only a fantasy, he reminded himself. He could have her any way he wished in his head but never in reality.

Dean's body relaxed as he imagined a version of Lucy he could pursue. His breathing evened as his conscious mind slipped into the fuzzy beginnings of a dream.

§ð.

Lucy and Thea strolled into the conservatory, where her mother chatted with Jonathan and Lord Winchester. Lucy smiled in greeting as the gentlemen stood and held out their chairs. She had herself in control once more, and she was determined to show Lord Winchester that she wasn't some witless ninny. She would give him very little of her attention, though.

"How was your ride?" her mother asked.

"Wonderful. How was Mrs. Farris this morning?"

"She is on the mend. She adored the novel you lent her."

"Oh, good. I will bring her the next book."

"A splendid idea. Her son will be arriving tomorrow to tend to her."

Lucy stiffened and caught her mother's eye. "How nice it will be for her to see her son again."

Lady Heath had that look. The expression that said she'd attended far too many weddings, and none of them for her own children.

The arrival of her father cut the tension, but only for a moment.

"What are we discussing?" he asked the table at large.

"Mother is trying to wed Lucy to Mr. Farris," Jonathan said before taking a bite of his chicken.

Lucy rolled her eyes. She didn't want to have this discussion, especially not in front of Lord Winchester.

"Mr. Farris is an amiable fellow," Thea said.

"His dogs have more wit than he does," Lord Heath put in as he spread butter on a roll.

"That isn't the least bit true," Lady Heath said.

Lucy wanted to get up and leave. She glimpsed Lord Winchester shifting uncomfortably. "Mother, we have a guest. Let us leave talk of my prospective witless husbands for another time, shall we?"

Lady Heath regarded her. "The gentlemen should invite him on a hunt."

"Shall we have a hunting party?" Lucy turned to her table companions, holding Lord Winchester's gaze.

"If you've already pushed one suitor into a fountain, I'm not about to hand you a pistol and have you face another," her father said dryly.

Jonathan erupted in laughter.

Lucy's cheeks burst into flame. "I... I wouldn't shoot a

man for asking to marry me. Jonathan, stop it." She would throw a roll at him if only Lord Winchester weren't present. "Though I am contemplating fratricide."

"I am interested in a good hunt, but perhaps we shouldn't invite this poor fellow. Mr. Farris, is it?"

She heard the pleasant rumble of Lord Winchester's voice, surprised he would join her family's antics. Maybe he wasn't as serious as he appeared?

"I'm willing to try. I haven't much experience with guns," Thea said.

"Well, I suppose we must teach our Dorothea to shoot," Lord Heath replied.

Thea seemed very pleased by this. She absolutely glowed whenever she was made to feel a part of their family. Lucy wished it could be true, and that they could be real sisters. Thea deserved a loving family more than anyone she knew.

Lucy took a deep breath, collected her nerves, and summoned her good humor.

"That's settled, then. We will teach Thea to shoot, and I won't shoot Mr. Farris, regardless of whether he asks me to marry him." She glared pointedly at her mother.

"I will send an invitation." Her mother seemed pleased.

"It will have to be in the morning," her father said. "We're going to the races in Newby tomorrow afternoon."

"Oh, may we come?" Lucy clapped excitedly.

He gave her an assessing stare.

She grabbed his hand. "Please, Father?"

He sighed. "Very well."

"So much for a pleasant day at the races," Jonathan mumbled.

"Thea and I will have a wonderful time, I'm sure. If you plan to be sullen, then stay home."

"Now, now." Her father could always sense a budding sibling squabble. "Lord Winchester, do you keep a stable?"

"I'm afraid not. I travel too often. I bring my own horse everywhere."

"What is his name?" Thea asked.

"Fenrir."

"Of the Norse legend?" Lucy asked.

"Yes. You know it?"

"I do. I find Norse mythology interesting."

He raised his eyebrows.

"Don't look so surprised. My governess taught me more than how to pour tea."

"I didn't say otherwise. Your brother speaks highly of you."

"Please remember *all* that your governess taught you," Lady Heath scolded her.

"Yes, Mother." She let the matter drop.

"It was Lucy who chose the name for Odin's pup," her father said. "We have a fair bit of Norse blood in the Heath line. Thor is the pup's name, and she named her kitten Freya."

"Then my horse will be in good company."

"Freya stays in our London residence," Lucy said. "The carriage makes her sick. She is a sweet little gray tabby."

Lord Winchester nodded. "I've yet to meet Thor and Odin."

"They spend their time in the kitchens begging for scraps," Jonathan said. "They'll be glad to come hunting with us and scare up some game."

From then on, lunch was pleasantly amicable. Lucy and

Thea had planned to sketch in the garden afterward, while the men went fishing. Although desperate to prove herself in front of Lord Winchester, she was glad to be alone with Thea. That was, until her mother decided to join their little party.

"I haven't sketched in years." She sat comfortably in the shade of a tree on a blanket shared by Thea and Lucy.

"I'm surprised you wanted to join us, Mother."

"Well, there was something I wanted to discuss with you."

Lucy gritted her teeth.

"Your father informed me of Lord Winchester's stay after I returned from visiting Mrs. Farris. I know little of the man, and he wanted to assure me."

"Assure you of what exactly?" Lucy focused on the bunch of roses she was attempting to sketch.

"His reputation," Lady Heath answered. "I know little of his family, though they hail from Yorkshire. He attended school with your brother, but otherwise, he remains in the wind."

As her mother fed her these little morsels of information, Lucy wondered what their purpose was. Was she encouraging her or warning her off?

"What exactly are you trying to say?" Lucy set her pencil down and twisted to face her.

"I just wanted to be sure he wouldn't be an unacceptable acquaintance for you or Dorothea. Your father assures me he is not, and I thought you ought to know."

"Jonathan wouldn't have invited him to stay if he were." Lucy wondered at her mother's strange tone.

"That is true. Your brother fancies himself your gallant protector."

That was taking things a bit far. Lucy narrowed her eyes, and her mother's glance darted away.

"What is it you are not saying to me?"

"Why would you think I'm withholding something?"

"Because you have that *look*."

"I don't have any such *look*."

"You have many expressions, Mother. One of them being that you are withholding something to trick me into admitting something."

Thea giggled. "You do have that *look*, Lady Heath."

Lady Heath scoffed and tossed her head. "Very well. Are you or are you not smitten with Lord Winchester?"

"I scarcely know the man," Lucy said. "I didn't even recognize him when he arrived. The beard certainly changed his face."

"Oh, yes, I remember now." Lady Heath nodded. "It suited him, but I favor a clean shave."

Lucy prayed that would be the last said of it. "Do you think mauve will be a popular color next season?"

"Lady Temple was stunning when she wore that mauve frock with the feather tassels," Thea said. "She is always ahead of the season's trends."

Lady Heath narrowed her eyes at both of them.

"You would be lovely in mauve, Mama. Perhaps a shopping expedition is in order?"

"Hmm." Lady Heath focused on her sketchbook once more.

Lucy shared a glance with Thea and then returned her attention to her own drawing. All she had managed to accomplish so far was a rough outline of a rose. At present, there was a small winged bug marching across the paper. She stared at it, but she didn't really see it because—once again—her mind wandered to thoughts of green eyes and a square-cut jaw. Lucy wondered if he knew his grin was crooked. He often only smiled on one side of his mouth, as if he couldn't commit to the full thing.

He also had crinkles around his eyes when he half smiled. In fact, it seemed as if he smiled more with his eyes than his lips.

Lucy paused on the mental image of his lips. She loved his lips and the way they formed words. They didn't match the gruff aura he presented. Instead, they appeared soft and versatile.

She sighed. She'd give anything to know the feel of them. Then she caught Thea and her mother staring at her.

"What?"

"You sighed, and you're smiling," Thea responded.

"Is something the matter?" Her mother studied her.

"There's a darling little bug on my paper. I can't draw, or I might squish him."

"Insects are distasteful." Lady Heath shuddered.

"We are in their domain, Mother. It only wishes to live fruitfully like us."

Lady Heath raised her brows as she gathered her sketch-book and pencils. "I suppose that is true. I forgot I must write to my sister. Carry on without me."

"We will." Lucy smiled cheerfully.

She watched her mother until she was out of sight—and well out of earshot. "Let's find something new to sketch."

"Like what?"

"The lake."

Thea stilled. "The lake? Or *the men* fishing on the lake?"

"What a lovely idea. My father would love for me to sketch him, doting daughter that I am."

Lucy could hear Thea grumbling as she gathered her pencils and charcoal. She gathered their blanket, and they made their way from the garden to the lake. Lucy wasn't so bold as to march right up to the three men. She chose a dry bank just within calling distance. She waved as the gentlemen took notice, but otherwise, paid them no attention, or at least, pretended not to.

"What are we doing here, precisely?" Thea asked.

"Drawing the gentlemen fishing. It's very serene, isn't it? The way they stand so still, I mean. The sunlight reflects off the water and creates a sort of glowing haziness."

Thea narrowed her gaze at Lucy but then glanced at the men, and her face softened. "I dare say it does. I've never noticed that."

"See? We are expanding our artistic experience. Observe the darling dragonfly on those reeds. Its wings are iridescent."

Thea didn't answer, but instead, took the blanket from under Lucy's arm and spread it on the ground. Lucy sat and curled her legs to the side. Then she peered out over the water, resisting the urge to peek toward the dock.

"What are you doing?"

"Oh!" Lucy cranked her neck over her shoulder to glare at her brother. "You frightened me."

He grinned. "I know. What are you doing here?"

"We're sketching," Thea answered calmly.

"The garden wasn't inspiring?"

"Not in the slightest. I thought to draw Father fishing." Lucy kept her gaze on her work as she idly sketched the bank upon which her father stood. She ignored the rustling beside her as her brother sat.

"You've got that air about you." He leaned into her and bumped her with his shoulder.

"I shall not pretend to know what you mean." Lucy scowled at the squiggly line she drew when he bumped her again. "See what you've done now?"

"Oh, I see what you're doing."

She turned her head and met his eyes. She kept her face carefully blank. "What, precisely, am I doing?"

"I've got a friend visiting. A new person of new experiences. You're going to pester us like you used to when we were growing up because you can't stand to be left out of the fun. Winchester isn't a new toy for you, though. Let the man be."

Lucy blinked. Her mouth slackened. "You think I'm going to be chasing your coattails, wanting you to include me in your boring activities?"

"My activities are never boring," he returned, without skipping a beat. "Some things we will do together—riding, perhaps a jaunt to the river—but he is here to recuperate, not pander to your distaste for idleness."

She rolled her eyes. "Go away, Jonathan."

He stood and dusted his hands on his breeches. "Do I have your word?"

"You're going to have my pencil jabbed into the toe of your boot if you don't leave immediately. I care not what you and your little friend are here to do. I've got Thea to *pander to my distaste for idleness*."

Lucy glared at her brother. Lord, if he only knew the infatuation burning inside her. Her anger must hide it well.

"God's speed, Thea," he muttered as he walked away.

Thea giggled. "He hasn't the faintest idea."

"He can be daft at times."

"Lord Winchester has glanced over here many times since we've settled here."

"Has he?"

Lucy had made a distinct effort not to look at him, not directly, anyhow. She was simply going to draw her father. Men like Lord Winchester hated to be ignored. The more she pulled away, the more he'd be intrigued. He expected to have to fend off the paltry affections of a friend's little sister, but she knew better. If she wanted his attention, she would have to gain it through the lack of hers. At least, that's what she hoped to do.

He was different from any man she'd met before. Where others pretended to be dangerous rakes, he actually was. His aura was one of power and wariness. He'd seen things, done things. He understood his place in the world and made the world bend to his will.

She wanted to move closer to him, study him, but he was so far removed from her he may as well have been a wild animal. She would have to bide her time and approach slowly and carefully. First, she would need to earn his interest and his trust.

CHAPTER 3

Lucy dressed for dinner with exceptional care. She wanted to appear alluring without the impression of trying. She wore a simple white gown—virginal but sumptuous in the way its sweetheart neckline cupped her breasts. Its gauzy outer layer shifted over the tighter, sheath-like dress just the tiniest bit suggestively. She left her hair partially down and used a bit of lip color to make her lips rosier and more plump. She draped one curl over her shoulder, where it would lay right between her breasts and draw the eye.

She hoped she wasn't being too obvious, but no matter what she did, she felt exposed. She felt like a fool.

Lucy made her way to the drawing room, entering as her family talked animatedly about a local fair their village had every year. She stayed quiet, making herself small as she sat in the corner of the settee and picked up a book she had left on the side table just the other day. It felt like ages had passed since she'd put that book down, a lifetime. She felt like an entirely different person from that absentminded girl with her frivolous romance novel. She had completely forgotten its existence.

Now she paged through it, the words a blur as she could think of only one thing—one *person,* to be precise. She was so intently focused on him and his presence in the room. She observed him as he adjusted his stance, refilled his glass, slapped her brother on the back, and laughed heartily. His head was thrown back, and he was laughing openly and honestly. She sucked in a breath and yanked her attention away.

"Lucy! Goodness, I didn't see you come in." Her mother turned to her.

Lucy schooled her features and set the book aside calmly. "You were all enjoying yourselves immensely. I didn't want to interrupt." She sounded melancholy even to her own ears. That wouldn't do at all, so she gave her mother a shining smile. "I missed the joke entirely, but it must have been brilliant."

"Your brother is telling us of his time at Eton with Lord Winchester," Thea responded.

"Wildly exaggerated stories, I'm sure." Lucy rolled her eyes.

"If you could attend university, little sister, your own exploits would put mine to shame."

She grinned at that. "No doubt."

"Thank heavens she can't," her father quipped.

Lucy glared at him.

"She can behave when she wishes," her mother defended her.

"No great story ever began with good behavior." Lucy patted her mother's hand.

Lady Heath harrumphed in her usual disapproving way. "You are incorrigible."

"Thank you!" Lucy laughed along with her brother and father. She was happy to see everyone in good spirits. She felt a peculiar warmth glide over her skin, like when a sunbeam unexpectedly broke through the clouds. Could it be the touch of someone's gaze? She courageously peeked at her prey, masking it with a playful glance at Thea, who was nearest to where he stood.

§

Dean pulled his focus away from Lady Lucy's décolleté. Instead, he peered down at his drink, which he'd only just poured. No rescue on that front. He sighed quietly and focused on her family again. He needed to put her to bed. He needed to put *it*—her growing infatuation—to bed. Her entire costume tonight, from the softly curling hair around her shoulders to the deceptively innocent cut of her dress, was meant to entrap him. He was sure of it. He'd seen it all before. There wasn't any sort of trick or subterfuge he hadn't already experienced at the hands of a woman. This girl—or woman—was a novice at best, but that made her all the more dangerous. She could ruin herself and put him in a very difficult position.

He needed to get her alone and deliver a quick and merciful death to her tender feelings. If she were all that Rigsby had said she was, then that should be all he needed to do.

Then the butler entered, and mercifully, dinner was announced. Dean moved slowly, deliberately catching her eye, and waiting until the others passed through the doorway.

She waited, too, hands fluttering at her sides, glancing nervously at the door.

He strode confidently toward her.

"Lady Lucy, I only need but a moment of your time."

"Yes, Lord Winchester?"

He moved closer to her, closer than appropriate, close enough to see her quick inhale and her pupils dilate. Close enough to smell the sweet scent of her perfume—some fruity blossom mixed with her skin. He let a familiar heat enter his voice.

"Whatever it is you think you feel, or may want…it will never be."

A little crease formed on her brow.

"We are from different worlds. You would do well to think of me as an ugly uncle far beyond your years."

"Different worlds?" She raised one brow. "I haven't the slightest idea what you mean, Lord Winchester. Are you feeling well?"

Dean smiled as he regarded his glass, swirling it gently. "Do you think I don't know? I know *exactly* what I do to women, the effect I have on them. I don't want to lead you on, or cause strife between your brother and me, so I will draw the line now."

She gave him an expression of utter puzzlement and then smiled beguilingly.

He frowned. "What?"

"You know exactly what you do to women?" Lucy snickered and patted his arm. "Far be it for me to ruin your self-esteem." She moved through the doorway into the hall.

"I beg your pardon?" Dean followed her, his entire plan unraveling. Was he wrong? No. His instincts in matters like this were always spot on. The hall was empty, so he snatched her hand and stopped her before she could escape down the stairs.

"Just a moment, Lady Lucy. Whether you can admit your attraction to me is not the point. What you need to know is that men like me are unsuitable for girls—or women—like you. Please don't waste a moment thinking I could be anything more than an acquaintance of your brother."

Now he had her attention. She appeared startled, her gaze dropping to their hands. He immediately let go of her, and her eyes slid back to his.

"Is that all?"

He nodded.

She turned away from him without another word. Dean let her advance farther down the stairs before following. He wandered into the dining room a moment after her and claimed his seat. She didn't seem affected by his little speech. He wasn't certain if that was a good thing or a bad thing. Perhaps she was not as naïve as he'd thought? Either way, he'd done all he could to discourage her, apart from leaving altogether. Truth be told, he didn't *want* to leave. This family seemed happy, and he could do with a little bit of happy right now.

৯১

Lucy retired that evening in an unusual state of lethargy. The entire night had felt like an awful play with no end. She had played her part admirably well, but it had worn her down. Only Thea could tell she wasn't herself. Lucy had waved off her curious glance and avoided her questions, but now that she was alone, she could properly reflect on what that oaf had said.

He was warning her away. Could anything be more humiliating? Probably. At least he'd done it privately. Presumably he wasn't confiding his suspicions about her to her brother. Be that as it may, Lucy was not dissuaded in the least.

Unsuitable? Bah!

Could someone explain to her why handsome rakes always thought themselves too dangerous for gently bred young ladies? Did they think themselves too worldly and over-whelming?

Well, perhaps this gently bred young lady was too dangerous for Lord Winchester. He obviously just needed more time to see that. Time, she could give him. She had a whole season to devote to that very thing. He hadn't glimpsed enough of her true character to realize she was more than a match for him.

There was no point in remaining shy now. He knew she liked him, so she wouldn't hide her intentions, except from her brother and parents. She would go after what she wanted—blast him, and she would win.

She climbed into bed after undressing and washing her face. She blew out her candle and stared at her canopy, blinking rapidly as the strain of the evening made her eyelids heavy and scratchy.

"Lord, grant me patience," she prayed and let her eyes drift close. She would need all her good humour and intelligence to make the man see sense.

CHAPTER 4

The next morning, the gentlemen decided they would all go target shooting before heading to the races in the afternoon. This update came from Thea, who had breakfasted with them while Lucy had slept in.

Lucy vaguely remembered a maid coming to wake her and then Thea tapping on her door. She rose refreshed and broke her fast in her room while Thea sat patiently.

"Are you feeling well?"

"Yes." Lucy yawned. "I was dreadfully tired last evening."

"I could tell," Thea agreed.

"My body needed more rest. That is all."

After Lucy finished her eggs, Thea returned downstairs while Lucy washed and dressed. When she was finished, she met them in the morning room.

"Good morning, everyone," she said with a sunny smile. Her attention settled on Lord Winchester. He held a cup of coffee, and it paused on the way to his mouth as she caught his gaze. She raised both brows ever so slightly and turned away from him and toward her brother, who read from the paper.

"Ready for shooting?" she asked Jonathan.

"Father will be joining us," he said from behind the paper.

"Why?"

"Because Mr. Farris will also be accompanying us, and he doesn't want you to shoot him."

Lucy scoffed. "I've no reason to shoot him unless he tries to trap me into marriage. It goes both ways, you know."

"I simply can't see why all these men want to marry you," Jonathan grumbled.

"I'm lovely, that's why," Lucy grumbled back. She turned away from her brother in annoyance. "Thea, would you care for a morning walk? I feel the need to move."

Thea nodded. "I'm looking forward to this morning. Lord Winchester promised to teach me to shoot."

"Nonsense. I can teach you to shoot. I'm a better shot than Jonathan, anyhow."

Thea hurried to catch up with Lucy as she bolted down the terrace steps.

"Must we run?" Thea asked.

"My apologies." Lucy slowed. "Isn't it a wonderful morning?"

"Are you positive you feel well?"

Lucy clenched her teeth. "Why do you keep asking me that?" She paused on the gravel walk of the rose garden and faced her friend.

"Your behavior is just a bit odd. It has been since dinner last night."

"Well…" Lucy glanced back toward the open French doors of the morning room. "Did you notice that Lord Winchester and I were delayed before joining you in the dining room?" she asked quietly.

Thea gasped. "Did he kiss you?"

"If only. He tried to warn me away."

"From who?"

"From himself! He informed me that even if I couldn't admit I was attracted to him, he was completely unsuitable for a woman like me."

"Oh," Thea said despondently. "What will you do now?"

"Well, I'm certainly not going to give up. I will show him how well suited we are. He is a peer, for goodness sake. How could he possibly be unsuitable?"

"Perhaps he has some deep dark secret?" Thea whispered.

"Wouldn't that be exciting? Like a lurid novel, but reality is never as interesting as fiction. He's simply acting the fool, as all men do."

"How can you be so certain? What if he simply doesn't want to marry you?"

"I'm certain. If it wasn't meant to be, then I don't think I would feel like this. Do you? My heart—my gut, is telling me so. He can choose to be obtuse for now, but in time, he will see."

Thea sighed heavily. Her sigh echoed the uncertainty Lucy felt but could not admit. There had to be something to all these uncomfortable emotions. No man had ever affected her in such a way before. She was not usually one to succumb to a handsome face or well-cut coat. Her judgment wasn't always what her parents wished it to be, but this was different.

This was fate.

The difficulty was in proving it somehow.

He wasn't immune to her, she knew that. He studied her, aware of her, just as she was conscious of him. She could still feel the caress of his gaze like a physical touch.

But now she had to remain focused. It was no time for daydreaming or fantasizing.

Lucy and Thea finished their walk around the garden, returning to the morning room just as her father arrived with Mr. Farris in tow.

Lucy greeted him cordially but remained somewhat aloof. They set out as a party and caravanned to the east lawn. Her father handed her the pistol he'd given her when she was sixteen, a flintlock inlaid with silver wire. She stood by as Jonathan and Lord Winchester argued about distance and placed bets with each other.

"Thea? Would you like me to show you? You may use my pistol," Lucy offered.

Thea was regarding the entire setup nervously. "Oh, I'm not sure I should try. Perhaps I will just watch."

"Nonsense. Shooting is a skill. You may need to defend yourself one day."

"From who?" Thea laughed.

"Most likely a man, but perhaps a rabid dog or—"

"Lucy," her father warned.

He was using the tone that suggested she close her mouth immediately.

"We will all educate Miss Manton with our collective knowledge," he continued. "First, let's begin with how to safely handle a pistol."

Lucy stood to the side while her father bent near Thea and showed her the workings of the pistol. She could hear Jonathan, Mr. Farris, and Lord Winchester murmuring to each other. When she glanced their way, they stopped. She glared at Jonathan, and he let out a patently fake cough.

"Are you ill?" She strode over to him and surveyed him.

"I'm feeling very well, thank you," her brother replied.

"Very well, then. Would you care to enlighten me regarding what was so fervently being discussed between the three of you?"

"What business is it of yours?" Lord Winchester asked.

Lucy was surprised to feel a bit of annoyance. Good. It would keep her from acting like a lovesick twit.

"Discussions about me are my business."

"How do you know we were discussing you?"

"I'm very observant."

"It so happens that I was warning Mr. Farris. I told him he better not propose, or you might shoot him. He has heard about the events with the fountain," Winchester said with a smirk.

Lucy tried not to react to her rush of embarrassment. She took a steady breath and turned to Mr. Farris. He wasn't a bad-looking fellow. His brown hair ruffled rakishly in the breeze, and his features held a cheery youthfulness.

"That is sound advice." She nodded to him.

He swallowed loudly as Lucy turned away and returned to her father.

She had that anxious feeling of being watched, a prickling right between her shoulder blades. When she turned around, Lord Winchester and Mr. Farris both stared after her. Lord Winchester with an amused smirk, and Mr. Farris with a dreamy expression.

Drat. So much for remaining aloof. If the threat of a gunshot wound wasn't enough, she would have to scare Mr. Farris off in some other way.

Dean shook his head as he turned back to the table where Rigsby primed his prize pistols. He caught sight of Farris still staring longingly after Lady Lucy. He pitied the man. He knew what Farris saw in her; she was charming and beautiful, with just enough of a hint of eccentricity to be interesting, instead of dreadfully boring, like most well-bred chits.

She would eat the poor man alive. Dean clapped him on the back and turned him away from certain demise.

Then he inspected his gun, and soon they were ready to begin shooting.

"Ladies first." Rigsby gestured to Lucy.

Dean noticed that she always scrutinized her brother, as if she couldn't tell if he were insulting her or not.

"I think Thea should try first," she suggested.

"Oh no. Please, lead by example."

Lady Lucy raised a single brow. "Are you sure?"

Miss Manton nodded in encouragement.

"Very well. Jonathan, watch closely."

Rigsby snorted. Dean enjoyed the way they affectionately teased each other. Lady Lucy picked up her pistol and took aim at the target, her shoulders relaxed and her stance casual. With its wide vertical blue stripes, her simple walking dress accentuated the dip of her waist and the flare of her hips. He tore his attention away. He shouldn't even be noticing such things.

He focused on the target instead, the rapport of the pistol following shortly after. Somehow, he was unsurprised by the resulting hole in the bullseye. He applauded her with the others.

Lord Heath beamed proudly. "Very good, my dear."

Lady Lucy set her pistol on the table and pulled Miss Manton to the designated line.

"Now you, Thea. I know you will be wonderful. It's in your blood!"

Miss Manton appeared nervous. She picked up a pistol and took aim, Lady Lucy using little touches to adjust her hold and stance before stepping back.

"Exhale as you pull the trigger, and don't close your eyes," Lord Heath said encouragingly.

Miss Manton did as instructed, the rapport snapping in the air, along with her gasp of surprise.

Then there was a shout from Rigsby. "My arm!" he cried and fell to the ground.

Miss Manton screamed. Lady Lucy colorfully cursed at her brother as he languished on the ground with an imaginary wound.

"Lucy! Jonathan! I don't know which of you to whip first," Lord Heath bellowed. "Jonathan, get up before Thea faints."

Rigsby got to his feet in fits of laughter and apologized. "I'm sorry. I just couldn't resist."

Dean felt a protective surge for Miss Manton. The poor girl was utterly horrified.

"Give me that. I'll shoot him for real," Lady Lucy said angrily and took the pistol from Miss Manton's weak fingers. Then she rounded on her brother. "She will never shoot a gun again, Jonathan, and she has you to thank for it."

Lord Heath stepped between the siblings and took the pistol from Lucy. Dean sighed in relief. Miss Manton gently shook, her face ghostly pale. He went to her side and draped an arm around her shoulders, turning her away from the squabbling and toward the target.

"You see that mark? That's yours. An excellent first shot."

She blinked rapidly and then focused on the target. "For a moment, I thought…"

"If you had, you'd be famous. He's done many things to deserve it."

She shook her head. "That can't be true."

Dean winked at her. "It's a little true. He doesn't deserve death, but a hole in the arm might do him some good."

"I beg your pardon?" Rigsby came around Miss Manton's other side.

"It's true and you know it."

Rigsby pursed his lips. "I apologize, Thea. It was all in jest. I didn't mean to frighten you. Please don't stop on my account."

"Thank you."

"How about you take another right now?" Dean suggested. "Rigsby, go stand by the target."

Thea laughed, as did everyone else.

Dean stepped back as Lord Heath handed the pistol to her. She turned to Dean with uncertainty. He nodded encouragingly, and she took her aim.

Dean felt Lady Lucy as she stepped beside him, the light breeze picking up the scent of her and wafting it before his nose. What was that scent? It was so sweet and elusive.

"Thank you," she whispered.

He acknowledged her words with a slight dip of his head.

The crack of the pistol filled the air, Thea's second hole closer to the bullseye than her first, and everyone cheered as she placed the pistol on the table with a big smile.

Lord Heath applauded. "Even better than before. You're a natural."

Lucy felt a swell of fondness so profound that her eyes

teared. Thea still shook like a leaf, but her smile was wide and joyful. If Lucy had learned anything this morning, it was that the man beside her, who proclaimed himself unsuitable for her, was, in fact, perfect for her. His inherent kindness toward Thea proved it. Most men ignored Thea. They let her fade into the wallpaper and didn't give her a second thought.

Did he somehow not know this about himself? This would take more investigating on her part. For the rest of the morning, they each took turns until the air was tangy with gunpowder and it was time to leave for the races.

CHAPTER 5

Lucy spun her parasol aimlessly as she strolled with Thea outside the stables. She wasn't fond of racing. She thought the sport unfair to the horses. It was wholeheartedly a male pastime, along with the betting. She lowered her parasol and stepped under the eave near the stall of a particularly fine horse. He nickered at her in welcome and huffed into her hand by way of greeting. Lucy fished a lump of sugar from her reticule.

"You shouldn't." Thea hissed in warning. "He may require a specific diet."

"A little sugar never hurt anyone."

"Come, before someone sees us." Thea looped her arm through Lucy's and pulled her away.

Lucy waved farewell to the horse. "We should return to the seating area, or Father will begin to worry."

"Since when are you concerned with worrying your father?"

"Since I've been banished from the season. What more

would it take for him to remove me from England altogether?" Lucy mused.

"You're right. It has absolutely nothing to do with you-know-who seated right next to your father."

"That, too, but he maddens me. It's frustrating trying to impress someone who is so *unimpressed*."

"Just be yourself."

"I *am* being myself."

"No. You're being a nervous ninny pretending to be Lady Lucy. The real you would never try to impress a man. The real you would trample him under the onslaught of your charms."

"That…doesn't sound complimentary."

"It is and it isn't."

Lucy clamped her mouth shut and thought about Thea's words. So she wasn't being herself? Was she afraid she wasn't interesting enough? That thought stung far too much. She pushed it away. Her entire life, she had never been *not* interesting. She'd been a trial for her nursemaid and governess, a delight to her parents, a pest to her brother, but never once had she been boring. She *was* interesting, so why didn't she feel like it when in the presence of Lord Winchester?

Her mood declined as they returned to their designated box. An attendant opened the curtain and held it for her, and she took her seat and faced the races.

Only the crunch of peanut shells broke the silence that surrounded them.

"May I have some?" Lucy asked her brother.

Lord Winchester glanced at her briefly and then back to the race that was about to begin.

"You'll ruin your gloves," Jonathan replied.

"You don't give a fig for my gloves. I simply want a few peanuts, you glutton."

Lucy pulled off her gloves and held out her hand. Jonathan obliged her, passing a handful to Lord Winchester, who took them, dumped them onto a folded square of handkerchief in his other hand, and then gave them to Lucy's father, who handed them to her.

"Thank you." She beamed at Lord Winchester.

"You are very welcome." He smiled back at her, but his mouth was pulled tight.

She faced forward again.

"Would you like a peanut?" Lucy offered to Thea.

Thea smiled her thanks and took one. Everyone quieted as the next race began. She set the handkerchief in her lap, noticing the initials stitched in the corner. She ran her thumb over them, her chest tightening oddly. She thought of the way he had smiled at her just a moment ago. She even peeked his way, but his attention was firmly on the track.

What did that smile mean? If she was going to be herself, they needed to move past all this awkwardness. It was uncomfortable to feel constantly on edge. Perhaps Thea was right. Lucy should just throw caution to the wind and admit that yes, she liked him. That would require her to not hold back, to let go of the fear of failure and humiliation. What did she have to lose?

Him.

But if she did nothing, that was already guaranteed. What did she have to gain?

Everything. Everything she had ever wanted in love. The risk was definitely worth the reward.

She would need to tread carefully, though. Her brother and parents could not know what she was up to, or the repercussions would be dire.

CHAPTER 6

That evening, Lucy prepared for dinner as she normally would, feeling both nervous and relieved. Thea had been right. She'd been playing a part and not acting like her true self. She'd never felt so vulnerable, so open to potential heartache. She'd cared for men before, nursed tender feelings and budding attractions, hoping they would grow into something real, but those feelings paled in comparison to what she felt now.

She surveyed herself in the mirror, her dress a deep red her mother wouldn't approve of. The color made Lucy feel bold, and that was exactly what she meant to be. She quit her room and headed for the drawing room with a stomach that floated uncomfortably as she bounced down the stairs. She entered quietly, seeking Thea's side as she chatted with her mother.

Lady Heath took in her appearance. "I don't recall that exquisite frock as part of your usual wardrobe," she said with a small frown.

"No, it's new. I meant to wear it at the Featherington Ball, but since I won't be in attendance, I didn't want it to languish in purgatory."

Her mother eyed her carefully, but then turned back to Thea and resumed their discussion. Lucy wondered at her mother's lack of censure. She'd anticipated a battle, but perhaps, because they were at home, sequestered away from the scrutiny of society, she'd earned a reprieve. Her father and Jonathan had a chess game going by the fire, and after a quick scan of the room, she saw there was no sign of Lord Winchester.

How dismal would it be for her to wear her best dress and he not be in attendance this evening to appreciate it? There wasn't anything she could do about it, either.

"How was the shooting today, my dear?" her mother asked.

Lucy pulled herself out of her musings and smiled. "Wonderful. Thea is a natural marksman."

"I had heard. How did Mr. Farris fare? No wounds?"

"None. He refrained from proposing. Jonathan warned him beforehand."

"Jonathan, you didn't!"

"I did," her brother said without looking up from the chess game. "He wasn't dissuaded in the least."

"I think it encouraged him. He followed her like she was a rare butterfly." Thea giggled.

"I *am* a rare butterfly," Lucy preened.

"The rarest of them all, my dear," her father agreed.

"Good Lord. This is why she is the way she is," Jonathan grumbled.

"You dote upon her just as much as your mother and I. You must accept some of the blame," Lord Heath urged.

"Goodness. What am I to do with you three?" Lady Heath said. "Thank heavens Thea is here to ease the trouble. The arguing would never cease otherwise. And what of Lord Winchester? Is he joining us this evening?"

Lucy could have kissed her mother for asking.

"I'm sorry to have kept you waiting, Lady Heath."

Lucy just barely caught herself from shivering with delight at the sound of his gruff voice. She twisted to face him, taking in his easy stride and the breadth of his shoulders in a perfectly tailored jacket. She smiled—she couldn't help herself—and she didn't hide any of the appreciation that was surely glowing in her eyes.

He greeted them all as he entered. As their gazes met, his changed. The smile creases disappeared, and a barely notice-able line appeared between his brows. Lucy doubted anyone would notice but her, because she was the only one paying such close attention. She raised a single brow in challenge. Could he be frightened so easily?

Then the line disappeared, and his expression hardened in answer to her challenge.

"Lady Lucy," he acknowledged, and took a seat on the sofa across from them.

"Lord Winchester. Dinner has not yet been announced, in case you were wondering."

"Thank you for informing me. I am relieved."

"Do you like my dress?"

"Your dress is lovely."

"As is your coat. Your green waistcoat brings out your eyes."

"Thank you, Lady Lucy."

"Please, call me Lucy. I hate formalities this far from London."

"Yes, as you said. However, I don't think it appropriate."

As of yet, they hadn't garnered much attention, but Lucy would swear her mother listened intently. Thea, too.

"Why not? Are we not friends?" Lucy knew she was toeing the line.

"My dear, don't pester Lord Winchester for having impeccable manners," her mother broke in.

"Impeccable? If he's befriended Jonathan, he cannot care that strongly for manners—*or* witty conversation."

She heard the rumble of his quiet laughter. Triumph filled her.

"Lucy, please. I already feel a headache coming on," Lady Heath begged.

Lucy reined herself in, but not before beaming a victorious smile toward Lord Winchester.

His lips twitched in return, but that was all. He was determined to resist her. That was fine. She didn't think she could win him in one night. All the best things were worth fighting for.

After a subdued dinner, her mother developed a headache and retired, leaving Lucy and Thea to their own devices. It wasn't long before Lord Winchester and Jonathan joined them, her father having retired, as well.

"I hope it is nothing more than a headache," Thea said with concern.

"Mother has a fierce constitution and is rarely ill."

"That is true," Jonathan agreed. "How shall we entertain ourselves? Cards?"

"If you will excuse me, I'm going to step out for a smoke while our evening's entertainment is decided," Lord Winchester announced and stood to leave.

"How about charades?" Lucy suggested while she

observed him depart out of the corner of her eye. Thea and Jonathan nodded in agreement. "I feel a chill. I'm going to fetch my wrap. Thea, would you like one as well?"

Her friend nodded. "I will come with you."

"Don't leave poor Jonathan alone. I shall only be a moment."

Lucy casually left the room while Thea and Jonathan discussed games to play. Once she was no longer in sight, she hurried toward the nearest location a man might enjoy a smoke. Her father's study was just down the hall, and light spilled out from the open door. She slowed as she neared and then paused beside the door. He squatted before the fire, using the poker to rearrange the logs. Then he pulled a cheroot from his jacket and lit it in the fire. She watched him, mesmerized by the flickering light over his profile. She wanted to touch his face, to feel the planes of his cheeks under her hands, the sweep of his lips under her fingertips.

"I knew you'd come," he said quietly.

Lucy wasn't sure he was speaking to her, but she entered anyway and closed the door softly behind her. "I felt in need of another lecture regarding how I shouldn't be attracted to you."

His jaw tightened as he stood, but she had a feeling she amused him.

"Ah, so now you *are* willing to admit it."

"Yes. You are the last person I should hide it from."

"The first being your parents, your brother, your friends… Did you stop to consider why you *should* hide it?"

Lucy stopped by her father's favorite chair and lightly fingered the worn seam on the top corner as she considered his words. She knew he was trying to force her to admit he was unsuitable, but she didn't believe that for a moment. It was *she* her family didn't trust, not him.

"It isn't for the reasons you'd like it to be." She caught his stare and strolled forward until she stood before him, hands clasped before her. She wanted to reach out and touch him but feared his rejection.

"What is the reason, then?"

She bit her lip to hide a smile. "The first reason is that it's clear *you've* yet to accept your attraction to *me*."

His lips twitched, but his face remained impassive. "Have I? Or am I only trying to spare your feelings?"

Lucy stepped closer, testing the invisible bubble of intimate space between them. "Don't do me the disservice of playing gently with my feelings. Nothing I'm feeling is gentle."

He was silent for a moment, the air between them heavy and warm. Then he sighed and stepped back, turning toward the fire. "You're putting me in a very difficult position."

"I promise it will be worth it in the end," she said with a flirtatious smile.

"What end? Our wedding? White tulle and roses, a sprawling country house, a passel of children in the nursery... Is that what you envision when you look at me?" he asked angrily.

"I hadn't gotten that far."

"Then what is it you want, Lady Lucy? A roll in the grass, a dalliance under the noses of your family? Is that what excites you? I know your kind. You snub your nose at your gilded cage, determined to destroy it with no real idea of what it is like to live outside it."

"You've come to such a conclusion about me in such little time. Is that what my brother told you?"

"Your brother is under the impression that you suffer from the burden of having beauty *and* brains."

"And you don't agree."

"I tried to warn you. I am not your toy. I am not your diversion. There are serious repercussions for your actions. Permanent. Life altering.

"I *am* serious."

"Prove it."

"Gladly." Lucy closed the space between them, stepping between him and the hearth. She put one hand to his chest and set her lips to his. There was no explosion of emotions or all-consuming passion. His lips didn't move against hers, but at least they felt soft and warm. He stood as still as a statue. She pulled away and hid her disappointment behind a confident smile. "Not the best kiss I've ever had, nor the worst."

He tugged her away from the fire and put distance between them again. "Little girl, you are in over your fool head."

He left her standing in the study alone.

❧

Dean quit the house, stepping out a side door and into the cool evening air. He relit his forgotten cheroot and puffed hungrily.

Goddamn it.

He kicked a pebble out of his path and started walking. He moved in whatever direction took him the farthest away from Lady Lucy. She had no right, but did she care? No. She was dead set on pursuing him.

And that kiss? It had been awful, yet the moment her lips

had touched his, eager and pliant, his body had gone rigid with arousal, his head roaring with lust. If it had been any more inviting, he would have pulled her against him and shown her what a real kiss was. She was dangerous—terrifying. She should fear him, and yet he was the one running away.

Damn her.

His legs pumped aggressively as he climbed an upward sloping path toward the edge of the property. How had he gotten so far so fast? He stopped and caught his breath.

He wasn't a man who ran from things, but this ridiculous situation possessed risks he didn't usually face. It galled him to admit it, but he was afraid. He hated being forced into action, but that was exactly what had happened with Lenora. His father had wanted to force him to marry her, and Lenora had paid the price.

But Lucy was not Lenora, he reminded himself. Lucy was strong, with a spine of steel, and her family loved her. Dean was certain they would never push her into a marriage she didn't want. Lenora had been meek and rather melancholy, and she'd buckled under the pressure of her family. If Dean had known she'd take her own life, he could have stopped her. He could have done something to save her.

Guilt stabbed at him; the memories of Lenora never ceased to haunt him. And that's why he was he going to put a stop to this situation any way he could. He couldn't go through the same thing all over again. Lucy didn't deserve such heartache.

He sighed and started back toward the house. The cool air calmed him, and thinking with a clear head again, he considered his options. He could leave, but he didn't want to. He was enjoying his time with Rigsby and the pastoral pleasures of the countryside. Would he let a woman chase him away? No. Never.

He'd tried honesty with her, and that hadn't been enough. So if she wanted danger, he would show her danger. He would prove to her that she wanted nothing he had to offer.

When he reached the house, he pondered whether to return to the drawing room, where she likely waited. It would be a gamble, but he was sure she wouldn't make a fool of herself in front of her family. He decided to pretend the entire scene in the study simply hadn't occurred. From now on, *he* would be in control, and he would be the one to seek her out so they could be alone. Then he would prove to her, once and for all, that she had no business toying with a man like him.

CHAPTER 7

Lucy entered the drawing room wearing a shawl, another one in her hand for Thea. "I've returned at last," she announced.

"What took you so long?" Thea asked.

"I couldn't find my purple wrap."

"It's around your shoulders," Jonathan said.

"Well, yes, I eventually found it." She handed the spare wrap to Thea and sat beside her. "What game have you chosen for us to play?"

"We decided on cards. Jonathan doesn't believe Lord Winchester will enjoy charades."

"Very well. Cards it is. Where *is* Lord Winchester?"

Thea caught her eye as she stood and took a seat at the card table.

"He's having a smoke," Jonathan said as he poured himself a drink.

Lucy moved to the card table and shared a speaking glance with Thea. "Shall we begin without him?"

"I'll go see where he is," Jonathan said, departing the room.

"What took you so long?" Thea whispered.

Lucy shuffled the cards. "Exactly what you think."

"I don't know *what* to think. Have you been with Lord Winchester this entire time?"

"Goodness, no. I truly did have trouble finding my purple wrap."

"It was in my room."

"I remembered that, eventually."

"So, what happened with Lord Winchester?"

"Nothing good. He called me a little girl and told me I was in over my head."

Lucy refrained from mentioning the kiss. That humiliation didn't need to exist outside of her own head.

Thea grimaced. "That doesn't sound encouraging."

"No. It was not, but that doesn't mean I'm giving up."

"I found him. Call off the dogs," Jonathan said as he returned with Lord Winchester on his heels.

"Lord Winchester, we were afraid you'd gotten lost." Lucy attempted to sound disaffected by his presence.

He took the chair beside her and smiled. "I did, but I found my way back."

"Oh?" She didn't know what to make of that smile. It was friendly and inviting. He was a master of deception, it seemed.

He addressed the table in general and released her from his regard. "I took a short walk."

"Weren't you cold outside?" Thea asked.

"A bit."

Jonathan dealt the cards while they chatted, and Lucy wondered what had happened to Lord Winchester on his walk. He acted entirely different now. Before, she could always sense his reserve whenever she was around, but now...he seemed somehow willing?

She took her cards and focused on her hand. She didn't care whether she won or lost, only that his gaze kept sliding her way. At one point, he leaned back in his chair, broad shoulders angled her way, one leg stretched under the table, invading her foot space. If she wasn't careful, she might kick him, but instead, she kept imagining sliding her foot along his calf...

He was up to something; he had to be. He had been forthcoming with his lack of regard, and now Lucy would swear he was behaving like a rake on purpose. He hadn't done or said anything remotely flirtatious—he was far too skilled for such obvious tactics. But now he oozed sensuality, and he was definitely directing it her way.

Preposterous.

She threw her cards down on the table. "I don't want to play this game after all."

"Jonathan picked up her cards in dismay. "You just won!"

"I did?"

"Shall we play something else then? It's too early to retire," Thea said.

"Can we play anything else?"

"Why do you want to quit when you're ahead?" Lord Winchester asked.

His voice caught her attention, quieting the thoughts in her mind. She focused on him.

"I need action, movement. Anything but staring at a hand of cards."

Jonathan rolled his eyes. "What, do you want to play Pickled, like children?"

Lucy grinned. "Yes!"

"What is Pickled?" Thea asked.

"A childish game," Jonathan answered, rubbing his face. "One person hides, and the others look for them. When one finds the first player, they have to hide with them until the very last person finds the hidden group."

Thea frowned. "Why is it called Pickled?"

"Because you end up packed together like pickled fish in a jar," Jonathan grumbled.

"Oh."

"It's very fun," Lucy put in.

"And not the least bit appropriate," Jonathan added.

"Who is going to know? Is there anyone here you can't trust to keep a secret?"

"Beyond you, no. But—"

"Are you afraid you will lose your head if squished behind a chair with Thea?"

"What! No—my apologies, Thea. You are lovely." Jonathan turned to glare at his sister.

"Are you afraid Winchester will compromise me whilst hiding behind a curtain?" Lucy continued. She braved a glance at Lord Winchester, who hid a smile behind his fist.

Jonathan scowled at her. "I'm more worried about *you* compromising *him*."

"I solemnly swear I will not compromise Lord Winchester. Is that sufficient? May we play now?"

"I'm going to play billiards. Coming, Winchester?" Jonathan pushed back his chair.

"Come on, Rigsby. It might be entertaining. I haven't played since I was a boy."

Jonathan froze and stared at his friend in shock. "You *want* to play?"

Winchester shrugged lazily. "It might be a good opportunity to compromise your sister…or Miss Manton."

"That isn't the least bit funny, and I'd be worried about your intentions if I didn't know you so well," Jonathan retorted.

"There you have it. Let's relive some of our childhood magic," Lucy coaxed. Internally, she was vibrating with excitement. "I'll go first."

Her brother finally relented. "Fine. Stay on this floor."

She hurried from the room while Jonathan counted. She knew exactly where she wanted to hide. She fervently hoped that only one person would find her.

She counted to herself so she knew when to expect the others to begin searching for her. Tucked behind the Chinese screen in her father's study, she eagerly anticipated the sounds of approaching steps. She didn't have to wait long before hearing the muffled slide of Thea's slippers. They paused at the entry to the study and then entered.

Lucy cursed in her head when Thea popped her head around the screen.

"Oh!" she squeaked.

Lucy sighed. "Would it be awful if I asked you not to find me so that someone else could?"

"Do you think that is a good idea?"

"I think it's a splendid idea."

"What should I do?"

"Pretend you didn't find me."

Thea sighed and backed out from behind the screen. Lucy listened to her steps retreat from the study. Then it was silent.

After a time, she felt him in the room, but she didn't hear him.

"If I was a bored young woman, where would I hide?" Then he came around the corner of the screen.

"Are you going to compromise me, or did you already compromise Thea?"

"I can't compromise two women in one night?" He filled in the small space behind the screen, crowding her against the wall.

Lucy moved to make room for him, their clothing brushing every time they moved.

"I will make you marry her. Her family is terrible to her," Lucy whispered.

"Will you?"

"Even if I have to hold a gun to your back."

He held a finger to his lips.

Jonathan's muttering echoed from the hall.

"I already looked in there," Thea said to him

They both moved on. Lucy studied Lord Winchester, not sure what to do next. Would he kiss her? This was a complete turnaround from his earlier behavior, and she wasn't sure she believed it yet.

Then he bent forward, bringing his mouth close to her ear. "Alone at last."

Lucy licked her lips. "For the moment."

"What shall I do with you?"

She bit her lip. He towered over her, shadowing her in the protection of his body. She wanted to snuggle closer and breathe in more of his scent, but she resisted. She wanted to see exactly what *he* planned to do.

"What happened during your walk? You seem…different."

He was silent for a moment. "I changed my mind. I had intended to leave you alone for the sake of my friendship with your brother, but why deny myself? I've had *so* many women. What's one more?"

Lucy steeled herself. "I'm only one more woman to you?"

"One more conquest," he clarified.

She scanned his shadowed, unreadable expression.

"And my brother?"

"I can make more friends."

Lucy didn't believe him for a second, not when it came to his friendship with her brother. She'd seen too much of his kindness in her short acquaintance with him to believe he could be so callous. She held her tongue while she marshaled her thoughts.

He brought his hand to her hip.

"Carpe diem, *oui*?"

She felt the hand on her hip tighten.

"Aren't you afraid?"

"Of you? Never."

"Why not?"

"I see the goodness in your heart. You won't hurt me."

"You don't know me at all. I've been callous with many hearts."

"There is always time to start anew. You could start with mine, for instance."

He blinked slowly. "How about I start with your breasts? Such ripe fruit, begging for attention." He trailed one finger along the edge of her bodice, teasing her bare skin. "Have you ever been touched here by a man?"

Lucy swallowed and nodded.

"You have?" He sounded surprised.

"You are not my first rake."

"I won't be your last, either. You've a penchant for trouble."

"I'd rather risk trouble than live a boring life of safe unhappiness."

"You are naïve."

"Perhaps."

His finger explored the valley of her breasts.

"What libertine defiled your tender flesh?" he asked gruffly.

Lucy took a shallow breath, aware of the fiery trail of his finger. She'd never understood why men fell over themselves for a pair of breasts. They were bothersome at times, useful at others, and ornamental at best. She'd been groped before, and while the experience was distasteful, it hadn't been horrible. She had made sure Sir Granger regretted taking such a liberty with her.

"Why do you wish to know?"

He didn't answer. He just pressed his palm to her chest, over her heart.

She tried to sense the direction of his thoughts. He must feel the pounding of her heart.

"Are you afraid?" he asked.

"No."

"Why not?" His voice was harsh.

"I want you to touch me," Lucy whispered breathlessly.

He pulled his hand away and let go of her hip. "You don't know what you're saying."

"I do."

"I won't be gentle. I won't be kind. I'm not a good man."

"I don't believe you."

"I know, but it doesn't matter what you believe in that fool head of yours. I will simply take what I want."

"So will I." Lucy lifted her chin defiantly.

"Sorry to intrude." Thea tapped on the screen. "I really must join you now." She edged around the corner into the small space. Lucy pressed against the wall, and Lord Winchester squeezed himself tightly into a corner. "Your brother isn't very agreeable this evening. I tried to give you as much time as I could to, um...sort this out." She looked back and forth between them.

Lord Winchester didn't answer. Lucy could see his face now that he wasn't towering over her. His lips were pressed tightly together.

"Thank you, Thea."

Thea smiled awkwardly and kept her gaze averted from Lord Winchester.

"I give up. I'm going to bed," Jonathan called from the hall.

They all heard the sound of him stomping up the stairs.

Thea sighed with relief and slipped out from behind the screen. Lucy followed, but Lord Winchester stopped her by grabbing her hand.

"This is your last chance to prove you've more brains than beauty. Tell me to leave you alone, and I will."

Thea waited by the door, but they were still hidden by the screen.

Lucy stepped close to him, brushing her bodice against his chest. She caught his quick intake of breath and smiled. She bounced up to kiss his cheek and then darted away. She was grinning as she met Thea at the door and linked arms with her as they hurried toward the stairs.

"What is happening?" Thea whispered. "I shouldn't have allowed you two to be alone. I don't like this," she panted as Lucy tugged her up the stairs. "He didn't appear very pleased."

"He's not. He's doing his best to frighten me away."

Thea dragged her feet until Lucy stopped. "He seems a nice fellow. Perhaps he truly doesn't want attention from you. I don't like lying to your family, not when they've been so kind to me."

Lucy sighed. "I'm sorry. I won't ask you to do anything that makes you uncomfortable."

"Simply knowing that the two of you are... What *are* you doing?" Thea frowned in confusion.

"I don't know. He will try to convince me he is all wrong for me, and I will do the opposite."

"How?"

"I haven't the faintest idea."

"What makes you think he wants this from you?"

"Because if he didn't, he wouldn't be so angry about it. He is fighting it."

They began to walk again.

"Should I ask what happened back there?"

"No. It was nothing to be scandalized by, but from now on, I won't involve you, so you won't feel obligated to help me make an utter fool of myself."

"Thank you." Thea gave her a swift hug.

CHAPTER 8

Dean didn't leave the study. Instead, he poured himself a drink and lit another cheroot before settling back against the deeply padded chair near the fire. He crossed his boots and glowered at the flames until his eyes glassed over.

Damn her.

She wasn't going to make this easy. He was done playing the rake, but if he had to do it one last time, so be it. Since leaving his mistress, Countess Clive, behind in London, he'd thought about taking a long holiday from the female half of his species. A bored widow was child's play compared to Lady Lucy. She was relentless. It wouldn't be so difficult to fend her off if she weren't so damned beautiful and alluring. Her skin was as soft as petals, warm and inviting. She was so confident about what she wanted from him. So sure that he wanted her.

And she was bloody right. He could *taste* his want. His blood hummed with it. But wanting things and having them were two very different things. He might want her, but he did not intend to have her. She was going to be sorely disappointed at the end of this farcical seduction when he left her still a virgin, still unwed. That was, unless Farris came up to scratch, but Dean was confident the lad would fall far short of Lady Lucy's expectations.

Lucy.

Such a simple and pretty name for a girl—*woman*—who was complex and contained so much more. She was bored and beautiful, determined to ruin herself—but it wouldn't be with him.

Maybe he was exactly what she needed. A man with the experience and control to force her into accepting her place in life. He'd give her a taste of what she thought she wanted, and then show her it wasn't what she'd wanted at all. She would be running away from him in no time.

"I thought I'd find you here. Did you even bother to search for my sister?" Rigsby slumped into the opposite chair and mirrored his mood.

"I found her. Right there behind the Chinese screen."

Rigsby scowled. "I was going to look there, but Thea said she already had."

Dean shrugged. "She joined us."

"Cheaters." Rigsby stared at the fire thoughtfully. "I trust you didn't compromise anyone tonight?"

"Both of them, actually. But I should like to marry Miss Manton. Lucy gave me the impression she needs to escape her family. I could be her heroic—if tarnished—knight."

Rigsby chuckled. "They are horrendous. It's why Lucy demands her attendance at everything. I imagine when my sister does marry, God willing, she will insist her husband allow Thea to live with them. I'd be surprised if it isn't part of her marriage contract."

"She hasn't thought of it yet, that's why."

"You called her Lucy," Rigsby pointed out.

Dean blinked. "So I did. My apologies."

"It's fine. Make use of it while you can. She's right, you know. It gets tiring after a while. For the longest time, I refused to call Thea anything but Miss Manton. But then she became ingrained in our family. I relented with Dorothea, but that was still a mouthful, and now it's just Thea."

"Perhaps you should marry her and change her name for good?" Dean teased.

Rigsby grimaced. "She's like a sister to me. I could never bed her."

Dean took a sip of his drink. "Your sister has taken it upon herself to be her protector."

"Yes. Lucy does that quite often." Rigsby folded his arms behind his head and closed his eyes. "She hasn't bothered you, has she?"

"I beg your pardon?" Dean finished the last of his drink in one swallow.

"If she fancies playing the matchmaker between you and Thea, it will make your stay here a chore. You can tell me if she bothers you. She bothers me to no end."

Dean snorted. "You love her."

"I have to."

"No, you don't. There are plenty of siblings in the world who only tolerate each other. You and your sister have something special."

"I suppose. She can be entertaining to have around. She has a special way about her."

Dean scrutinized the bottom of his empty glass. "Yes, she does."

"But I'll be glad when she takes a husband. I won't have to

worry so much. As strong as she can be, there is always someone stronger."

Dean glanced at Rigsby, but he still had his eyes closed.

"Have you ever had to defend her?"

Rigsby furrowed his brow. "Once. Lord Harris. Do you remember him from university? He always had a mean streak. During her first season, he tried to drag her someplace private. Luckily, I was already down that path with Lady Walters." He grinned for a moment, then sobered. "Lucy fought him off, and he hit her."

Dean's hand tightened around his glass. He imagined planting his fist in Lord Harris's face. "What happened?"

"I met him at dawn and put a bullet in his shoulder."

Dean smiled. "That's how he lost the use of that arm?"

Rigsby grinned without opening his eyes. "Yes."

"Does she know?"

"No, but I did show her a few new punches after that, and lectured her about entering gardens with men until her ears bled. She still does it, but I haven't had to shoot anyone since then."

Dean chuckled as he stood to refill his glass. Then he changed his mind and set it down. He wasn't in the mood to drink anymore.

"I envy your family," he said thoughtfully.

"How is your father?"

"Still a righteous arse. He's been ill for years, but I'm convinced I'll die before him." Dean retook his seat.

Rigsby studied him now. "You still won't share why you hate each other?"

Dean shook his head. "I don't like to relive the past."

"Is it the past if it still hangs over you like a dark cloud?"

"Yes, because I refuse to discuss it. There's no changing it."

Yet despite his best intentions, the past regularly intruded into his life. Dean's relationship with his father was the exact opposite of Rigsby's and Lord Heath's.

Rigsby relented. "Fine. I won't ask, but I will say this. It's not the past if it's still hurting you."

Dean didn't respond to that. Instead, he relaxed back in his chair.

"Will you ride with us tomorrow?"

Dean nodded.

"Good. I'm off to bed. We'll go after breakfast."

"Sleep well," Dean muttered. He knew *he* wouldn't. He resisted the urge to go to bed. He wanted to avoid lying there staring at the canopy, his father's harsh voice ringing in his ears, Lenora's pale face circling his thoughts. There were only two remedies for his current problem, whiskey and sex, and he only had one at hand.

He pushed thoughts of his father away, and instead, called to mind an image of Lucy. Soft, sweet-smelling Lucy. He would ride tomorrow. And then he would take any opportunity that put her in his path and give them a chance to be alone.

§•

Lucy woke as the sun penetrated her curtains, the tendrils of a wonderful dream just leaving her consciousness. She'd been riding, soaring over the hills and mountains on a horse with wings. What a perfect way to begin the day.

Then inspiration struck, and she quickly devised a plan and bathed before slipping from her room to Thea's. She tapped on her door before entering, tiptoeing inside when there was no answer.

"Rise and shine, dearie. I've a marvelous plan."

Thea sat up in bed and blinked. "What are you doing in my room so early?"

Lucy tossed a garment on the bed.

Thea picked it up and inspected it. "These are boy's breeches."

"Jonathan's, to be exact. We're going riding."

"In breeches? No. Absolutely not." Thea dropped them in distaste and climbed out of bed.

"I promise you, it's extraordinary. The freedom of movement, the sensation, the power of being one with your horse."

"It doesn't surprise me that you've done this before, but I have not, and I don't intend to start this morning." Thea went to her washbasin and splashed water into the bowl. Then she rubbed it on her face aggressively. When she reached for the cloth, Lucy held it out to her.

"Please try them on, and then decide. I know you don't feel the same urge as I do to throw caution to the wind and experience new things, but this is—"

"Secretive and deceptive, or else you wouldn't be waking me at this hour. Did you concoct this plan with Winchester?"

Lucy sighed. "No." She followed Thea to her vanity and stood to the side while her friend brushed her hair.

"This has nothing to do with him." Lucy leaned on Thea's vanity. "Yes, I've done it before, and it's absolutely wonderful. I had a dream, Thea. I was flying on a winged horse, and this is as close as we will ever come to such a dream. Ride with me, please."

"This is madness."

"Try them on at least. Feel how much freedom they afford you before deciding. You love to ride as much as I do. There is nothing like riding astride in breeches after living in the prison of skirts."

"Fine. I will try them on."

Lucy jumped to her feet and fetched the breeches. She hurried Thea behind the dressing screen and waited. Eventually Thea came around the screen, clearly not pleased.

"Show me."

Thea shook her head. "It's indecent."

"Men wear them every day, and we have less to fill them with."

Thea gathered the hem of her nightgown to her waist. "That isn't true for all of us."

Lucy clasped her hands over her mouth. "You're a pocket Venus! I knew it!"

"What does that even mean?" Thea dropped her nightgown in shame and covered her lower extremities.

"It means you are lusciously round in all the right places."

Thea went behind the screen. "I've tried them. I still reject them."

"Wait," Lucy urged. "You have to walk around, feel the difference. Enjoy the freedom."

Thea sighed. She lifted her nightgown again and held it bunched around her waist. She paced around the room in jerky, agitated strides.

"Sit down and stand. Hop over that stool," Lucy instructed her.

Thea grudgingly obliged.

"Well?" Lucy was grinning.

"They *are* comfortable. And they do keep my legs warmer than stockings."

"Imagine riding astride. Jumping, galloping. Thea, there is nothing like it." Lucy walked forward and took her friend's hands. "Ride with me. We will leave right now, before my brother wakes. No one will see us."

"Except the grooms in the stables."

Lucy shrugged. "They've seen me do it plenty of times, and are easily bribed into silence."

Thea sighed. "Fine. Let's go ride in breeches like hoydens."

Lucy hugged her tightly and then stepped back to remove her dressing gown, already dressed in her own shirt and breeches.

"Does Jonathan know you pilfer his clothing?"

"He hasn't worn these since before he left for university. I've got more stashed in my room."

"Dare I ask why?"

"You don't really want to."

❧

Dean caught up with Rigsby on the stairs, and they entered the breakfast parlor together. The room was empty except for a lone footman, who promptly handed a note to Rigsby after they had taken their seats.

"What's this about?" He opened the note and scowled. "Bloody hell. What is that minx up to now?" He tossed his napkin from his lap and stood.

Dean sipped his coffee. "Something is wrong, I take it?"

"She's gone riding again without me." Rigsby bolted from the room.

Dean hurried after him in puzzlement. "Is there something dangerous about her riding alone on your father's land?"

"Yes. *Lucy* is dangerous. Any moment she chooses to slip her leash has great potential to be dangerous," Rigsby growled.

Dean bit back a smile. He couldn't wait to see what shenanigans she'd gotten herself into now. He kept a hearty stride while Rigsby hurried from the house in a flat-out run. How much trouble could she cause before ten in the morning?

When they reached the stable, they discovered that neither of the women were immediately present.

"Jenkins, where is my sister?"

"She's just outside, sir." The groom blushed and kick at the dirt.

"Ready our horses immediately. She's likely to bolt."

"Yes, sir."

Rigsby strode to the other end of the stable and pushed open the door.

Dean imagined that his friend's prediction would hold true, and he readied his own horse in giddy anticipation of chasing Lucy across the countryside. Hurrying outside, he froze in the open door of the stable as Rigsby confronted his sister.

"What in the—bloody hell, Lucy!" Rigsby threw his hands up in exasperation. "Thea, *you as well*? Father is going to keel over."

"Calm yourself, brother," Lucy said. "You act as if you didn't realize women have legs."

"I know very well that women have legs," he retorted, dragging his hands down his face. "What I don't understand—

Lord help me—is why you think it acceptable to traipse around in breeches? In front of Winchester, no less!"

Lucy threw him a mischievous glance, but Dean averted his gaze, heat climbing his neck as he fought the urge to ogle her lithe form in the soft buckskin breeches that begged him to run his hands over her curves.

"Interesting," she said, cocking her head to the side. "I was given the impression that Lord Winchester couldn't be scandalized. Look, Thea, we've embarrassed a notorious rake. Bravo!"

Thea turned three shades pinker and cowered behind her horse. "I wish to change immediately."

"There, you see? At least one of you has sense," Rigsby said through clenched teeth.

Lucy stepped nearer her brother to whisper something. Dean was just barely able to hear them.

"She does not like her figure. Compliment her."

"You want me to ogle Thea? Are you mad?" he whispered back, aghast.

"Heavens no. Just…appreciate it."

"I—" Rigsby snapped his mouth shut. He turned sharply and strode to where Thea stood beside her horse, her forehead pressed against the mare's neck.

Since they were out of earshot, Dean took his time, while Lucy's back was turned, to indulge himself, admiring the feminine curve of her hip, the tight breeches lovingly displaying her womanly-yet-athletic hips and legs. He hadn't considered dresses such a hindrance to women before, but as she mounted her horse, it occurred to him how heavy and confining those skirts must be. Much like the societal constraints she tried so valiantly to defy. No matter their differences, he understood that much about her, and if he were in her place, he'd rebel, too.

Rigsby marched back to his horse, his face set in a stony mask and his ears tipped with red. Dean hid a smirk and remained silent as Rigsby climbed into his saddle. Lucy and Thea rode off ahead and Dean and Rigsby followed, the space between the two sets of riders growing.

He watched her crest a hill and ride out of sight. She rode wild and free, a beautiful sight to behold. Without speaking, he and Rigsby had moved away from the direction of his sister but still circled around to keep track of her whereabouts.

Rigsby was in a foul mood, and Dean wondered if perhaps he was having conflicting feelings about Miss Manton. She did have a charming figure in breeches, he had noticed, but it was Lucy who had held his attention. Where Miss Manton had cowered in embarrassment over being so exposed, Lucy had strutted with confidence. His gaze had followed her whenever she and her brother were not looking.

She was not as voluptuous as Miss Manton. She was taller by half a head, and her build was more svelte. She still had sweetly curving hips, however, with an inverted, heart-shaped derriere, but her legs were lean and strong, unusual for a woman of her station. She must do a lot of riding and other physically enduring activities. He pulled his mind away from that thought before he went too far into imaginings of the physically enduring activities that he'd enjoy performing with her.

When he turned his horse down the hill and rode into the small valley, Rigsby was resting his horse by a small copse of trees at the bottom. Dean reined in beside him.

"Are we going to follow them?"

Rigsby shrugged.

"Are we going to discuss why you're acting so sullen after speaking with Miss Manton?"

"No, we're not."

"Let me guess. She is everything you ever wanted, and you are only now just realizing it?"

Rigsby scowled at him. "Bite your tongue."

Dean chuckled.

"There is nothing remotely amusing about that scenario. Yes, she has the curves of Aphrodite but, good God—I don't even want to acknowledge that about her any more than I want to acknowledge my sister's feminine anatomy. They are the same in my mind, but somehow I can't stop seeing her in those bloody breeches!"

"Miss Manton is not your sister. She is a perfectly eligible wife for you."

Rigsby gawped at him in horror. "Don't ever say such a thing to me. She is very much my sister in spirit, and I don't want that to change." He shuddered. "If I close my eyes, I can see her bottom half, and my head and other parts are quite pleased, but then I see her face and—"

"She isn't a startling beauty, but don't be unkind."

"It's not that. She's too familiar to me. I become disgusted with myself."

"I see," Dean said, though he didn't, really. He didn't have any sisters. He vaguely remembered his aunts and cousins from his childhood. His father had done an expert job at pushing everyone away after his mother had died. She had been the one to insist on the importance of family.

"Perhaps if you spoke to her honestly about your brotherly regard for her, then you might become comfortable in her presence, regardless of what she is wearing. I've no doubt she views you in the same light."

Rigsby was silent as he stared in the direction his sister and Thea had disappeared. "Perhaps."

"Let's catch up with them. The sooner this awkwardness is over, the better."

Dean wasn't sure why he was in a hurry to be near them again. With Rigsby and Miss Manton present, he wouldn't have a chance to be alone with Lucy.

"All right. They won't be too far ahead. Those clouds closing in are not promising for further riding, anyhow."

CHAPTER 9

"Does it hurt very much?"

Thea clutched her hand to her chest. "Of course! A bee stung me! It's bloody dreadful!"

"Bravo!" Lucy smiled. "I've never heard you swear before."

Thea sniffled.

"Oh, dear. Return without me, and I will walk back. Gibbs has a salve for the horses that is marvelous for stings, as well."

"I don't feel comfortable leaving you. It's going to rain."

Lucy scanned the darkening sky. "Yes, it is, but a little rain never harmed me."

"A little lightning might."

Lucy grimaced. "I will be fine. It's *you* I'm worried about."

"That's all very well, but it's you *I* worry about because you never worry about yourself," Thea said testily.

"Fine. We will walk back together."

"'Tis my fault Penny startled when I screamed. I feel so terrible she's sprained her leg. I can endure the discomfort if she can."

Lucy patted her horse's neck. She held the reins of both horses while Thea remained on her horse and started the trek back toward the stables. They weren't that far away, but there was no chance they would beat the rain at this pace.

Eventually they settled for silence. The only sounds were those of nature and Thea's gentle sniffs. Lucy knew her friend was doing her best not to cry. She was grateful for her breeches and boots as she hiked across the field with greater strides than a heavy riding costume would have allowed.

"We could both ride Esmerelda," Thea offered.

"Yes, but I'm enjoying the walk. And we'd still have to go just as slow for Penny's sake."

"That is true."

Lucy paused. She could here other riders approaching. "We may have company."

Thea twisted in her seat to look. "It's Jonathan and Lord Winchester!"

Lucy felt a buzz of excitement go through her. She waited for them to approach, trying to compose herself enough to appear unaffected by his presence.

***

"What happened?" Jonathan asked after they rode up, inspecting both women in alarm.

"Thea was stung by a bee, and Penny has a sprain," Lucy answered with a sigh.

"A bee! Where?" Jonathan edged closer, and Thea held out her hand. The back of it was growing swollen and red. He grimaced. "We need to get you home immediately."

"It only hurts a little," Thea lied, her discomfort evident by her red nose and teary eyes.

"That was what I advised, but Thea refused to leave me, and Penny can't do more than walk."

"Have you been stung before, Miss Manton?" Dean asked. He'd heard of some people dying from bee stings.

Thea shook her head.

"Are you feeling all right other than your hand being hurt?"

"I believe so," she said, still sniffling.

"Rigsby, you should escort her back quickly. I will make the slower return with Lady Lucy," he recommended.

Jonathan nodded. "Can you hold the reins?" he asked Thea.

"Yes, I think so."

"Let's be off, then. We'll see you back at the house. I'll send a groom with another horse to trade places."

"That isn't necessary." Lucy sighed. "I can walk back with Penny. Don't make a poor groom walk in the rain. He doesn't have access to a warm bath like I do."

Jonathan nodded. "My thanks, Winchester."

Then he and Thea took off at a trot.

"That was very considerate of you."

"What was?" Lucy squinted up at him.

"Thinking of the groom's comfort."

She shrugged. "I suppose I could always request a bath be heated for him, but I can just as easily walk my horse back myself and spare everyone the extra trouble."

Dean looked up at the sky. When he glanced back at her, she had walked her horse a ways ahead of him, so he caught up with her. "You should ride, and I'll walk," he suggested, as he dismounted and walked behind her. He took a moment to let himself appreciate the view of her backside.

"I'm fine walking."

He moved to walk beside her, sandwiched between their horses. "How did Penny sprain her leg?" he wondered aloud.

"She startled when Thea screamed."

"Ah. I sincerely hope Miss Manton is not allergic to bee venom."

Lucy frowned in concern. "I didn't know that was possible."

"It is. How many times have you been stung?"

"Three," she answered.

"Three?"

"Mm-hmm. Twice on the foot, and once on the arm."

"The foot?"

"I enjoy walking barefoot at times, especially during the summer, when the lawn is freshly cut. Have you ever been stung?"

"Six times. All on the hands."

"Six?" She laughed in surprise. "What were you doing?"

"Stealing bits of honeycomb from the hive." He glanced at her sideways and grinned, surprised at how comfortable he felt with her right now. This was their first unguarded conversation about things other than boring pleasantries. They were alone, and yet he was perfectly at ease.

"How many times has Rigsby been stung?" he asked her profile.

"To my knowledge, none."

Dean chuckled. "To my knowledge, once."

"When and where?" Lucy demanded, smiling back at him.

DAYNA QUINCE

He sucked in a breath. That smile of hers was dangerous. It was genuine and…wicked. A shiver went down his spine. If she kept smiling at him like that, he wasn't responsible for the things he might do. He exhaled slowly.

"We were on break from school and he was stung on the —" He stopped and coughed. "Never mind."

"No. You brought it up. You have to tell me now." Lucy shoved him playfully, but he didn't budge.

He gave her a wicked grin. "He was stung on the arse while swimming nude."

Lucy threw her head back and laughed.

They had stopped walking, and he hadn't realized that laughter could increase a woman's beauty, but like everything she did, Lucy laughed without restraint, without concern for the judgment of others. She did it with her whole being, with pure delight.

He wanted to kiss her and swallow all her lovely laughter, but then he instantly sobered. He shouldn't be thinking like that. His plan was to appall her out of her infatuation with him, not kiss her, or any of the other things that kept devilishly slipping into his mind when he thought of her.

When she finally stopped laughing, he saw her throat move with a swallow as she collected herself. Wariness crept into her gaze. Good. She should be guarded. He turned and started walking again, expecting her to follow. He needed to get ahold of himself.

He paused when she didn't immediately follow. She was scrutinizing the sky, holding out her hand. The light had a strange luminosity, and it made her skin vibrant and soft. Clouds smothered the sun, and a drop of rain slid down Dean's neck even as one landed in her hand. Rumbling thunder echoed in the distance.

"You should take my horse back," he said angrily, not feeling like himself, now that there was the threat of a proper storm brewing.

"No." She frowned. "Penny is my horse. I will take care of her. You're welcome to return home if you're afraid of a little rain." She walked past him.

He scowled after her and caught up with her. He let his irritation smother the other emotions that had taken hold of him. He could think clearer that way. She stumbled over a molehill, and he grabbed her arm to keep her from falling.

"I'm fine." She pulled her arm away.

They had stopped again and were facing each other. The rain had begun to fall in a light drizzle around them.

"Do you think I would let you walk back alone?"

"I don't know what you would do. First, you want to get away from me, and now you are acting differently. I'm trying to ferret out what is real and what isn't. I don't know you well enough to tell the difference."

"That is precisely my point."

"I'd be happy to discuss it with you once we've reached shelter, but for now, I'd like to keep moving. I'm sure you would agree." She turned to walk again.

The sky was growing darker, but the misting rain had ceased for a moment. She was right; whatever he had intended to achieve with her would not happen out here in a field with the threat of a downpour. He shook his head and followed her. There was a crack and then the rumble of thunder, closer than before. Her horse shied right, knocking Lucy to the ground.

Dean cursed and ran to her.

"Penny!" Lucy glared at her horse from the ground as it bolted to the shelter of a tree a few meters away.

He offered her his hand, and she let him pull her up. What she didn't expect was for him to put his arms around her.

"You're walking trouble. I cannot let you return alone."

"I didn't foresee Penny being spooked again, but other than that, what could possibly happen?"

His hand swept over her rear, brushing off the dirt. "A man will see you and want to ravish you."

"That is absurd," she said, scoffing, but her voice had gone weak and breathy.

"It's not. That very thought has crossed my mind a dozen times in the last hour."

Her gaze moved from her hands on his chest to meet his. "You're lying. You just want to frighten me."

Dean wished that it were true. But try though he might to separate what he wanted to do and what he was trying to do to frighten her, things had become muddled in his mind. Both involved him seducing her to some degree.

Then their weight shifted, he lost his balance, and they both toppled to the ground. He retained enough control to guide her down gently, but he still landed on top of her, holding her with one arm and catching himself from falling on her with the other.

She gasped as she hit the ground, but Dean guessed it was more from surprise than hurt. "You must have been standing over a burrow, and it collapsed."

"That's very plausible, but it doesn't explain why you are still on top of me."

He smiled crookedly. "Because I want to be."

Her breath was coming in short pants. He adjusted himself on top of her, their legs tangling together, their hips lining up naturally. He wanted to groan in pain and pleasure. He could almost mistake the flash of fire in her eyes for arousal.

"Let me tell you exactly what a man like me does with a woman like you underneath him. I've got you in my arms. I can feel the cradle of your body in these damned breeches. Do you know what that makes me want to do?"

She shook her head and licked her lips.

He bit back a groan. "It makes me want to bed you, Lucy. I'd like to be in a literal bed, bending you over the coverlet and slowly peeling these breeches over your hips until I have you bared just enough to take you, but here we are in a field. I could still flip you over and take you from behind, like our ancestors would have done. Quick and rough. You'd cry my name and startle the birds from their nests with moans of ecstasy. Or, I could take off my jacket and lay it on the ground. Peel the clothes from your body, making love to you slowly, keeping you warm and sheltering you from the elements while I leaned over you, your thighs open beneath me, welcoming my thrusts. If I took you like that, with you naked beneath me, I could enjoy the sight of your breasts, taste them like delicacies set out before me."

He moved his hips just barely enough to enunciate the pressure of his groin against hers. "Would you like that?"

She took in a shaky breath and nodded.

Dean clenched his jaw. He dipped his chin and hid his expression from her, a swell of acute need overtaking him. She felt so damn good under him, radiating heat from her sex straight to his manhood, and it took everything in his power not to respond, not to feed the beast inside him that wanted to do everything he had said. He was losing. He pushed himself away from her, falling back on his haunches.

She slowly sat up and dusted off her hands. "You didn't have to stop," she said quietly.

"I know I didn't."

"Then why did you?"

"Because I know what I'm doing, and you don't. You're a naïve virgin who doesn't get the simple fact that you are at the mercy of the world."

"And you want to show me that?"

He stood and pulled her to her feet, not pulling her against him this time. "I want to show you how cruel it can be."

"You mean how cruel *you* can be," she stated.

He paused and then turned his back to her. "Yes."

He knew when she started to walk away, and he followed her to collect her damn horse. She was soothing her mare when he joined her under the branches of a tree.

"It would be faster to ride back with you given the circumstances. She certainly had no trouble getting here swiftly, but I don't want her to bear any extra weight."

He eyed her horse with dislike. She was right, of course. The patter of rain on leaves filled the silence.

"Let's be quick about it," he growled.

He mounted his horse and pulled her up. The breeches tightened over her rear as she settled back against him. There may as well have been nothing between them. He immediately dismounted.

"What's wrong?"

He ripped off his jacket and tossed it to her. "Put this

around you. We're going to be cold and wet by the time we get back."

She did as she was told, and he climbed back into the saddle, bunching the tail of his jacket between them. "Are you ready?"

"Yes."

He walked his horse to hers and she leaned over to grab the reins. Then they left the shelter of the tree and raced the raindrops back to the stables.

§⁂

Lucy ignored the drops that pelted her face and focused on the experience of his body cradling hers. His smell, a heady mixture of leather, wood smoke, shaving soap, and horse, filled her head. The jacket rode up between them and her hips slid back into his. They moved in one motion, a rolling jolt, and each time, her bottom rubbed against his groin. His hold around her tightened, his knuckles turning white as they gripped the reins. The firming ridge of his manhood became impossible to ignore.

It was the best ride of her life, and it ended far too quickly.

When they arrived at the stables, he rode directly inside as a groom held the door. The rain fell heavily now, and their clothing had soaked through. He dismounted as a groom took their horses' reins. Shockingly, he did not help her dismount, but went immediately to the tack room.

Lucy jumped down ungracefully and followed him. She found him drying his hair with a blanket. She tossed his jacket on the bales of straw beside him and folded her arms. "You're really doing a poor job of convincing me."

He turned slowly to face her, holding the blanket in front of him. Lucy was dying to see what he might be hiding.

"I beg your pardon?"

"You want to convince me that you're too old for me, too worldly and experienced to trifle with a mere girl like me." Lucy rolled her eyes. "It's not working. I can see that you want me. I can *feel* how much you do. And as much as you wish otherwise, I'm not fooled, and I'm not scared."

She closed the tack room door and stepped closer to him. What she was doing was absolutely mad, but she was emboldened by his words, pushed to act by the proof of his desire for her. He had tried to push her away, but now she was pushing back.

"You said things that you thought would frighten me, but I'm not frightened. I like it." She stepped forward. "I may be a virgin, but I believe that, at the right time, with the right man, all the things that are supposed to scare me won't. Because I will know, in here"—she put a hand to her heart—"that it is right."

His gaze dropped to her hand. He stared at her so intensely her skin grew hot. Then he dropped the blanket. Lucy sucked in a breath and glanced down. She could see the rigid evidence of his manhood. She brought her gaze back to his, but the look on his face was furious and wild. She had a moment of panic when he strode forward, backing her against the tack room door. He touched his forehead to hers, the only part of him to touch her, and yet she couldn't move.

"You think you have any idea what I'm feeling based on what *you* see and feel?" He took her hand and brought it to his manhood.

Lucy gasped, shock and delight filling her.

"Touch me."

"I—I don't know how—"

He molded her fingers around him, closing his eyes briefly as he squeezed her hand around him. Then he opened them again. He let go of her hand and brought his to her breasts. He cupped them, dragging his thumbs over her erect nipples. He clamped his mouth over hers, taking advantage of her surprise. He swept his tongue over hers, pulling away the second she tried to engage him back.

"You think what you see and feel here is based on tender emotions? That is where you and I differ. I'm a man with a large sexual appetite. Being close to any woman of passable beauty, especially dressed in revealing clothing, will stir my arousal. But the truth is, I don't care who that woman is, only that she is willing and that I will be satisfied adequately."

He pressed his lips to her neck and closed his eyes again.

She was still gripping his manhood, albeit weakly, but if she had the inclination to do more, to run her hand down his length and squeeze, he might well spill his seed all over himself. He was only holding on by a prayer, but she took her hand away, and he could suddenly feel her withdrawing from the moment.

"You're a dog."

"Yes." He pulled away with relief, stepping back to pick up the blanket. He handed it to her. "Though a dog might have a tad more loyalty than I do."

She threw the blanket around her shoulders and pulled it tightly about her. Dean was feeling better by the moment. The more she closed herself off from him, the better he could temper his own desire. He gathered another blanket from the shelving and covered himself. He heard her leave the tack room without uttering another word. Then he collapsed onto a bale of straw and put his head in his hands. If she pushed him any further, she would surely be the death of him.

CHAPTER 10

Lucy sat in her bath with her fist curled tightly. She could still feel him in her hand, and though she ought to be disgusted with that entire scene in the tack room, she wasn't. She was actually beginning to think something was wrong with her. Yes, his words had stung. The bitter feelings they had evoked had not waned, but at the same time, she still yearned for all the things he had said, for the way her body had felt when she'd touched him and he'd touched her.

After seeing to Thea, who was recuperating with a cup of tea and poultice in her room, Lucy had gone to her own for a hot bath and session of sulking. She stared at the rain falling on her window and willed herself to cry, to feel ashamed of her behavior. The most she accomplished was a bit of mistiness in her eyes and not an ounce of shame. There had to be something wrong with her. She was a shameless wanton. This explained why she couldn't behave like a proper young lady, why the worst sort of men always sought her out.

She closed her eyes and sank lower in the water, but it was

no longer hot enough to soothe her. She climbed out of the tub and toweled herself off, putting on her dressing gown and standing before her mirror. She studied her reflection and tried to reason with the woman who stared back at her.

"Who are you, and what have you done with the charmed life I had before?"

Things had been easy before Winchester arrived—boring, even. Did she want that again? She hadn't been unhappy, but she had been aware that something was missing. And then when Winchester had arrived, she'd been sure it was him.

Her heart had shifted to make room for him. Now that room was empty, an open wound she didn't know how to heal. She focused on her reflection and tilted her head to the side, pulling the ties of her robe loose and separating the halves slowly. She saw her body in a way she never had before, as a woman, the type of woman Lord Winchester would take to bed.

He'd touched her breasts. She imagined him doing so now, but without clothing, or the filthy tack room around them. She remembered the feel of his hands. She recalled the hot press of his lips on her neck and pictured them moving down to her breasts. She'd never known that could be pleasurable. Twice now he'd touched them, and she wanted him to do it again.

Lucy jumped when a knock fell on her door and swiftly tied her robe. "Come in."

Her cheeks burned as she sat at her vanity and brushed her hair. Marigold smiled in greeting and waved in the footman to remove the tub. Normally, they talked, but this time, Lucy remained quiet. Marigold departed after helping her dress, but Lucy didn't feel the urge to leave her room just yet. Hunger gnawed at her, but she didn't want to see Lord Winchester yet, not when she didn't know how to behave around him after this morning. She needed time to come to a resolution over her muddled feelings.

She decided to set her feelings aside enough to visit her mother. Her father sat with her on the bed reading the paper.

"Are you unwell?" Lucy asked.

"Just a small chill," Lady Heath replied.

"It's nothing concerning," her father assured her.

Relieved, Lucy left her mother to rest and went to see to Thea, who was still in her room, nursing her swollen hand.

"Does it still hurt?" Lucy asked.

Thea sat on her bed and paged through an old newspaper. "It throbs and aches, but not as painfully as before. Did you get terribly wet walking back?"

Lucy bit her cheek. Thea had said she didn't want to know about things between her and Winchester, so she swallowed the urge to tell all. "A tad. We ended up riding back together after Penny got spooked again and knocked me down."

"On the same horse?"

Lucy kept her features composed and nodded.

Thea blinked. "That's all?"

"What do you mean, *that's all*? What did you hear?"

Thea leaned forward. "Is there something worth hearing?"

Lucy folded her arms. "You said you didn't want to know."

"Yes, but I didn't think you'd be able to resist informing me."

"Well, if you *must* know, he tried again to persuade me to abandon any sentiments I may or may not have toward him."

Thea frowned. "May not have? Have you had a change of heart?"

Lucy shrugged.

Thea set the paper aside. "Really?"

"I'm beginning to think I have poor judgment, or perhaps I'm just broken."

"Broken?" Thea asked in alarm. "What on earth did he say to you?"

"I'm not going to repeat it. It was very distasteful."

"He hurt you."

"He certainly tried."

Thea crossed her arms. "I won't stand for that."

Lucy smiled at Thea's militant frown. "He is only being honest about who he is. Most men we've crossed paths with in London would not be so forthcoming."

"I won't tolerate someone calling you broken."

"He didn't *say* I was broken. Upon reflection of the whole scene, I came to that conclusion myself."

It surprised Lucy when Thea leaned forward and covered her hand with her own. "You are *not* broken. You are a wild and colorful bird. It isn't fair how we're sorted into boxes of what is proper behavior. You are so many things—courageous, lovely, stubborn, but never broken."

At that, Lucy cried. She'd always felt like she was Thea's protector, but it was apparent that Thea was actually hers, as well. She mopped up her tears with her sleeve and gave her friend a swift hug.

"Thank you."

Thea sniffed and wiped her nose with the sleeve of her dressing gown. "This weather is dismal, but I bet we can find a way to entertain ourselves in the house."

"We can have a special dinner in the conservatory and listen to the rain?"

"And Marigold can teach us more dancing here in my

room!" Thea added.

"That is a splendid idea—but what shall we do until then?"

Thea shrugged. "Marigold said moving my hand will help dissipate the swelling, but it's not pleasant."

Lucy thought about what could keep Thea's hands moving without causing too much discomfort. "Let's see what fun can be had in the music room."

After they spent a lovely afternoon playing music, Lucy excitedly planned a special dinner for just her and Thea. She could completely relax and be herself. She didn't want to admit that she was avoiding Lord Winchester, but she was. She wasn't sure how to handle him after the incident that morning, and she wasn't yet ready to try.

She met Thea at the stairs, and they made their way to the conservatory in companionable silence. When they entered, Lucy halted in surprise.

"What are you doing here?"

She wasn't sure whom she'd meant to address, as both her brother and Lord Winchester stood from the table.

"Dying of starvation waiting for you," Jonathan returned.

She focused on Winchester, her heart thudding painfully, and Thea had to tug her into motion.

Lucy could not look away from him, the vibrant green of his gaze so intense it pulled her to him by some unnamable kinetic force. She hadn't realized she'd grabbed Thea's hand until her friend patted hers in reassurance.

Whatever he'd made her feel with his callous words, she longed for him still. She wanted to be near him, to collide with his body over and over, like the waves on the bluff, as long as it meant she was still near him.

She was being ridiculous, she knew. All the things he'd

said were painfully true, but still, that wouldn't stop her. She couldn't give up what her heart wanted so badly. She yanked her attention from him, not bothering to greet him or her brother, and took her seat at the small, intimate table.

"I didn't realize this was a private engagement. I was only alerted when the dining room was devoid of food and a footman directed us here," Lord Winchester said.

"It's nothing, just something out of the ordinary to do since Mother and Father are not dining with us," Lucy replied.

"I checked on her before I came down," Jonathan said. "She will be back to full health in no time at all."

Lucy nodded and remained quiet as the footman poured her wine and set out the first course.

"Is your hand much improved, Miss Manton?"

Winchester's deep voice snagged her attention. She studied him more carefully now that he wasn't looking directly at her.

"Yes, thank you," Thea answered. "I hope the return walk was not horribly uncomfortable."

"Not at all."

He lies so easily, Lucy thought. Though what did she expect him to say? The truth? She returned her attention to her food, not hungry anymore. The tapping of the rain on the conservatory glass was exactly as she had hoped, rhythmic and soothing, but not enough to lift her mood. Her bother kept shooting her odd glances, and worse still, Winchester appeared completely at ease. It annoyed her to no end.

"Lucy, would you stroll with me?"

She turned to Jonathan and blinked. "Stroll?"

"Around the conservatory."

"If you insist."

Her brother offered his arm and waited until they had moved far enough from the table to talk privately.

"She'll be fine."

"Who?" Lucy still couldn't wrap her mind around the fact that her brother had asked her to stroll with him. Did he know something? Had Winchester spoken to him about her?

"Mother."

"Of course," she answered, relaxing at his reply.

As they moved along a wall of panes, Lucy watched their reflection.

"You are quiet tonight," Jonathan remarked. "I thought perhaps you were worried."

Shamefully, she hadn't given her mother very much thought at all. She checked in on her periodically, but deep down, she was certain she would be well again. As certain as she was that the sun would rise tomorrow. It was thoughts of Winchester that plagued her. She'd revisited their conversation and the whole awful scenario over and over, reliving his touches, loathing the words that had stolen the pleasure from the moment. Seeing him so soon was salt in the wound, but it also proved something. These feelings she was having—they were unshakable. What did that mean? She'd told Thea she was in love, but perhaps she was only being dramatic. Was this what love felt like? She swallowed back a sigh of defeat. Jonathan was speaking to her, but she hadn't heard a word he'd said.

"I have faith," he said simply.

"Yes," Lucy said absently. "Mother will be better in no time at all."

"Lucy." He turned to face her and grabbed her shoulders, giving her a little shake.

She blinked up at him in annoyance.

"What the devil is wrong with you? Are you ill?"

"No! Take your hands off me before I blacken your eye."

He obeyed, but he rolled his eyes as he did so. Then he folded his arms and tried to appear intimidating.

Lucy sighed. He hated when she ignored him. She saw the reflection of Thea and Lord Winchester at the table, their heads bent together.

Her brother stepped into her line of sight.

"Why are you acting so strange?"

"I can't have an off evening? What do you expect of me? Perhaps I'm entering my feminine time." She enjoyed his immediate expression of distaste. Talk of women's issues always frightened him away.

"I'm sorry I asked or even showed the slightest interest in your emotional well-being. I stupidly thought you were worried over Mother, and only sought to comfort you."

"You did?" Lucy asked, startled. "Thank you, but I'm entirely capable of managing my own emotional state."

"Very well." He took her hand and set it on his arm.

She glanced past him as they turned to finish their circuit of the room and found Thea and Lord Winchester still bent with their heads together. Thea spoke vigorously, but so quietly that Lucy couldn't hear a word.

※

"I'd like to have a word with you, my lord."

"Certainly, Miss Manton." Out of the corner of his eye, he tracked Lucy's progress around the room.

Miss Manton had leaned closer, so he did as well.

"You hurt her," she said simply.

Dean contemplated pretending he didn't have a clue whom she was talking about and then abandoned the idea.

"Her? You mean Lady Lucy?"

Miss Manton glared at him. "I won't pretend to know precisely what is happening between the two of you, and I don't want to. Lucy is and always will be too exotic for the role she must play in society, but I trust her—that is, until today. She said something that broke my heart to hear."

"My apologies. I don't mean to hurt her." He didn't know what else to say. He wasn't sure how much Lucy had confided in her friend or how detailed she'd been. He kept his expression carefully impassive.

Miss Manton leaned forward farther. "I believe you, but I don't think you truly understand her."

"What was it she said that you found so alarming?"

She pressed her lips together in a firm line. "She said she felt broken."

"Broken? Because of me?" A shudder of self-loathing moved through him. "I'm trying to save her from herself, not break her."

"You *didn't* break her, but she's decided she is broken because of what she feels for you."

He slumped back in his chair.

"Whatever it is you said, find another way to say it that doesn't destroy who she is...or I'm afraid I will be inclined to kill you."

He had snorted at that, but a small part of him believed her. When he caught sight of Lucy again, she snapped her head forward.

"Billiards?" Dean suggested to Rigsby as he returned to the table.

"Excellent idea. Will you join us, ladies?"

Lucy shook her head. "I'd like to read. Thea?"

"I, as well. I may retire early. The rain makes me sleepy."

The men bid them goodnight and departed.

CHAPTER 11

Dean held the match to his cheroot and took a long draw and then tossed the match in the ashtray. He thanked the heavens the ladies had chosen not to join them at billiards. He needed to think without distraction. He didn't want to hurt Lucy, and he didn't want to damage his friendship with Rigsby, but this was all her fault, really. The moment he'd arrived, she'd targeted him and refused to take no for an answer. And now she felt broken because of her misguided infatuation with him? She had forced his hand, and the last time a woman had done that, it had ripped two families apart.

He remained lost in his thoughts as they began their game, but Rigsby didn't seem to mind. They played a few rounds and then retired. Dean climbed the stairs behind Rigsby and headed toward the guest wing. A lone candle stood guard over the dim hall from a side table. He stared at it dubiously and blew it out. Then he entered his room, closed the door, and unbuttoned his jacket.

"Don't," a feminine voice said. *Her* voice.

He turned toward the hearth, where she sat in a chair, her brown wool dress disguising her.

"Are you out of your mind?" he growled at her.

"I'm starting to think so."

"What are you doing in my room? Trapping me into marriage? Is Miss Manton leading your parents this way at this very moment?" he asked, furious. He was deliberately keeping his voice low, when what he really wanted was to roar in anger at her.

"Calm down. I wouldn't do anything so malicious. I just want to talk."

He glared daggers at her, but she didn't flinch. He turned and removed his jacket anyway. Then he prowled the room, lighting more candles.

"You've five minutes, and then I will escort you back to your own room."

"Fine, but the escort isn't necessary."

He didn't argue with her. The less time spent alone together, the better.

"Out with it."

"Thea told me what she told you."

"And?"

"And I thought we should discuss it."

Broken. She felt broken for wanting him. Was there any greater insult? It only proved everything he'd said. He was bad for her.

"I don't believe there is anything more to say. I've proved my point." His gaze wandered over her. She looked warm and inviting in the firelight—in *any* light. When she was present, he simply gravitated toward her. Now he turned his back to her instead, determined to keep as much distance between them as possible.

"What Thea said… I've changed my mind."

"Have you now?" he tossed over his shoulder. "And what does it have to do with me?"

She stood up from the chair. Dean cursed the air he breathed and prayed she kept her distance. He watched her as she circled around the chair and stood by the window. She touched the glass with one finger and then pressed her palm to it.

"I know it's possible you won't feel the way I do, maybe ever, but I'm not done experiencing these feelings. I'm not finished with *you*. I will keep trying to convince you, because deep down, I feel this could be something great. You *must* feel it, too. How can anything so lovely, so momentous, be completely unrequited? This is my chance for…"

He heard her voice catch, and he could feel the tension between them, a live current of emotion. It pulled at him again, but he resisted—he *must* resist her. Her words struck him like lashes from a whip, but he waited for her to finish, sensing what she would say next would be an even bigger blow.

"My chance to have great love."

He closed his eyes, nearly shaking with the effort it took to not react.

Love.

Such an awful word. It changed people, chewed them up and spit them out.

Please, God, don't let her fall in love with me.

"I can't give up so easily," she said.

Dean took a breath. "I *will* break you. A dalliance with me

—which is all it could ever be—will ruin any chance you have at the life you deserve."

She turned away from the glass and stepped toward him. He turned away from her, gripping the edge of his dresser with white knuckles.

"I'm not the girl you think I am. I'm beginning to believe I'm not meant for the placid, genteel life I've been born to. I want more than that." Her voice rose. "I know I won't regret risking it all for love, but I *will* regret not trying."

"Is that all you wanted to say?" He schooled his features into a bitter, hard mask and turned to face her, arms folded. "Your time is up," he said.

She stood there, lips pinched, eyes snapping with fire. Then she exhaled. It was shivery and light, and Dean imagined she would make the same sound if he trailed kisses down her naked spine.

"One more thing." She moved to the door and put her hand on the knob. "When you're ready to face all that you fight so valiantly to deny both of us, I'll be waiting for you."

He focused on the fire as the door closed behind her, waiting until the urge to break everything within reach passed before he moved, and then he promptly began to pack his clothes.

❧

Lucy had only just returned to her room when there was a pounding on her door. She threw her dressing gown over her dress and wiped the tears from her cheeks before opening it.

"Jonathan?"

"It's Mother. I've summoned the doctor."

Lucy's knees went slack, and Jonathan caught her arm and slowed her as she hit the floor. Then he squatted before her and took her face in his hands.

"Lucy. Can you hear me?"

She stared at him, but his voice was so far away. Then Thea's face appeared beside his and Lucy closed her eyes to stop the world from spinning before her. When she opened them, Jonathan lifted her under her arms and helped her to the bed.

"I don't understand," she said. "She was fine earlier. How could that have changed so rapidly?"

"Her cough has worsened. Father had me send for Mr. Mallock."

"That old fool?"

"Dr. Bradley is not in residence," Jonathan replied, grimacing.

"I want to see her," Lucy demanded.

"I thought you might. Father said you shouldn't, though, until we are sure it isn't catching."

She grabbed his sleeve. "Don't let them send me away. If I'm not here and... I will never forgive you."

"You will do as you are told to do for once in your life," he snapped back at her. "Thea. Stay with her. I will await Mr. Mallock and see that he doesn't make things worse. I will inform you if anything changes. Otherwise, try and get some sleep."

As if that were even remotely possible now.

"Did he wake you with that unnecessary banging upon my door?" Lucy asked Thea.

"He did, but I wouldn't call it unnecessary. You sleep like the dead."

"I wasn't asleep. I'm not even in my nightgown." She stood and removed her robe.

"Whyever not? What were you—" Thea clamped her mouth shut. "I suppose I can hazard a guess."

"Good. Then nothing need be said further."

Thea sat back on the bed and opened a book from the pile on the nightstand. Lucy paced the room, chewing at her nails while she waited for Jonathan to return. After enough time had passed for her to lose her sanity, he finally knocked on her door.

"Why aren't you sleeping?"

"Don't be daft. How could I possibly sleep when Mother is sick? May I see her now?"

"She's sleeping. It's almost midnight, after all. Mr. Mallock gave her laudanum."

Lucy sat at the foot of her bed. "Well, what did he say?"

Her brother stood before her with his hands on his hips. "It's Duncan Lung. You both have to leave until she recovers."

"Why?" Lucy cried. "She needs me to help care for her."

"You've never had Duncan Lung, and neither has Thea, since she didn't grow up here."

"Neither have you. I've never even heard of Duncan Lung. Why do you get to stay?" she retorted.

"Mr. Mallock says it is catching for women because of their weaker constitutions."

Thea and Lucy glared at him.

"I don't make the rules, but Father insists that you go to Aunt Harriet's until Mother is deemed recovered."

"How long will that take?"

"Three weeks, approximately."

Lucy scowled. She would bet her left arm Duncan Lung was as real as unicorns. "Thea will stay with me?"

Jonathan nodded.

"Must we leave tonight?"

Aunt Harriet's was only a four-hour carriage ride, but Lucy didn't want to make the journey in the middle of the night.

"I've yet to ask Winchester to escort you, but you will leave first thing in the morning. Go to bed before you weaken your constitution any further," Jonathan decreed.

Thea squeezed her hand as she passed and returned to her own room. Lucy undressed slowly when she was alone, fresh tears of worry falling for her mother. The one silver lining was that Lord Winchester would be accompanying them, and that meant more time with him. Mostly blind and deaf, Aunt Harriet was as good a chaperone as a blindfolded horse.

Dean had finished packing and now sat slouched in the chair Lucy had vacated earlier, an empty glass dangling from his hand. The knocking on his door jerked him into alertness.

"It's Rigsby."

"If you've come to shoot me, I don't blame you," Dean muttered, opening the door.

"Beg pardon?" Rigsby frowned at him. "Did you say something?"

"Is something amiss?"

Rigsby moved past him into the room. Dean closed the door.

"I've come to ask a favor. My mother has Duncan Lung,

and Lucy and Thea must vacate the house. I need you to escort them to my Aunt Harriet's."

"Duncan Lung?" Dean had never heard of it. Frankly, it sounded like malarkey.

"Will you do it? You'd leave with the girls at first light. It's only four hours by carriage."

"Of course," Dean said automatically. How could he refuse? Never mind that he had been planning his own escape only moments ago.

"Thank you. It is a weight off my shoulders to know Lucy and Thea will be in your care. Aunt Harriet is rather…eccentric and inattentive. Lucy would try to escape at the first opportunity and return home, and Mr. Mallock was adamant they not remain in the house."

Dean hesitated at the prospect of having Lucy placed directly in his hands—unchaperoned—but Rigsby wouldn't ask it of him if he didn't trust him. Dean would not betray that trust, no matter how much Lucy tempted him.

"I'm honored to help in any way I can. I'm certain your mother will recover swiftly, and your sister and Miss Manton will return soon."

Dean wasn't certain he'd remain after that. He needed to get away and purge these unsettling feelings, but for the time being, he'd view Lucy and Miss Manton as under his protection.

"Mr. Mallock estimates three weeks before they can return."

Son of a bitch, Dean swore in his head. "I am at your service for however long I'm needed."

"I am forever in your debt." Rigsby clapped him on the

shoulder. "I won't keep you from your bed any longer. I'll have everything ready for tomorrow morning."

Dean nodded and closed the door behind his friend. He picked up his glass from the floor and refilled it. He gulped it down and then poured another. He didn't know what to expect on the morrow, but he was certain it would be the greatest trial of his life.

CHAPTER 12

Lucy and Thea were already inside the carriage when he hefted himself in the next morning. They were huddled together under a blanket, looking fresher than meadow flowers after a spring rain.

"Good morning." His voice sounded like gravel under a boot, so he cleared his bone-dry throat.

"You reek of liquor," Lucy said.

"Thank you. You smell of..." He leaned forward and sniffed. "Orange blossom?"

"Very good," she said, smiling.

He managed to crinkle his eyes in return, but even that hurt. His whole body ached like he'd traded places with a rug for a beating.

Then Lucy turned and whispered something in Miss Manton's ear, and they both giggled, stopping only when he squinted at them.

"Are you not scared for your mother?"

Lucy sobered instantly. "Yes and no. Mr. Mallock is a

crackpot. His brand of medicine frightens me, but I'm certain my mother will improve."

"How?" He genuinely wanted to know. He'd been certain as a boy that his mother would never leave him, but then she had. Illness didn't care for the prayers of children.

"I just know. I know it in my heart," she answered him.

He raised his brows and hoped she was right. Then he covered his eyes to block out the light and closed his gritty lids. If God had any mercy left for him, he would sleep the entire trip.

§**.

Lucy grinned as she watched him. She thought she heard a faint snore.

"Is he asleep?" Thea whispered in her ear.

"I think so."

"Why do you suppose he drank so heavily last night?"

"Because he's going to be alone with us—mainly me—for three weeks."

"And your Aunt Harriet," Thea reminded her.

"My Aunt Harriet is mostly blind and half deaf. She has very little furniture or rugs, and everything is situated in a precise manner so she knows exactly where it is."

"Oh dear. Who is going to chaperone us?"

"We don't need a chaperone."

"Well, I don't, but you certainly do."

"And somehow that task has fallen to poor Winchester."

His snoring grew louder.

"He has the right idea. I didn't sleep well, did you?" Thea asked.

"Of course not. I snuck into my parents' room to see my mother."

"You didn't! You could get sick!"

"Unlikely. I had to see her. She was sleeping soundly, and her color was good. I predict she will be better much sooner than three weeks."

"I hope you are right. I don't think Lord Winchester and I are up to the task of keeping you out of trouble for that long."

"He's the only trouble I want to get into, Thea." Lucy sighed, leaned back against the squabs, and closed her eyes.

Thea yawned. "That's what I'm afraid of."

§🍃

Dean woke when the carriage made a sharp turn. The crunch of crushed shell under wheels revealed that they had reached their destination. He peered out the window, charmed by the thatched-roof cottage that greeted him. Across from him, Lucy and Miss Manton slept soundly. Miss Manton's glasses were askew. He reached across and gently plucked them from her face, setting them on the seat beside him. When he looked back up, he found Lucy smiling at him.

"Careful, your kindness is showing."

He shifted uncomfortably. "I never said I wasn't capable of kindness."

"No, but you've tried very hard to mask it from me."

"We need to set some rules for how we are to comport ourselves around each other."

"You sound like my governess."

"An admirable woman, I'm sure."

"What's that?" Thea asked, stretching and rubbing her eyes.

Dean held her glasses out for her.

"Oh, thank you."

"Good morning, Miss Manton."

"Good morning, Lord Winchester. We are here?"

"Yes."

A moment later, the carriage rocked to a halt, and Dean kicked down the steps and stepped out. He turned to hand Lucy down and then Miss Manton.

"It's lovely!" Miss Manton cheered.

"It is. It's my favorite of all the properties," Lucy said.

"Your father owns the land?" he asked

She nodded as she took in the surroundings. "I used to spend summers here as a child, and we frequently visit when not in London. As my aunt's vision has deteriorated, she's requested that things be kept exactly as she remembered them. The same flowers replanted every year, the same round shrubs instead of ornamental characters. It's not entailed. He bought it for her, and one day it will be mine."

Then her aunt's butler stepped out to welcome them.

"Stow, please forgive the intrusion. My mother has taken ill, and we've been banished from the house."

"We are always ready to accommodate you, Lady Lucy. Your aunt will be thrilled to have you."

"Lord Winchester is an acquaintance of my brother's, and agreed to be our escort." Lucy turned to Winchester. "Will you be staying?"

"Your brother entrusted your welfare to me. I will be staying until I return you to your family."

Stow waved them inside. "I will show you to the parlor."

"There is only one footman, Gregory, and two maids," Lucy said, waving to encompass the sparse front hall.

Stow waited by the open door to announce them. "Ma'am, Lady Lucy, Miss Manton, and Lord Winchester have arrived," he said loudly.

"Oh?"

A woman with white frizzy hair and fine wrinkles lacing her face turned at the announcement of visitors with surprise. "How delightful!"

"Aunt Harriet." Lucy came forward and took her hands. "I've a letter to read to you from my father."

"You've come to stay for a time?"

"Three weeks, approximately. Mother is sick, and the surgeon recommended Thea and I not stay."

"Oh, dear. Will she be all right?"

"I have every faith she will be fine," Lucy reassured her.

"How are you, Miss Manton? Married yet?"

"No, not yet, Aunt Harriet."

"The right one will come along soon." She patted Thea's hand. "It is so good to have you here. Did I hear Stow correctly? There is a gentleman among you?"

Dean wasn't sure how much she could see, or if she could see anything at all. "It is a pleasure, ma'am. I apologize for the sudden intrusion." He stepped forward and bent over one of her hands.

"Oh my," Aunt Harriet gasped. "Your voice is so deep and masculine," she said, tittering.

He smiled. "Thank you." He could hear Lucy and Miss Manton giggling behind him.

Aunt Harriet put her hand up near his face. "May I?"

"She wants to touch your face to feel what you look like,"

Lucy informed him over his shoulder. She moved to sit beside her aunt, and Thea moved behind the settee to watch.

Dean shifted uncomfortably.

"Certainly," he agreed.

She put her hands to his face delicately and examined his features. Then she stared vaguely over his shoulder with a growing smile.

"Oh my. You are a handsome one," she said, as she finished her inspection.

He stepped back in relief and stood by an upholstered chair.

"Which of you are going to marry him?"

Thea and Lucy both sputtered and blushed, and Dean coughed to cover his laughter.

"He's only here as an escort, Aunt," Lucy replied, giggling.

"Well, what is the problem? Are you already betrothed?"

"No." Dean cleared his throat.

"He is perfect for you, Lucy. Wild and handsome, just like you."

Lucy turned three shades redder. "That's enough, aunt. You've embarrassed poor Winchester."

"Ah, perhaps he is afflicted with ideas of permanent bache-lorhood. I shall do my best to convince him otherwise."

"I'm sorry," Lucy mouthed silently to him.

He cracked a smile and nodded.

"I'm so excited you're all here!" Aunt Harriet exclaimed.

*

Later that afternoon, Lucy found him smoking a cheroot on the small terrace at the back of the cottage.

"Still here, I see."

"I'm not scared away so easily."

"That's encouraging." She leaned back against the wall, just as he was doing.

He glanced sideways at her. "That reminds me. We didn't finish our discussion this morning in the carriage."

"What discussion?" Lucy feigned innocence and examined her nails.

"The discussion about your behavior."

"My behavior? Was it I who—" She stopped. She couldn't finish the sentence.

He turned to her, leaning one shoulder against the wall. He crossed his feet and folded his arms. "You were saying?"

She gritted her teeth. "I was going to say, it wasn't *I* who pinned *you* to the tack room door and took liberties."

"Granted, but it is *you* who wants *me* to take liberties, and it is *you* who puts yourself before *me* like a worm dangling above a hungry fish."

She turned to face him with a smug smile. "Are you saying you can't resist me?"

He straightened, taking one more pull on his cheroot and then stamping it out with his boot. "That isn't what I meant."

"A worm dangling above a hungry fish. Your analogy is awful, but I do believe that is what you meant, or you wouldn't have said it."

"I misspoke," he ground out.

Lucy stepped closer and put a hand on the lapel of his jacket. "Shall I test you? Actions speak louder than words, you know."

He scowled at her. "You can't test me or any man. We will always take what is offered to us."

"By that reasoning, if my aunt slipped into your bed tonight, you'd be overcome with animal tendencies?"

"That's not the same."

"What if Thea did it? Is age a factor, then?"

His scowl deepened. "If you try to slip into my bed tonight or any night, I will drag you out by the ear. Like a child."

"But you said—"

"You are under my protection. I will not forsake my honor."

"Now you're honorable *and* kind? You're doing a very poor job convincing me how bad you are for me."

"Damn it. Have you heard a single word I've said? Are you that spoiled—that manipulative, that you disregard my every attempt to convince you that your admiration is not wanted? Has no one ever told you no?"

Lucy stepped back. His words struck a painful chord. "I've been told no many times. It's my father's favorite word."

He moved closer to her, so close his forehead almost touched hers. "But has a man told you no? Has a man ever refused your advances?"

"According to you, that is an impossibility," Lucy returned smartly. "Either I am irresistible—which I've never considered myself to be—or it is *you* who cannot resist *me*, and that scares you. It can't be both."

He stepped back. She would have called it a revelation, but his expression of astonishment quickly switched to one of anger.

"Even if I wanted to bed you, consider this. Not only would such an event destroy your reputation, because there would be no offer of marriage, but it would also destroy the standing of your family and my friendship with your brother—

something I hold in very high regard. Are you willing to hurt so many of the people you care about for your selfish desires? Before you answer, let me tell you one thing. I've done that very thing, and more than ten years have passed, and I still can't face them. Are you really ready to give up everything you love for one brief moment?"

Lucy was about to say yes, but then she clamped her lips shut. The pain etched into his face said far more than his words. What had he done?

"No."

"Good. That is the smartest thing you've ever said." He turned away from her and peered out over the garden.

She saw him wrestle his emotions back into place. She'd never seen him so vulnerable before.

"I'm sorry," she muttered as she turned away and slipped back into the parlor.

CHAPTER 13

A week passed, the most boring week of his entire life. Lucy had been on her best behavior. She didn't smile at him or lean in close and say things that set his skin on fire. Instead, she read, played the pianoforte for her aunt, and sang with her angel's voice. She rode daily, took long walks, and at the end of the evening, she retired early. It should have been heaven, but it was hell. When she wasn't paying any attention to him, Dean found himself so entranced by her he could barely walk without bumping into walls. Thea had trumped him in games of chess every evening, because whenever Lucy played or sang or read aloud to her aunt, he was watching her, distracted.

Every other day they received a letter about her mother. This day was no different, but this time, she was not smiling lightly as she read it. Instead, a line appeared between her brows as she moved her lips. He waited for her to inform them of the trouble, but she only stood and walked to the window. Afternoon rain hammered on the roof while they lingered over tea. Dean finally set his cup down and went to her side.

"Is something wrong?"

She turned away from him and left the parlor.

"Where has she gone?" Aunt Harriet glanced around in confusion. "What is in the letter?"

Thea patted her hand. "I'm sure it's nothing."

"Go find her, Winchester!" Harriet demanded. "She mustn't go outside in this weather."

Dean frowned. *He* shouldn't be the one to comfort her. "She wouldn't go outside, would she? She clearly just wants some time alone."

Thea shook her head at him.

"She fancies the bench under the arbor when she's upset," Aunt Harriet said, shooing him away.

He sighed and went to fetch his great coat. Then he grabbed an umbrella and ventured out into the rain. The arbor was just out of view of the cottage, and as Aunt Harriet had predicted, there he found Lucy, shivering on the damp bench.

"You'll catch your death." He held the umbrella over her. "You should come inside at once."

"Please go away."

He crouched down in front of her and peered into her face. Raindrops and tears merged into rivulets as they raced down her cheeks.

"I've been sent to rescue you. I cannot return without you."

He shrugged out of his coat and swirled it over her head and shoulders. He tried to position the umbrella over them both, but while his head remained dry, his back did not.

"Come inside on your own, or I will toss you over my shoulder and carry you in."

He saw her lips twitch, and his gut tightened.

"I don't need a hero."

"I'm not trying to be heroic."

"And yet here you are, braving the elements to save me from the evil rain."

He chuckled. "Call me your knight in dripping armor."

She laughed, but then sobered. "I thought she'd be better by now."

"The doctor said three weeks."

A sob broke through her voice. "I wanted him to be wrong."

"Hold this." He handed her the umbrella. Then he stood and bent to scoop her up into his arms.

"What are you doing?" she said, gasping.

"Rescuing you, and myself. My arse is freezing."

He carried her back into the parlor, but Thea and Aunt Harriet were nowhere to be found. The fire had been built up nice and high, so he set her down in front of it and poured her a cup of tea. The pot was fresh and hot. What was going on here? He shivered, reminded of his wet backside. He poured himself a cup and went to stand near the fire.

"What did the letter say?"

She took a sip before answering. "She isn't worse, but she isn't better. Mr. Mallock wants to bleed her—the imbecile—but Father and Jonathan refuse. I want to be there."

"She's well taken care of."

"Yes, but if something changes—if I weren't there to say goodbye…"

The cup shook in her hands. Dean took it from her and set it on the mantle. He stepped close and rubbed her arms and then impulsively hugged her, resting his cheek on her head. She was the perfect height for it.

"I would get you there in time. By horse, we could cut the

time in half, if not more. But it doesn't matter, because she will be fine."

She nodded and sobbed. He let her cry, but just as quickly as she had begun, she finished. He fished his handkerchief out of his pocket and handed it to her. She thanked him with a watery smile and dabbed at her remaining tears.

"Your nose is red," he told her. He didn't know why, but he found it adorable.

"It does that on occasion."

He snorted.

"Are you laughing at my nose?"

He poked it. "It's cute."

She swatted his hand away. "Don't do that."

"Did it hurt?" He grabbed her chin and kissed the tip of her nose. "Is that better?"

Color filled her cheeks. He'd touched far more than her nose before, and yet she turned bright pink now.

He began to chuckle. "Now your cheeks are pink. Do they hurt, too?" He kissed one, and then the other. They were chaste kisses, kisses he'd never given a woman before, and yet he no longer felt his cold, damp clothing. Warmth gathered in the pit of his stomach, like he'd just downed a glass of whiskey.

"What are you doing?" she asked, followed by a sigh.

He grabbed her chin again and tipped her face up to examine it. "If you're not careful, you'll soon be the shade of a raspberry."

"I dislike raspberries. They're sour."

"Ridiculous. Raspberries are delicious. Plump and sweet." As he said the words, his thumb brushed her bottom lip, and his gaze dropped to her mouth.

She released another sigh. He licked his lips and reversed

direction. He'd been moments away from kissing her. He let go of her chin and stepped back.

"I've got to change." He paused before turning away from her. "Will you be all right?"

She nodded.

§&

Lucy pulled his coat tighter around her and breathed in the scent that clung to the inside. Her patience had been rewarded. The entire week she'd done nothing to warrant even a raised brow from him, and look what it had revealed? He'd kept his distance but watched her constantly. Now he was kissing her? Those kisses were so telling.

Joy bloomed inside her. Her fears of unrequited love gasped their last breath. He wanted her, it was undeniable. His behavior didn't come from an admission of love, but it was a seed upon which something could grow.

He'd been so tender just now. She was giddy at the memory of his touch. She entered the hall and hung his coat to dry and then climbed the stairs to her room and found Thea there, reading.

"What are you doing in here?"

"There's a leak in my room."

"Oh dear. Well, the bed is roomy enough for both of us. What is my aunt up to?"

"She is resting. She is determined to see a match between the two of you. It was her idea to send him to you, and then we left the parlor so you would be alone when you returned."

"Well, her tactics are working. I thought he was going to kiss me—and, he did, on my nose and cheeks—but those were nothing compared to the kiss he *wanted* to give me. I'd become worried that the affection I felt really was one-sided, but after today…"

"He is stubborn, just like you. He has to come to his own conclusions."

"I suppose, but restraining myself is so difficult."

"I know, dear. Your aunt and I can tell. What of the letter?"

"Oh! I almost forgot." Lucy lost some of her joy. "Mother isn't worse, but she isn't better. I was expecting more encouraging news."

"So soon?"

"That's what Winchester said, more or less."

"Well, as long as we keep ourselves busy, time will move quicker."

"Have you heard from your family?" Lucy wondered.

"No, but the season is about to end. It's a busy time."

"So it is," Lucy murmured. She kept her judgments about Thea's family to herself now.

"I did receive a letter from Heather. She returned to Scotland early. She says the season is not as enjoyable without us. She will return to debut Violet next year."

"I don't doubt that. I can't remember the last letter I received from Rose or Charlotte. It worries me."

"I received a missive from Rose," Thea admitted.

"When?"

"At the start of the season."

"Why didn't you tell me?"

Thea set her book down. "She asked me not to."

"Why?"

Thea looked down for a moment. "I'm not sure I should say."

"I don't understand. I thought we were all friends?"

"We *are* all friends, but our circumstances are vastly different. Heather is a duchess, while you and the twins are daughters from wealthy families."

Lucy had a sinking feeling. "Is she in trouble?"

"No." Thea sighed. "She is a companion now."

Lucy chose her words carefully. "That isn't so terrible."

"From the perspective of someone who doesn't have a family to support her and no marriage prospects, it isn't so lovely. She will never marry. She will forever be indebted to caring for someone."

Lucy sheepishly glanced away. She couldn't help the family she'd been born into. She'd never put herself on opposite spectrums from her friends, but it seemed as if Thea had.

"She shouldn't be ashamed," Lucy murmured as she changed her dress. She didn't know what else to say, so she chose to return to the parlor rather than remain in awkward silence with her friend.

CHAPTER 14

The awkwardness remained for another week. The house was silent and dull, even when the rain departed and the sun returned. Lucy set out for a walk, past the grounds of the cottage garden and well into the surrounding rural hills. She knew her surroundings, as she'd marched these hills with Jonathan many times. The ground was soft from the rain, squishing beneath her feet as she slogged up one hill to its crest. She peered down at the old ruins of a mill where nothing stood but some stubborn walls, but it was picturesque enough to invite her to sit for a spell.

She carefully picked her way down the slope. Reaching the bottom, she found the remnants of a stone wall low enough to sit comfortably. A valley stretched out before her, fresh and green. She tried not to think of bothersome things—she'd done enough of that while at the cottage. Instead, she took a deep breath and valiantly tried to clear her mind.

"You shouldn't be out this far alone," Winchester said from somewhere behind her.

"Did it ever occur to you that I came all the way out here to be alone?"

"Yes, but that doesn't make it any safer."

Lucy looked around. "Is there anyone here to hurt me?" she called out.

Silence.

"Are you satisfied? I can find my way back, thank you."

"You know I won't leave you here alone."

She could hear the clop of his horse's hooves coming down the damp hill. He rode through the ruins slowly, coming up behind her. She would ignore him, even though she knew he wouldn't go away. She was going to sit here and enjoy the view for as long as she wished. She'd been a bloody saint for the past two weeks, and she didn't have any more patience.

"I've news from your brother."

"I've already read the letter."

"No, you haven't. It just arrived."

She bolted to her feet as dread filled her. "What did it say?"

He grinned. "You may return home."

Lucy almost collapsed from relief. She could have sworn the earth under her feet moved. "Thank heavens. She is well, then?"

"Well enough to demand your return, or she'll come and fetch you home herself."

Lucy giggled. "She *is* well, then." She tried to step forward, but her foot had sunken into the mud. She wheeled her arms to regain her balance, stumbling backward when she managed to yank her foot from the mud, only to find herself in deeper in it.

"Are you stuck?" he asked, dismounting from his horse.

"I think I'm sinking. I—" The ground buckled, and her

scream was drowned out by a loud, sucking noise. She threw herself forward, terror seizing her as she slid down into a void with nothing to cling to but slippery mud and clumps of grass.

He leapt over the wall and slid forward to catch her hand before she was out of reach and the earth had a chance to swallow her.

"I've got you." He wedged his boots into the mud, finding a thicker layer of clay and rock to hold him. "Give me your other hand."

"I'm trying," she cried. She kicked at the cloying mud, searching for leverage. She managed to claw her way up enough to give him her other hand, her torso level with his boots now.

He sat back into the mud and pulled her up to his chest, wrapping his arms around her.

They rested for a moment, panting from exertion.

"We're not safe yet," he said. "Use me to climb out."

"What about you?" she asked as she clung to him, her arms looped around his neck.

"I'll get out after you."

Lucy briefly pressed her forehead to his and said a prayer and then shimmied her way up his body. In any other time and place, she would have loved this moment, but the rancid taste of mud was still inside her mouth. He helped her up, gripping her waist and then her hips to give her a boost. Her dress made it difficult, as it was weighted by the wet mud. She lifted her knee to his shoulder, and then he pushed her up over his head to dryer ground.

She was finally free and holding onto the wall. She turned to help him as he flipped himself over and climbed out of the sinkhole. From this perspective, she felt lucky to be alive.

What had once been an open clearing of grass was now a gaping hole. Thank God he'd come along when he had, or she might not be here anymore. Her heart throbbed as he staggered toward her, boots and clothing caked in mud.

"Are you all right?" he asked hoarsely, his hand cupping her face, his thumb sweeping over the arc of her cheekbone.

Lucy nodded, her throat tightening with emotion. "And you?"

He'd risked his life for her, coming to her rescue without any hesitation. Was it her specifically that he cared about, or was it just his innate goodness? She wanted to be the reason. She wanted his heroic action to be driven by his need for her... or his love of her. Her eyes burned with the threat of tears. She sucked in a breath and reined in her emotions

"I'm well, but we should move farther away. We don't know how much more will cave in." He pulled her to her feet and helped her to the horse, which stamped in fear as Winchester helped her into the saddle and climbed up behind her.

"Here we are again," Lucy commented, though she felt wildly shaken and significantly more unattractive this time, caked as she was in smelly mud.

He didn't comment but just charged the horse up the hill.

"What on earth was that?" Lucy asked as they reached the top and she took a relieved breath. She leaned back against him, still needing to feel his strength.

"Underneath could have been a natural cave or a cellar of sorts from long ago," he answered, his tone unreadable.

"It used to be a mill," Lucy murmured.

"I see. You shouldn't venture there again," he said, this

time with an edge to his voice, as if he were disciplining and errant child.

"I won't, I assure you."

They had quite the story to tell Thea and Aunt Harriet when they returned. It served to ease the tension between herself and Thea, and now that Lucy was out of danger and in a hot bath, she could think more about Dean and his stoicism on the ride back. Had he been as afraid as she was? She'd glimpsed a flash of emotion in his eyes when he'd held her face and stroked her cheek. But what was it? Fear? Love? Relief? She wished she could be as circumspect with her emotions. Instead, they spilled out of her in torrents, sweeping her away in floods of angst, joy, and unbridled lust.

She sank farther into the steamy water.

Why did love always sound so wonderful in poetry? It was horrid, akin to repeated stabs with a sewing needle over one's entire body and then being dipped in lemon juice.

Feeling homesick on top of lovesick only made it worse. Lucy eagerly awaited the journey home. Winchester had said they would leave tomorrow morning if there was no more rain. The roads were still horrendously muddy, and she could appreciate the wisdom in choosing to wait another day.

Being that it was their last night, Aunt Harriet wanted to make it a special occasion. They dined in a sea of candlelight, and after dinner was over, they pushed the parlor furniture aside for dancing. This Lucy relished the most. As Winchester was the only gentleman about, it was up to him to dance with all of them.

Dean scanned the room dubiously. Lucy caught his eye, and she grinned playfully as she took her seat at the pianoforte. A brutal pang of want startled him. Today's events had shaken him to his bones. The sight of her clinging to the mud, about to disappear before his eyes would torment him for a thousand sleepless nights.

He could admit now he'd been afraid, even as he'd helped her to safety. He'd wanted to crush her to him and hold her for hours, assuring himself of her continued existence. What would the world be without this vibrant and enchanting woman?

As much as he wanted to deny his feelings for her, she'd somehow slipped under his guard and demanded access. And when denied, she'd simply scaled the wall, picked a few locks, and made herself comfortable in the hallowed recesses of his heart.

In the beginning, he'd set out to keep her from being hurt, but what he hadn't realized until now was how much leaving her would damage *him*. The only way he could still go through it was remembering that it was the best thing for *her*.

"Aunt Harriet will have the first dance."

"A waltz will do," the lady chimed in.

Dean wanted to groan, but he'd become quite fond of Aunt Harriet, and if it was dancing she wanted, it was dancing she would get.

"Do you waltz, Lord Winchester?" Lucy asked.

"Of course. Can you play a waltz?"

"Of course," she answered smugly.

He took his place in the middle of the open floor with Aunt Harriet and bowed. She curtsied and then she stepped close to him. *Too* close. She put one hand in his, the other on his shoulder, and laid her cheek upon his chest. He could hear giggling in the background as the music started. He moved in slow revolutions, unsure Aunt Harriet would be able to keep up, but she kept pace with him, and surprisingly, Dean enjoyed the dance immensely. As the music came to a flourish and ended, he bowed before her and kissed her hand.

She batted her eyelashes at him. "You rogue."

He chuckled as he awaited his next partner. He turned to Miss Manton and held out his hand. "I do believe the next dance is mine?"

"Oh no," Thea said, shaking her head. "I'm only here to spectate."

"*Everyone* will dance," Aunt Harriet decreed from her throne-like chair.

"I'll play a reel, Thea. You love those."

Thea reluctantly stood from her chair.

"You wound me." Dean put a hand to his heart.

Thea took her place. "Wait until I trample your feet, and then see how you feel."

It was odd only having two people on the floor for a country reel, but they mucked their way through it, finishing with more laughter than proper dance steps.

࠙

"Another!" Lucy cheered and played another reel. Winchester and Thea obliged. She hoped if she kept playing, they'd simply grow tired of dancing before it was her turn. She longed to dance with him, but at the same time, she was afraid. It was easier to hide behind the pianoforte and poke fun than to look him in the eye, let alone touch him. Her heart had begun to ache for him. These two weeks of holding herself back had shown her how vulnerable she felt not engaging him.

What would she feel if he left? What would she do? Pine for him? She had never liked the heroines in books who did so, but she feared she would soon learn what it meant to have to love someone from a distance and survive on memory alone.

But if she thought she would escape a dance with him, she thought wrong. She'd forgotten how conniving her aunt could be.

"Lucy, don't think you will escape the festivities. Thea can play just as well as you. Young ladies should dance at every opportunity."

She hesitated with her fingers on the keys as everyone's attention turned to her, including Winchester and his vivid green eyes. "I really am enjoying playing for you."

"But I'd so love to see you dance, my dear," Harriet said sweetly.

"You can't *see* much of anything, aunt," Lucy muttered quietly.

Then Thea came to take her place.

"What would you like?"

"A waltz," Winchester answered, his voice startling Lucy.

"Lovely!" her aunt replied, cheering.

"Go," Thea whispered as they changed places.

Lucy didn't know why her nerves were on edge. It wasn't as if she were in a crowded ballroom with a hundred people's eyes on her. Only Thea and her aunt would witness her spin around the room with her heart on her sleeve.

And Winchester. He would have the best view of all.

"Don't look so frightened. I won't bite," he murmured as he bowed over her hand.

"What a shame," she answered.

He gave a crooked smile in return and placed his hand on her waist. They waited as the music began and then moved into the steps. Lucy counted in her head. She could waltz in her sleep, but being so close to him made her head woozy. She lifted her gaze to his nose and then his mouth. He was biting his bottom lip, and she had such a strong urge to kiss him, she had to rip her attention away from his face.

"Are you all right?"

"I'm fine."

"You seem distracted. Am I such a bad dancer?"

She pulled her gaze back to his. "No, I'm just tired, and anxious to return home. You must know how that feels."

"Not particularly."

"You don't have a place of comfort? Sanctuary?"

He spun her around before answering. "No. My home stopped being a home long ago. I like to live a nomadic existence."

"Oh."

"But I can see why you are so attached to your home and family. You are very blessed."

She grinned. "I am. Even with Jonathan as a brother, I'm luckier than most."

He snorted. "It's clear there is a strong sibling affection between you, even when you're threatening each other with bodily harm."

Lucy thought about that. She supposed there would always be a bond between them, no matter how many years passed or how they grew and changed.

"Have you any siblings?" she asked him.

"No. My family has been rather good at pushing each other away."

"Oh." She didn't want to pry, not when he was finally speaking to her so easily. She didn't ask any more questions, but she didn't look away from him as his gaze trailed over her face. Her cheeks warmed under his inspection, though, and she licked her dry lips self-consciously.

A little line appeared between his brows, and he tore his stare away from her.

Lucy bit her cheek in annoyance. Why did he do the things he did, if he didn't return her feelings?

"What are you thinking?"

Her face blanked. "What?"

"I could tell you were thinking about something interesting. Your eyes lose focus, and you bite on the corner of your bottom lip."

"I—I do?" She blinked. She couldn't consciously recall doing anything of the sort.

He smiled smugly. "Yes, you do."

His smugness irritated her. He thought he knew her so well.

"Why do you watch me so incessantly?"

He furrowed his brow. "I don't. I'm just highly observant of my general surroundings."

She pushed at his shoulder, and they stopped dancing as the music ended.

"You stare at me all the time. Thea tells me so, and half the time I see you do it with my own eyes. Then you make comments like you just did about some quirky thing I do with my lip that I don't even realize I do."

He put his hands on his hips and tried to glare down at her. "I *have* to keep an eye you. It is my job to keep you out of trouble while we're here, because apparently, it follows you to no end."

"It does not. You are watching me because you want to. You are exhibiting all the things a man does when he wants a woman, but yet you still refuse to acknowledge such things."

"Don't—" He glanced around. Thea and Aunt Harriet had slithered from the room. They were alone again. He cursed.

"Diabolical, aren't they?" Lucy muttered.

"I can't marry you," he said quietly.

"I didn't ask you to."

He pinched his nose. "Everything that is happening here is a result of a simple infatuation. Yes, you are beautiful. You don't need me to tell you that, but there is one immovable fact that will never change. You and I are from different worlds. I don't want to marry, and it is your destiny to marry. You will have a grand house, a nursery full of children, and all the trappings that go with it."

"You don't want to marry? Ever?"

"I'm hardly the first man to choose the bachelor lifestyle in lieu of the parson's mousetrap."

"I see." She tried to marshal her thoughts.

"I'm sorry," he said quietly. "I wanted to spare you this hurt."

She shook her head. "You can't spare me. It's not your place. I did this to myself, or perhaps it is just fate."

"I don't believe in fate."

"Bully for you." Lucy wiped at a tear. Embarrassment and a swell of other uncomfortable emotions took hold of her, resulting in more tears that made her feel like the typical weeping female.

She never wanted to be typical. *Ever.*

"Please don't cry." He wiped his thumb across her cheek and caught a tear.

"I don't want to. I don't want to be standing here, feeling this way, dreaming of an outcome that I'll never have. I don't want to be just *anyone's* wife. I needn't marry if I don't wish to."

She moved away from him and sat in her aunt's chair, kicking off her slippers and tucking her feet under her skirts.

He remained standing in the middle of the room.

"I've never been comfortable with the assumption that I wanted these things—I do, but I want them on *my* terms. A husband, yes—a partner to have adventures with. Children... eventually. I want to do things first, things I'm not allowed to do now. I can either find a man who meets these needs, a man like you, or I don't marry, wait until I'm of an age that no one cares what I do, and do it all."

He chuckled and shook his head. "Do you think it's that easy?"

"For you, yes. You're a man. You can do as you please."

"No, it isn't easy. Part of the reason I avoid society is because there is still an expectation that I must marry, that I need an heir."

"Then you understand, don't you? You didn't want it, and yet you've managed to find happiness outside the walls of society."

"I didn't choose this life. It chose me."

Lucy tensed. "What do you mean?"

"It's not up for discussion."

"I think I deserve an explanation."

He snorted. "Why?"

She stood up from the chair and slowly approached him. "With every word, you've tried to persuade me not to like you, but your every action has brought me closer to you than before."

"It doesn't matter. We can't always have the things we want."

"It *does* matter. A life of repression and regret isn't worth having."

He sighed. "What can I say that will end this? I don't want to hurt you."

"Tell me why you won't consider love. What happened?"

"Don't you dare say what you feel is love," he growled.

"How could it not be? I've never felt like this before. How do I know what it is and what it isn't? All I can do is trust my heart, and my heart says that you are my match."

He scrubbed his hands over his face. "I told you, I don't believe in love."

"Then what is this?" She grabbed the halves of his coat. "Tell me what this misery is!"

"It is lust, infatuation, and obsession. It afflicts us all. Sometimes all it takes is a night of passion, but sometimes it demands something more."

She rubbed her thumb over the velvet lapel of his coat. She believed the "sometimes more" part. There was no chance she would ever be satisfied with one night. Not with him.

"Prove it to me."

"No."

"How else will I know?"

"You won't."

She smoothed invisible wrinkles on his coat, enjoying the

freedom of touching him. "There has to be a way that won't harm either of us."

"You've already done enough harm."

"Me?"

"I've told you from the first night to let it be. You didn't do what you ought to do. What is best for you."

Lucy scowled at him. She dropped her hands to her side. "Everyone always tells me what is best for me. Shouldn't *I* be the one to know what is best for me?"

"Not necessarily."

"This is exactly what is wrong with our society. Women are treated as property, as unintelligent breeders, and look what you men have done? You bring about war, famine, and death. I don't believe for one moment that another person should decide what is best for another—not when it comes to this. If it affects the rest of my life, *I* should have the ultimate say, and everyone else can damn themselves to hell."

He raised one brow. "Impressive speech, but you won't change anything. This is simply the way things are."

Lucy lifted her chin in challenge. "Watch me."

She turned on her heel and left him standing alone in the parlor.

CHAPTER 15

They arrived midmorning, and Dean handed Lucy and Thea down. Her father, brother, and mother waited happily on the steps. He held Lucy's hand a moment before she could move away. She hadn't spoken to him since last night, and that was probably for the best, but he had one last thing to tell her.

"I'm leaving," he said, low enough for only her to hear.

She turned to him in confusion. "What?"

"I'm part of this problem, so I'm withdrawing from the situation entirely."

That was all time they had to speak privately before her family descended upon them.

Rigsby clapped him on the shoulder. "My thanks, Winchester. I will never be able to repay you for the trial you must have suffered."

"It was nothing. Your Aunt Harriet is very entertaining."

"That she is."

"By the way, an acquaintance of yours has arrived fresh from the season. She awaits you inside."

"She?" Dean asked curiously.

"The Countess of Clive," Rigsby replied, smirking.

Dean's face fell. "No."

"Oh, yes. I tried to spare you, but my mother, fresh from the boredom of her sickroom, insisted the countess stay, and assured her you would return posthaste."

Irritation filled him. The nerve of that woman. How had she found him?

"Unfortunately, I can't stay. I was planning to return Lucy and head home to check on my father."

From the corner of his eye, he saw movement on the steps. He turned slightly.

She descended with that predatory air of hers, shimmering in the sunlight, her gown far too elegant to be a day dress, but Lisbeth didn't care. She always wanted to shine, to be the center of attention. She smirked as she caught his eye. Her expression said she knew precisely what he was thinking and feeling. Her raven hair was radiant and bounced perfectly as she moved forward with the grace and tenacity of a huntress.

He broke eye contact with her, his focus moving to Lucy, who was also witnessing the glorious arrival that was Lady Lisbeth St. Andrew, the Countess of Clive. He swallowed back an urge to snarl. Lisbeth had turned her attention to Lucy, as well, and her eyes gleamed like a predator who smelled blood. Dean unconsciously moved forward, thoughts of his escape vanishing from his mind. A protective instinct swelled inside him. He must shield her from the venomous snake that was Lisbeth.

Lord Heath greeted him first, thanking him for his escort, and then Lady Heath went so far as to hug him and kiss his cheek.

"You are forever in my prayers, Lord Winchester. My deepest thanks for the safety of my daughter and dear Thea."

"It was my honor," he said, sheepishly.

"He rode in a carriage. He didn't fight off a dragon," Lucy said.

"*You* are a dragon," Rigsby quipped.

Lucy grinned. "I shall take that as a compliment."

Lady Lisbeth sauntered over to their group. "Lady Lucy, it is a pleasure to see you again. You were sorely missed during the season."

Lucy turned to face her, hiding her surprise. "How good of you to visit, Lady Lisbeth. I can't say I've missed the season, though. The country has been very diverting."

"I dare say it has." Lady Lisbeth's gaze cut to Dean for a moment. "I'm sorry to intrude on this little family reunion. I only arrived yesterday."

"Let's move to the drawing room where Lady Heath can rest while we chat," Lord Heath bid them.

"I should change," Lucy said, separating from the group at the stairs.

Dean followed everyone into the drawing room and took a stance by the mantle. Lisbeth had taken Lady Heath's arm and led her to a sofa, where they sat and chatted like old friends. He had no misconceptions about why she was here. He had a rat in his employ.

"What brings you to Yorkshire, Lady Lisbeth?" he asked.

"I was having a post-season tour of the homes of my friends when I suffered a disaster with my carriage. Luckily, I knew Lady Lucy to have a home nearby, and sought refuge."

With all attention tuned to Lisbeth, Dean openly scowled at her. Only she was aware of his skepticism.

She raised one brow in challenge. "I had no idea you were acquainted with such an admired family," she taunted.

"We've known each other since university," Rigsby spoke up.

Dean marshalled his anger. It wouldn't do to cause a scene in front of Rigsby's family. Lisbeth was a remarkable actress when she needed to be.

"University? How spectacular. I thought I knew everything about you, Winchester."

He bit his cheek. He couldn't think of anything to say that wasn't outright insulting.

"How goes the carriage repairs, Lady Lisbeth? My man says your steward left to fetch the needed part?" Lord Heath asked.

"Yes, mine is a very special carriage. He should return within the week."

"We'd hate to delay you from friends that are expecting you. You are welcome to our travel coach," Lady Heath continued.

"Oh no, I couldn't. I have a very special coach designed just for me. I can't travel in any other conveyance. But thank you for your generosity. I hope I can someday repay you in kind."

All of a sudden, Lucy burst into the drawing room. She came to a halt and then managed to continue at a reasonable pace.

"My goodness, that was fast!" Her mother said with a laugh, which turned into a gentle cough.

❧

"What brings you to Yorkshire, Lady Lisbeth?" Lucy asked, taking note of the other woman's companionable place beside her mother.

Lady Lisbeth never did anything not calculated to suit her in some way. In the three seasons Lucy had spent with her, she'd garnered enough impressions of her to know this.

"Lord Winchester only just asked that very thing," her mother informed her.

"Oh?" She turned to him.

He had his back to her, pouring himself a drink at the sideboard. She raised a brow at that and turned back toward Lady Lisbeth. She was also watching Winchester and smiling secretly.

"Lady Lisbeth?" Lucy asked again. "I'd still love to know what has brought you to our little piece of York."

Lisbeth's gaze snapped back to hers. "My carriage broke down. My steward has gone to fetch the piece necessary for its repair."

"Oh. What's wrong with it?"

Lady Lisbeth's expression hardened. "I won't pretend to understand the workings of my carriage, Lady Lucy. It's a very special carriage, one of a kind."

"How interesting. How long do you plan to stay?"

"Would you like to further our friendship? I can stay as long as you wish." Lisbeth smiled charmingly.

Trapped, Lucy thought. "Of course. We must take advantage of your time here. However, my mother is still recovering from her illness."

"If it pleases you, it pleases me, my dear." Lady Heath patted Lucy's hand.

"Wonderful. I will stay the week, and we can truly get to know each another."

Lucy grinned, but she wanted to gag.

"It will be a miniature house party," Lady Lisbeth beamed.

Everyone was forced to happily agree, but there was an obvious lack of enthusiasm.

"Now that it's all agreed, shall we go for a ride? The weather is lovely and Penny will need the exercise." Lucy stood. "Do you ride, Lady Lisbeth?"

"Of course!" She stood. "But only gentle mares. Do you have a suitable horse?"

"Alexandria will suit you perfectly. Right, Father?"

"She will suffice for a leisurely rider," Lord Heath advised. "My son will escort you about the estate."

"We'll return here after changing," Lucy said.

"I think I will rest while you ride." Lady Heath rose with the assistance of her husband.

"Winchester, will you join us or retire?"

"I will join you, but I, too, must change."

"We'll meet here again in a quarter hour," Lucy decided.

"How lovely! I'm enjoying myself already," Lady Lisbeth sang.

❧

In the end, the ride was brief. Moments after leaving the stables, Lady Lisbeth had claimed cramping in her leg and said she needed help returning. Lord Winchester had walked her back to the stables. Lucy had fought a jealous urge in her heart and continued to ride for another quarter hour before returning.

"Well, this was a colossal waste of time," Jonathan fumed.

"What is she doing here?" Lucy hissed at him as they walked back to the house.

"She's chasing Winchester and nursing her battered ego."

Lucy's stomach clenched. "What do you mean?"

"She's the woman he came here to escape."

"The mistress?" Lucy felt sick now. Winchester and Lady Lisbeth were lovers?

"Yes. She turns rabid when her affairs end. I tried to warn him, but…"

Affairs, plural, Lucy thought. She shared a glance with Thea, who grimaced.

As they climbed the steps, the very steps that he had been climbing when she lost her heart to him, she saw them on the terrace. They sat beside each other at the table, just as she and Thea had. They were leaning close and talking. If the ground below her feet chose to give way and swallow her at that moment, Lucy might have welcomed it.

"How are you, my love?" Lady Lisbeth purred.

She reached out to rub his thigh, but he caught her hand and pushed it away.

"I'm not your love. I told you we were done weeks ago."

"So coldhearted. Imagine my surprise when I learned you were here at the bosom of Lady Lucy."

He glared at her with warning. "I'm here to recover from your poison. It is *Rigsby* I came to visit. His sister's presence is coincidental and insignificant."

"Liar." She winked at him and sipped her tea.

"I beg your pardon?" he growled.

"She reeks of infatuation."

"Don't make trouble, Lisbeth," he said, darkly.

"Aw, was that so hard? I love how you say my name."

Dean moved away as the scuffle of footsteps heralded the others' return.

"Here comes the little wife now," she sneered.

"Feeling better, Lady Lisbeth?" Rigsby asked as he walked up.

"Much improved, my lord. Winchester took exceptional care of me. Sit and have tea with us, Lady Lucy. You may sit beside me." She patted the chair.

Lucy smiled and did so, Thea taking the chair beside her.

Rigsby was left standing, so he leaned back against the balustrade. "Bring me a cup, will you, Winchester?"

Dean filled a cup, splashed in some milk, and brought it to him. "How was the ride?"

"Short. I'll go again this afternoon. Join me? We'll go all the way to the cliffs. It's a rough ride."

"We should join them," Lady Lisbeth said, turning to Lucy. "What's a party if the gentlemen are not present?"

"You would not like it," Lucy warned. "The going is rough and chilly."

"Oh." Lady Lisbeth pouted. "Then we shouldn't let them go." She twisted to face the gentlemen. "I won't let you go, Winchester. It sounds dangerous."

"You are not my mother, Lisbeth," he said tartly.

"We don't need them," Lucy said. "Winchester and Jonathan are boring."

"Oh, Winchester is never boring, as long as the activity suits him." Lady Lisbeth turned back to Lucy and winked.

"There you have it. He—I mean—they, would rather ride

than spend the afternoon with us. I wouldn't want to keep someone against their will, would you?"

"I… If that is their wish, then no." Lady Lisbeth frowned in puzzlement.

Lucy smiled. "We don't need gentlemen to entertain us. Right, Thea?"

Thea nodded.

Lady Lisbeth didn't appear pleased at all. "If you say so."

"Let's go shooting!" Lucy offered.

"No!" Rigsby and Dean said at once.

"Father sent all the pistols for cleaning," Rigsby blurted.

"All of them?" Lucy said in disbelief.

Rigsby nodded. "Every single one."

"Shooting is barbaric," Lady Lisbeth said.

"It is not. It's an important skill, and very invigorating," Lucy said, unfazed by Lady Lisbeth's noninterest.

"We could take a walk or play charades, shuttlecock, or bowls," Thea suggested.

"Those sound like childish things." Lady Lisbeth pouted again.

"What would you like to do, then?"

"I don't want the gentlemen to leave."

Lucy shrugged. "Shall we tie them up?"

Her brother scowled at her.

Lady Lisbeth sighed. "I've yet to see your village. Perhaps an afternoon of shopping will be an adequate diversion?"

"If that is what you wish," Lucy said, sharing a glance of annoyance with Thea.

CHAPTER 16

Lucy dressed for dinner and mused over the afternoon. If there was an unseen benefit, it was that the village shops earned significant profit from Lady Lisbeth's shopping expedition. The woman bought everything she saw. She'd barely spoken to them as Lucy and Thea followed her from store to store, but she was doted on by every shopkeeper, and my, how Lady Lisbeth loved the attention.

Lucy shuddered, hoping she never appeared as such. It reminded her of what Winchester had said about her own need for attention. She hated to think she resembled anything of Lady Lisbeth.

She finished dressing and knocked on Thea's door. Thea opened it and joined her in the hall.

"What do you think dinner will be like tonight?" Lucy wondered.

"Interesting, but I'm not confident if it will be a good-interesting or a bad-interesting."

"Well, we will soon find out."

Lucy had a burning question for Winchester. Why hadn't

149

he left? He'd come here to escape Lady Lisbeth, but now that she was here, he remained for some reason.

"My appetite has returned with gumption," her mother said as they joined the others in the drawing room. "I lost one stone, and I fear three will return."

"I will sorely miss your curves if they don't return," Lord Heath said from her side.

Lucy made a face at her parents. "Stop that right now, or I won't be able to eat a thing."

Jonathan joined them. "What are they doing?"

"I won't repeat it."

Their parents snickered.

"Do you think a stork delivered you upon the steps, Lucy?" her brother teased.

Lucy covered her ears and turned away. She could hear her father and brother laughing while Mother scolded Jonathan, so she withdrew to where Thea stood by the window, conversing with Winchester.

Thea smiled at Lucy's disgusted face. "What's going on?"

"Nothing," she said, focusing on Winchester.

He raised a brow in question.

"What are you still doing here?"

"I'm waiting for dinner to start, just like you."

"That's not what I mean." She lowered her voice. "You said you were going to leave."

"So I did, but I changed my mind."

"Because of a certain young widow, who used to be your mistress?"

"Who told you that?"

"If it were a secret, you never should have told Jonathan. His mouth is like a sieve."

Winchester growled. "I'm here because I know she is only here to make trouble. She's vindictive."

Lucy folded her arms. "What is it that she wants?"

"Me," he grumbled.

"So she's playing the part of a scorned lover?"

"I did not scorn her. I—I'm not going to divulge the details to you. The sooner she departs, the better for all of us."

"I have to agree."

As if summoned by their discussion, the woman herself appeared in the doorway. She wore a vibrantly red dress cut dangerously low. Lucy pretended not to notice her, and instead, turned back to Winchester. He had done the same, which left them staring at each other.

Lucy swallowed uncomfortably.

"There is something else I should tell you. It's more of a warning."

"Yes?"

"She's taken it into her head that we...that I am courting you."

"Well, that's absurd," Lucy scoffed, but then inspiration struck. "Would that drive her away?"

"A stake through the heart wouldn't drive her away," he quipped.

They heard Lady Lisbeth greeting Lucy's parents first, but she was talking inordinately loud and shooting looks their way.

"I'm serious."

He pinned her with his gaze. "Only a fool would agree to such a thing."

Thea spoke up. "It is a good plan, my lord."

Lucy had forgotten she was even there. "You see? Thea is

far more intelligent than I. If she says the plan has merit, then it does."

§.

Dean wanted to curse. Court Lucy? Openly? That was the worst idea he'd ever heard. He didn't need closer proximity to her than he already had. He'd been a bloody saint since that afternoon in the stable, and he meant to keep it that way.

Rigsby appeared at his side. Lisbeth still sat with Lady Heath, but she watched their group closely.

"Tell Winchester that pretending to court me to drive Lady Lisbeth away is a brilliant idea," Lucy pleaded to her brother.

Rigsby brightened. "That *is* brilliant."

"You want me to court your sister?" Dean asked in alarm.

"It wouldn't be real, Winchester. And it would drive the vermin from the house."

This time, Dean did curse. He strode away from them and poured himself a drink. It was only a second before said vermin appeared at his side and simply waited for him to pour her a drink.

"You know exactly what I like, don't you?"

He poured her a sherry and shoved it into her hand.

She moved closer to him, brushing her bosom against his arm. "What's the matter, Chester?"

"You know I hate that name. Only you dared to call me that."

"It's my pet name for you," she purred.

Dean wanted to snarl at her. He'd had his fill of conniving women, but she took the medal for worst of them all. Compared to—no, he stopped himself. He would *not* compare them. There was no reason to. Lisbeth was his former mistress and Lucy the sister of his friend. The two should never have crossed paths, but here they were, the room rife with tension, as they all pretended to enjoy each other's company. Perhaps he *should* leave. He would if he was certain Lisbeth wouldn't punish Lucy out of sheer vindictiveness. That was the crux of things. She wanted revenge, and she believed Lucy to be the new target of his affections. It was laughable.

Lisbeth had never truly had his affection. It was only sex, but when she wasn't ready to let go, it was hell on earth for her lover.

"You're wasting your time here," he said to her.

"Why do you say that? I'm having a lovely time, aren't you?"

"I would if you weren't here."

"That isn't very nice," she hissed at him.

"Then leave."

"No. I'll either have you, or enjoy the misery on your little wife's face."

Dean turned to face her. "If you so much as make her frown as a result of your venomous presence, words, or behavior, you *will* regret it."

She smiled at him gleefully. "How?"

He narrowed his eyes dangerously. "Use your imagination, Lisbeth. What do I know about you that will ruin you?"

She dropped her cheerful façade. "You wouldn't."

"Only if you make me."

"We'll see about that. Why do you care what I do or say to the chit? She's no meek mouse fresh from the nursery. Lady Lucy reminds me of myself during my best years. She can handle a little competition, can't she?"

"Do not compare yourself to Lady Lucy. You will be found wanting."

Lisbeth sucked in a breath and bared her teeth at him. "How dare you."

"You were right earlier. She is to be my wife, and I won't tolerate your filthy presence around her. Leave."

She glared at him with hatred. "You're lying."

"It isn't official. I've only just begun to court her. I will speak to her father tonight."

"She can't have you, not until I'm finished with you," Lisbeth spat and walked away.

Dean leaned on the table as a wave of disbelief swept through him. Dear God, what had he done?

CHAPTER 17

Lucy followed the group into the dining room. She nearly jumped out of her slippers when Winchester appeared at her side and put her hand on his arm.

"I will escort you in," he said quietly.

She blinked. "If you insist…"

"I do. After all, I will be asking your father for permission to court you this evening."

"That was a rapid change of heart."

"I'm only doing as you suggested," he whispered as they followed the others far enough behind to speak privately.

She yanked him to a halt. "You cannot ask my father for permission to *pretend* to court me. Do you realize how ridiculous that sounds?"

"Yes, but I can't not ask him for permission when it becomes obvious that I am courting you. How will we explain that?"

She sighed. "You're right."

"This plan is horrible enough as it is, but I will not pull the wool over your family's eyes. They trust me, and I intend to keep that trust."

"I admire that about you," she grumbled, somewhat reluctantly.

He chuckled beside her, the velvety sound spreading warmth through her body. After all they'd been through and expressed toward each other, somehow they'd accomplished an odd sort of friendship. She'd never mention it to him, though, sure he'd deny it vehemently.

They entered the dining room and took their places. She made eye contact with Jonathan and Thea. She hoped that was sufficient to pass along the new situation. Her brother raised a brow in question and Lucy sighed. At times, he was brilliant, but at others...

As for Lady Lisbeth, Lucy gave her a friendly smile. "You look radiant. Is that a new dress?"

"Why, yes, Lady Lucy. I noticed you wore that same adorable blue frock last season. It suits you so well."

"Thank you, Lady Lisbeth. It was a gift from my father."

Lucy kept her smile as Lady Lisbeth's faltered. If she meant to insult Lucy by pointing out last season's dress, her remarks fell flat. Lucy cared not for the wasteful practice of only wearing a dress once. She chose her wardrobe with care and love. Each piece she wore for years, regardless of the current fashions. She also took part in a charity with her mother that refashioned and repaired dresses for women less fortunate. If a dress no longer fit her or needed significant repair and resizing, she donated it, sometimes doing the sewing herself.

§♠

The women retired to the drawing room after dinner while the men shared cigars and port. Lucy sat beside her mother, while Thea tinkered on the pianoforte. Lady Lisbeth was surprisingly quiet and sat motionless while staring at the fire.

"How are you feeling?" Lucy asked her mother.

"Tired, but I am enjoying myself. Missing the season has made me long for company and the chatter of friends."

"There is always next spring," Lucy murmured. She hadn't missed the season at all. She had barely thought of it since her banishment. All her friends had remained cloistered away with new husbands or far away with family. Only Thea would have remained, if Lucy hadn't begged for her to join them in the country. And in truth, her family relished the opportunity to not fund another season.

"I've noticed the attention Lord Winchester pays you, my dear."

"What?"

"Lord Winchester, he pays you marked attention. Haven't you noticed?"

"No." Lucy shook her head. "It's not what it seems."

Lady Heath tilted her head to the side. It was her skeptical look.

"Really, Mother. He and I..." Lucy lowered her voice. "He claims we are too different."

Lady Heath brightened. "Then it has been acknowledged?"

"Not just acknowledged, more like discussed...at length." Lucy snorted over the absurdity of how that sounded. They'd *talked* so much, when all she wanted to do was to throw her arms around him and kiss him madly.

Her mother nodded sagely.

"He doesn't want marriage."

"No man does until he meets the right woman."

But how was she to know if she was the right woman for him? How did he? And more to the point, could she help him come to that conclusion, or was she completely impotent in the matter?

"I'm afraid I don't understand."

"Love is never easy to understand. It appears first as lust—"

"Mother!" Lucy said in a whispered gasp. "Please don't say such things." She used her eyes to indicate the elegant form of Lady Lisbeth sitting by the fire.

Lady Heath giggled like a young girl now. "Why not?"

"How much wine did you have at dinner?"

The giggling only grew louder. "I don't remember. Not nearly enough as I usually do, but perhaps I'm a bit delicate for the two glasses I had."

Lucy helped her mother stand. "Oh, dear. Let's get you to bed."

"Send me your father," Lady Heath tittered.

❧

He sat back and drew from his cheroot. The table was quiet, the women having left them to their port. Lord Heath swirled his glass and belched. Dean leaned forward in his chair, alert and uneasy. He didn't have the right words for what he was about to say, but he hoped with Rigsby's help, Lord Heath wouldn't have him thrown out of the estate.

"We should discuss Lady Lisbeth, my lord," he began.

"I know she is a viper." Lord Heath leaned back in his

chair and stretched. "I don't know why my wife is entertaining such a woman."

"She's here because of me, and for that, I apologize."

"We've all got a past." Lord Heath took a sip of his port. "What do you plan to do about it?"

Dean hated what he was about to say next. He turned to Rigsby for encouragement, but his friend only shook his head.

"What the devil is going on?" Lord Heath asked.

Rigsby shrugged. "Nothing."

"It's *not* bloody nothing if Winchester here is all tied in knots about it."

"We've devised a plan," Dean said.

Rigsby coughed, and it suspiciously sounded like the word *no*.

Dean exhaled. "I'm going to court Lady Lucy in front of Lady Lisbeth to drive her away."

Rigsby slapped his hand to his forehead.

Lord Heath's eyes narrowed to slits as he looked between the two men. "You call that a plan? It sounds like something Lucy would concoct."

"That is because she did," Rigsby admitted.

"You want to toy with my daughter's affections to drive away your nasty mistress?"

Dean swallowed, the heat of shame climbing his throat. "No, sir. She is aware of the fabrication. It was her idea to pretend so that Lady Lisbeth will concede defeat and move on."

Lord Heath turned to his son. "And you thought this was a clever idea?"

"I did, but I don't now," Rigsby blundered.

"You boys have a lot of growing up to do." Lord Heath

stood from his chair. He faced Dean first. "I *do not* give you my blessing to *fake* a courtship with my daughter." Then he turned to Rigsby. "*Protect* your sister. Even from herself. I'm going to bed." He turned and left them in stunned silence.

"I feel like a flogging would have been less painful." Rigsby rubbed his face. "What did he mean 'protect her'? I *do* protect her."

Dean cursed himself. "He means from me."

"He said from herself."

Dean stared down at the floor. "I'm going to retire. Tomorrow I will leave, and then maybe Lady Lisbeth will depart, as well."

Rigsby shook his head. "Bloody hell. Maybe I will just throw her out. Half the *ton* already doesn't care for her."

Dean stood and put out his cheroot. "Goodnight, Rigsby."

He climbed the stairs in a daze, wishing he could fall into bed, close his eyes, and wake up with a plan to fix everything. He turned down the hall and noticed a shadow of a woman leaning against the wall.

"Curse you to hell, Lisbeth, and leave me alone."

The lady stepped into the light and he stilled.

"That is not very nice, though I agree with the sentiments."

He hesitated to move closer.

"Perhaps you think I'm a ghost?"

Lucy stepped farther into the light, moving closer to him until he put his hand up to stop her.

"What are you doing here?"

"I escorted my mother to bed, and thought to walk the halls for a bit. Thea retired, too, so there is only Lady Lisbeth downstairs."

"You should go."

"Why?"

"I spoke to your father, and he declined to bless our *fabricated* courtship. I think that is answer enough."

"That isn't surprising. My father doesn't enjoy larks the way I do, or my mother does."

He cocked his head to the side. "Your mother?"

"Where do you think I received all my wildness? It's hereditary. My father tries to pretend to tame my mother's, but he loves it."

"What are you doing here?" he asked again.

"I'm proving a point," she said coyly.

"And what point is that?"

Lucy bit her lip. Was she nervous? Good. He wasn't in the mood to play the gentleman, not when he could still feel the sting of her father's words. He shouldn't care. It was all for pretend, but deep down, he knew the truth. His sins still followed him. He could try to be a better man, but in the end, he was only as good as his past deeds.

Now she stood before him, the embodiment of temptation. She knew it, and he knew it. What would he do? A surge of lust tore through him, as well as a surge of anger. He wasn't good enough, that's what he'd always been told. He shouldn't touch her, but the devil inside him wanted to, *demanded* it. Damn the consequences.

"If you dare, come a little closer…."

It was his turn to tempt her. He remained completely still, and predictably, her arms came around him and she pressed her lips to his.

He folded his arms around her, lifting her off her feet. It was time he gave her a real kiss. He wasn't allowed to court her—or pretend to—as it happened to be, but dammit, he was going to kiss her for *real* this time.

Tomorrow, he would begin again as a good, honorable gentleman, but tonight, he felt like the rogue he claimed to be, the unscrupulous bachelor, and that meant he could kiss a noble daughter and not think twice about the consequences. He could kiss her until she lost her will to stand if he wanted, until she saw stars behind her lids.

He moved down the hall until the shadows hid them. Then he lowered her slowly to her feet, sliding her down the front of his body and enjoying every inch of it. He cocked his head to the side and deepened the kiss.

She opened her mouth for more, and he eagerly gave it to her, tasting her at last. Their first kiss, he had purposefully starved himself. He had resisted the enjoyment for fear of loving it too much. But now he feasted. He didn't care about the emotions involved. He wanted to sweep her off her feet and claim her as his, if only for a night.

He pushed her against the wall, unwinding her arms from his neck and pinning them above her head. Then he placed his knee in between her legs, until her skirts gave way, and she parted her thighs. Now he could step in between them with just one leg. He held himself against the length of her body, taking in each panting breath, each heavenly sigh. He laid claim to all of them.

He pressed his thigh between her legs until she rode upon him, coming to her toes. She needed him to hold her up now, and all the pressure of her weight centered on the delicate treasure between her legs. She shivered and broke away from the kiss to gasp.

He pressed his lips to her neck, licking the soft skin, tasting the essence of her on his lips. He explored her neck all the way to the small lobe of her ear, taking it between his teeth and softly biting it. Her breath shimmered out in a sigh. He relished it. He relished knowing he could give her more pleasure than she could dream of. He would be the only man to do so, the only man to own her, heart, body, and soul.

He closed his eyes, breathing deeply against the valley of her breasts, taking in the scent of her and searing it into his brain.

🙚

Lucy shuddered as his thigh pressed against her core and tried to resist the begging of her body to move. She didn't know if she should, but dammit, she wanted to. Sensations ricocheted inside her. Her skin tingled excitedly, her heart pounded, her head felt fuzzy, and the place between her thighs...well, that felt delightful. She tried to resist squirming, but when she moved, it was like heaven inside her, the sensations so sweet she didn't want to fight them.

She wanted *more*.

He flexed his thigh and she gasped. "Yes." She sighed. *Yes, please.* She had no command over herself when he did that. He took her wrists in one hand, and with the other, he lifted her skirts. Unable to hold still, Lucy moved against his thigh and cried out with a moan.

"I've got you," he said. His voice was deep and rough. It moved through her like a caress.

His hand reached the back of her thigh, squeezing her as his wicked fingers moved to the front and slid in between her and his leg. He touched her there, and she thought she might die from the exquisite pleasure. She moaned again, deep and throaty. She'd never heard herself make such a noise. But never had she experienced such piercing bliss.

"Hush," he said, before he took her mouth again. He stroked her with his fingers and his tongue, and all at once, she felt like she was coming apart. She shook with the force of it, rocking her hips against his hand shamelessly, and crying out into his mouth.

She squirmed until he released her arms, and she collapsed against him, her body limp, but her emotions roaring to life inside her. She wanted to cry and laugh and smile like a lunatic. She pressed her face into his neck and breathed in the salty mix of skin and cologne until she could regulate her breathing, and think up some sort of response for what had just occurred.

She still hadn't recovered when he pulled away.

He stepped back slowly, still holding her, letting her dress fall around her again.

Lucy pressed her forehead to his chest, too scared to meet his gaze just yet. She kept her eyes closed as he lifted her chin up.

"Open them," he whispered.

She shook her head.

"Open them, Lucy."

She blinked at him. "It's too dark to see." Her voice scraped her throat, raw and dry.

"I can see them." He lightly kissed her lips. "I will take you back to your room now."

"No, you won't. I can walk myself."

She gently pushed away from him, her legs weak as soft butter, but they held her up sufficiently. She didn't want to encourage too much talking. Actions seem to suit them far better.

She turned down the hall. "Good night, Winchester."

"Call me Dean."

"What?" She paused. He'd spoken so quietly, she wasn't sure he'd meant for her to hear.

"The next time I have you pinned against a wall, you will call me Dean."

"Dean," she said softly and turned back down the hall.

He watched her disappear and then turned toward his room. It was the first time he'd let a woman use his given name.

CHAPTER 18

Lisbeth sat alone beside the fire in the drawing room. She *hated* being alone.

One by one, the other occupants had dwindled, and the men never returned. This house was a bore, and the only person she wanted to spend time with was so smitten over Lady Lucy he couldn't even see it. She shuddered.

Love.

She'd been foolish to believe a man like Winchester was as immune as herself. But she'd been proven wrong before. But he had shown such a severe aversion to the state of love. He'd scorned affection and sought only physical pleasure and satisfaction. He'd mastered the art of both, but now love was suddenly on his horizon? She wouldn't stand for it, not when his touch was still seared into her skin. No man would leave her until *she* was done, and Lisbeth simply wasn't done with him yet.

She made her way to his room, despite the servant's reluctance to give the direction when her maid, Agnes, had inquired. But Lisbeth had Agnes figure it out herself, and now she knew exactly where to find him.

The house was dark in the guest wing reserved for bachelors. Lisbeth slinked along the hall, pausing before the door she knew to be his. She turned the handle slowly, but it was locked.

Insufferable man.

She scratched at the wood lightly. She could hear movement within as a curse was muttered, and then heavy footfalls prevailed before he opened the door.

He stood there, barely more than a dark silhouette. "What do you want?"

Lisbeth set her hands on her hips and jutted her breasts forward in a tantalizing display. "I've waited long enough for you to greet me properly, Chester. I don't know that I can forgive you for that."

Her gaze lingered on his bare chest. She reached out to touch him, but he stepped back. She clenched her jaw and slipped past him into the room.

He prowled around her. "Get out, Lisbeth. I'm not doing this with you tonight, or any other night."

His anger excited her. She wanted more of it, to feel his hands pawing at her skin as he took her aggressively against the wall or on the floor.

"What is the matter, Chester? You don't sound like a man satisfied with the company he keeps. Did you think a virgin of noble birth could satisfy your desires as I could?"

She saw him pause in his gait and change direction. She smiled triumphantly.

He threw the question back at her. "At one time, you were a virgin of noble birth, or have you forgotten?"

Lisbeth smirked at his dangerous scowl. "I have not. I paid my dues, and so shall Lady Lucy."

"What is that supposed to mean?"

"She can't marry a man like you. You will destroy her. It takes time and experience to satisfy a man of your passion. Sleep with her when she is ready and capable, after she has put her husband to rest and taken a few lovers."

He didn't speak as he circled around her.

Her eyes, having adjusted to the darkness now, could see the shifting planes of his abdomen as he moved. Two of the buttons of his breeches were unfastened. She licked her lips in anticipation.

"Mr. Peters would be a good beginning for her. He's gentle and sweet, and a very patient teacher. Sir William could be her second. He's a bit more adventurous, but he won't hurt her. Then perhaps Mr. Halstead, or maybe Colonel Dickens—"

"Don't utter another word," he said, his voice deadly.

Lisbeth sat upon the bed and ran her hand over the sheet. "Does the thought of it upset you?"

"Get out. Leave this house before you stain it."

She smiled, tasting the bitter taste of bile in her mouth. "How dare you judge me. What mark will *you* leave on this house? On Lady Lucy? If her family knew of the shame you have brought to your own family…the blood on your hands. They wouldn't *let* you have her, or lick the filth on her shoes."

She grew angrier when he didn't respond to her taunts. She could feel the empty chasm between them, as well as his disdain for her. She pushed herself off the bed and approached him, emboldened when he didn't back way. She dragged her nails along his chest as she walked a circle around him.

"Let's not fight anymore. I want to make up." She faced

him. "People like us don't belong here. We're different. We're like animals controlled by our passions."

"I don't want you, Lisbeth. I've already told you I'm done. We had our time, and now it's over."

"It's over when I say it's over."

He shook his head.

"You think you can deny me? I *know* you. I know everything you love, and everything you need to find complete, utterly decadent satisfaction. You won't find another woman like me, Chester."

He went and stood by the door, waiting. "I can only hope that is true."

She glared at him and didn't move. "What will you do? Toss me out like garbage?"

"If need be."

She stalked forward, pausing at the door to give one last warning. "I don't know what it is you see in the chit. She isn't anything like us. When she sees the dirty, worthless soul you carry inside you, she won't touch you. But I will be waiting for you to return to your senses and realize how bored you would be with a woman like her. It shan't take long, I think."

He folded his arms. "You're right, Lisbeth. She isn't anything like us. It's her best quality." Then he put his hand to her back and pushed her out the door, closing it swiftly and quietly behind her.

For a moment, Lisbeth considered making enough noise to wake the others, so it would be known that she was leaving his room—but no, she calmly returned to her own. She retained a respectable place in society, and she wanted to keep it. There were always whispers circulating about her, but without any substantial proof, they only served to make her more popular. She wasn't going to give that up in a fit of jealousy.

ॐ

Lucy woke the next morning with a huge smile on her face. She bathed and then dressed. Then quickly made her way to the morning room, where she hoped to find the man who had filled her thoughts and dreams. Things would be different today, she could feel it. She could hear the pleasant chatter before she entered the breakfast parlor, and it only fueled her delight for the day ahead.

"Good morning, everyone." She smiled cheerfully as she went to fill her plate. She met Winchester's gaze last, but didn't find anything to encourage hers to linger.

She didn't know what last night had meant to him. That was the problem. She took her plate to her seat beside Thea. The chatter continued, and Lucy wondered if perhaps he wasn't acting differently toward her because he was used to conducting his affairs discreetly.

Affairs? Heavens no. This was *not* an affair. This was the beginning of her life, the start of their shared life. What had she expected him to do when she'd entered? Burst to his feet and declare his love? She giggled to herself. While an enchanting thought, it wasn't like him. He was, by nature, not publicly expressive, and that suited her just fine.

Her mother called to her. "Dear?"

"Yes?"

"Is your breakfast amusing?"

"Beg pardon?"

"You've been staring at your food and giggling," her brother said from her other side.

"I have?"

Thea leaned over and peered at her food.

"It isn't my food." Lucy playfully nudged her. "I'm simply happy." She glanced around at her table companions. Her father peeked over his paper at her. She grinned at him. He chuckled and resumed reading.

"Isn't today just lovely?"

Everyone else blinked at her, but as she caught Winchester's eye, she saw him smile as he took a sip of his coffee. She didn't care how strangely she behaved. She would infect everyone with her joy if she had to.

"Well, I think it's marvelous you woke with such a sunny disposition," Thea commented.

"Thank you, Thea. Did you sleep well?"

"I did."

"I feel a hike is in order. The ground must be dry enough for a pleasant hike. Jonathan, Winchester? Would you like to join us?"

"Actually, we're leaving with Father."

Lucy's joy faded. "What?"

"It's his annual trip to check the other estates, remember?"

"But that isn't for another month. You never leave this early."

"I've decided to change my plans. I want to get it done with sooner rather than later, especially since Lord Winchester has offered to assist me."

Her father resumed reading the paper.

"You're going with them?" she asked Winchester.

"I've been invited, and am honored to help in any way I can."

"You will be counting cows."

He smiled crookedly. "And I shall do so with joy."

"Keep your chin up, Lucy. Mother is taking you to Bath," Jonathan put in.

Lucy smiled tightly. She didn't *want* Bath. She wanted Winchester, alone, all to herself. As quickly as her dreamy day had begun, it was over. Her father always spent at least two months away when he toured their properties.

"Why don't you wait until the end of the week at least? We have a guest, after all." Lucy had almost forgotten about Lady Lisbeth. She was absent from the table.

Her father coughed. "Um… We've had a record number of calves born this year. I want to get an early start before the heat settles in."

Lucy sighed. She knew there wasn't anything more she could say to alter her father's plans. "Very well. You must name a calf after me, then."

Her father chuckled.

Lucy poked at her eggs for a little while longer before convincing Thea to take a walk with her.

"What was that all about?" Thea asked as they descended the steps leading toward the stable. They wouldn't be riding, but instead, visiting the pond to see the ducklings.

"Something happened last night that boosted my spirits, and now it seems that it was all for naught."

"Do I wish to know what the something is?" Thea said with trepidation.

Lucy thought about telling her but decided not to. "No, but I thought it meant things had changed between us."

"Perhaps he was only behaving like a typical rake?"

Lucy pondered that. She *had* been waiting outside his room. Could he have just taken advantage of her? No. *No.* There had been so much feeling in that moment, such heady emotion. There was far more going on than simple lust. She'd been alone with enough rogues to know the difference. If he hadn't cared for her, he would have taken things much further. Instead, he'd taken her to heights she hadn't known existed and taken nothing for himself.

"There is so much more to him than what he wants to show me. I won't get a chance to discover what it is if he is away with my father."

"I'm sorry," Thea said.

They found the pond and cooed over the little ducklings, but it wasn't long before Lucy wanted to return to the house. She needed to speak with him. He couldn't just leave without explaining last night. But when they returned, they found Lady Lisbeth in the drawing room.

"Good morning," Lucy greeted her with reserve.

"Good morning, Lady Lucy." She indicated the grass-stained hem of her gown. "I can see you've been enjoying the outdoors."

"Yes, I have."

"I'm disappointed to hear our gentlemen will be leaving us."

"My father and brother do it every year," Lucy responded.

"How nice of Lord Winchester to join them."

"Yes." Lucy wondered where this conversation was going.

Lady Lisbeth smiled serenely. "You know, after I spoke to Winchester last night in his room—oops. Pretend you didn't hear that." She winked. "He and I are very old friends, you see.

Well, I've decided it is time for me to depart, as well. I have friends waiting for me. Fortunately, my steward has the part for my carriage and will be returning to repair it today. I will leave tomorrow."

Lucy returned her smile, but on the inside, a chill swept through her. *Last night in his room?*

"How fortunate. We usually visit Bath and take the waters while my father is away."

"Lovely. Bath is a wonderful alternative to London."

"Yes," Lucy agreed. "Now, if you will excuse me, Thea and I must meet with my mother to plan our own trip."

"Just a moment, Lady Lucy. If I could have a private word with you?"

"Certainly."

Lucy shared a glance with Thea. Thea moved to wait outside on the terrace, surveying the gardens with her back to them.

"Woman to woman, I think you could have a very rosy future if you followed the right path, my dear," Lady Lisbeth whispered, nodding toward the terrace doors.

Lucy twisted to see what she was looking at. Winchester was now out there with Thea.

"Men like him aren't suitable for a novice. One must begin slowly, with a marriage to an older man. Get rid of the annoying burden of virtue the respectable way." She winked and covered her mouth while she laughed huskily.

Lucy frowned at her.

Lady Lisbeth swatted her knee playfully. "Don't make a face, dear. You'll give yourself wrinkles! It's not so terrible, wedding an older man. You close your eyes, and it's over quickly. But the important part is, after it's over, you can move on to younger men, men with skill, and men with talent."

Lucy summoned all herself self-control to keep herself from reacting. Women like Lady Lisbeth *wanted* a reaction. They fed off the attention from others. What Lucy didn't understand was why she felt she could say such disgusting things to her.

Lady Lisbeth leaned in closer, but her eyes were on Winchester. "Men who don't want to trifle with virgins."

Lucy caught herself falling into the trap set for her, or perhaps she had set it herself. She had believed she could charm him into falling for her.

Now he glanced in their direction, but Lucy presented her back to him, her heart thudding painfully. Lady Lisbeth continued to boldly examine him, her gaze wandering over him in obvious carnal familiarity.

Lucy swallowed back her rising fury. She took a deep breath and leashed her emotions. "That is not the kind of future I want, or the kind of marriage I want."

"What a foolish thing to say. You'll never taste the delights of a man like Winchester any other way."

Lucy bit her tongue. She remembered such delights vividly.

"Your mother told me about Mr. Farris. He seems safe and boring. You should marry him, but that means your life will also be safe and boring."

"As opposed to…" Lucy couldn't help asking.

"A life like mine," Lady Lisbeth preened. "I can have my pick of men, and I have."

Lucy shrugged. "I suppose that is one way to look at it."

The other woman blinked. "I beg your pardon?"

"Having men, rather than having been *had* by so many of them."

Lady Lisbeth's gaze narrowed. "Semantics."

"If you say so."

Lady Lisbeth pursed her lips. "I need to prepare to leave. Good day, Lady Lucy."

"Good day, Lady Lisbeth."

Lucy exhaled slowly as the woman disappeared into the hall. She wanted to cry—or murder her.

"What did she say to you?" Winchester and Thea asked in unison behind her.

Lucy turned to find them standing before her, with twin expressions of concern on their faces.

"Nothing of importance," Lucy lied. She would not show how hurt she could be by Lady Lisbeth, and in essence, by him. He would only use it to further his notion that he was out of her league. Her doubt clamped around her heart like a vice, but she was not ready to concede. She let her anger override the sadness and come to the forefront.

Lucy stood. "What is it you're afraid she told me? That you and she have had an affair? Am I supposed to be shocked?"

"She's upset you."

He seemed angry, too. Was it on her behalf? She didn't want it. She didn't even want to look at him right now.

"I'm not a child, Winchester. I can handle women like her. She isn't the first or the last of her ilk. Thea, let's prepare for our trip."

He reached out and took her hand. "Wait."

Lucy glanced down at it with disdain.

"I'll give you a moment." Thea hurried to the hall and closed the door.

Lucy pulled her hand from his.

"Have I convinced you, then?"

"Of what?"

"Our differences. We are two people who can never be one in marriage. We're like fire and ice."

"Am I supposed to be ice? Cold and pure as snow?" She walked around him. The day had been so beautiful when it had begun, but now the sunlight made her angrier. She turned back to him. "I feel like fire, actually. I'm hot, and I want to burn you so you know exactly what I'm feeling. It is *you* that is cold. You refuse to feel, refuse to go any deeper than carnal cravings. You are the one devoid of color and warmth, not I."

He scowled at her, but remained silent.

"Have you nothing to say?" she taunted him, poking him in the chest.

He grabbed her hand, threading his fingers through hers so she couldn't pull away. "You are innocent. You shouldn't have to face the ugliness that lives inside me or Lady Lisbeth. You're right. I *am* ice, and you are fire."

"Don't you dare call me innocent. I am anything but innocent. I may not have your disreputable history, but nor do I deserve to be treated like some fragile creature, protected and preserved like a specimen in a jar. I want to live, I want to make love, I want to see things I've never seen before, and do things I shouldn't be doing. I won't be caged. I won't be cowed by people like you, Lady Lisbeth, or anyone else. You still refuse to see who I am, and that is your fault, not mine. Have you convinced me?" she mocked him. "You've only convinced me how much of a coward you are."

He let go of her hand then, and his face hardened. She waited to see if he would say anything, but he didn't, so she left the drawing room, her heart tearing in two. She had to let go of her dream of him, and it hurt more than she could bear. She hated herself. She hated that she was giving up.

CHAPTER 19

Two months went by, and after some convincing from Lord Heath, Dean returned to the place where he had left his heart. He studied the lonely house that sat at the top of a hill, looming over the valley and its village with condescension. That was how he always felt when he stood in its shadow. He wasn't good enough. He'd failed to live up to the house's expectations—as well as his father's. He hadn't realized that, after all these years, he could still feel like a boy of twelve.

Rigsby snored beside him, and Lord Heath sat opposite, staring out the window as the carriage climbed the hill toward the house. Dean would never have come back here if not for Lord Heath's insistence. The man imagined some sort of peace could be salvaged for Dean by mending the riff with his father before his death, but Dean knew the truth. Not even his looming mortality would change his father's stone-cold heart. But Dean had relented, purely to appease Lord Heath, a man he respected not only for his title and wealth, but for his wisdom and compassion.

If only *he* had been born to a father like Lord Heath, his life would have been entirely different.

Dean stared out the opposite window, but he only looked north. If he glanced east, he could see the roof of Abbey House, and all the reasons he hated coming home would suddenly rush back. His father he could deal with—maybe, but not Abbey House. Not those memories.

When the carriage pulled up to the house, Lord Heath stepped out and Dean elbowed Rigsby awake.

"We're here."

Rigsby rubbed his eyes and followed him out. "Don't sound so bloody excited."

Dean inspected the windswept grounds. There was nothing here but grass. No gardens, except the kitchen garden in the back, no lush lawns for games, or fanciful statues to greet you. Chickens pecked at the dirt in the small courtyard—they, at least, appeared happy.

He approached the door and it opened, a hunched old man pushing it against a current of wind. Dean rushed forward to help him. The man glanced up in surprise and gave him a weathered smile.

"Is it really you, or have I died?"

Dean chuckled. "It's me, Mr. Hale."

"By golly, look at the mountain you've turned into. What a sight you are." Mr. Hale waved them all inside. "Shall I have rooms prepared for your guests, sir?"

Dean hesitated to commit to staying. He didn't know what sort of temperament he would find his father in. "I haven't decided yet. Mr. Hale, Lord Heath and Lord Rigsby," Dean introduced them.

"Welcome to Winchester Manor, my lords. Let me show

you to the drawing room, and I'll have Mrs. Hale put on a fresh pot of tea."

"Very good, Mr. Hale." Dean followed the man into the great hall and into the drawing room, which was exactly as he remembered. The decor was the same, but that wasn't surprising. The house had always had a medieval flare. Battle-axes, suits of armor, and barren wooden chairs littered the house. There wasn't a single embroidered pillow in existence that he could remember. The place was stark, uncomfortable and cold, exactly like his father.

Mr. Hale threw another log on the fire, stoking it into something that could compete with the ever-present chill in the room.

"This house is like the inspiration for a gothic novel," Rigsby said.

"Or nightmares," Dean muttered.

"I hope we are not imposing on your father," Lord Heath said as he warmed his hands near the fire.

"My father wasn't expecting us, but you will be welcomed all the same," Dean replied.

"What about you?" Rigsby whispered as he moved past Dean to the decanter.

"I'm not certain of my reception."

"A father always rejoices the return of a son," Lord Heath said with his back to them.

Dean didn't believe this would be the case, but either way, it was time to put the past to bed.

Mrs. Hale carried in the tea tray. She beamed at Dean, her face still full and round with her cheerful smile, but also carved with the lines of time and strain.

"It is good to see you again, Mrs. Hale."

"Oh, how we've longed for your return, my lord."

Dean stood and hugged the woman. "Thank you."

She dabbed her eyes before pouring them cups of steaming tea and retreating.

Mr. Hale returned shortly after. "Your father is awake now, and I've informed him of your arrival. He would like to see you."

Dean's stomach clenched uncomfortably, but he stood and nodded to Rigsby and Lord Heath. "This won't take long."

Lord Heath gave him a meaningful look. "Take all the time you need."

Dean followed Hale up the stairs. He didn't need an escort to his father's rooms. He'd been there frequently enough, for lectures and floggings. Even before his father had become ill, the anteroom to the master bedroom saw more use than his study. He had eaten there, worked there, took meetings there, and punished his son there.

Dean's eyes adjusted to the dim corridor as they made their way down the silent, bereft hall to the door.

Hale knocked twice and then turned the knob, holding the door open.

Dean felt twelve again, called to his father's chamber for an offense he was never aware of. His feet dragged as he strode forward, the years of his manhood, confidence, and experience stripping away as easily as a silk scarf falling to the floor. He was a boy again.

A man of wilted stature and thinning hair awaited him. He bowed to Dean.

"Sir, I am Mr. Fisher. It is a pleasure to converse with you at last after exchanging so many letters regarding your father's estate."

"Good afternoon, Mr. Fisher. Your letters have been most informative."

"Thank you, sir. It is wonderful that you have finally come home. The reins of Winchester may now be firmly clasped in your hands."

"He isn't dead yet, is he?"

"No, sir!" Mr. Fisher blushed. "I only mean that, as your father's health has declined so significantly, it has become increasingly difficult to manage the estate to its fullest capabilities."

"I understand, Mr. Fisher." His father had a tight fist on the affairs of his estate. Things could improve, but his father refused to change his ways.

Mr. Fisher opened the door to the bedroom and waved him through. Dean entered slowly, surprised to find the room filled with pleasant sunlight, the curtains wafting in a gentle breeze. A woman hummed lightly as she rocked in a chair beside the bed, knitting a garment. She smiled in greeting. The room even smelled of freshly baked bread.

The maid leaned over and gently shook his father's arm. Dean froze. The man in the bed was a pale copy of the man who had terrified him most of his boyhood. His hair was white and thin, and his once-thick square jaw was now bony, with hanging bags of skin. His sideburns stood out comically, like two bushy columns framing his face.

Dean relaxed, a sense of himself returning enough to feel comfortable. This man couldn't hurt him anymore.

His father blinked and focused on the maid, smiling at her. "Mary?"

She nodded toward Dean. "You have a visitor, my lord."

Dean stepped closer to the foot of the bed. "I'm here… Father." The word tasted unfamiliar on his tongue.

The old man turned to him, blinking milky green eyes. "Is that so?"

"Mr. Fisher has kept me apprised of everything."

"He's told me as much."

Dean restrained the urge to walk out. "I've come to see how you're faring."

His father raised an eyebrow. "I'm faring quite well, thank you."

Dean raised a brow in return. It didn't appear as if he could even leave the bed.

"Mary, will you leave us a moment? This is my nursemaid, Mary. She is a balm to my soul."

Dean nodded. She was not young, but nor was she old. She smiled at his father and retreated from the room.

Dean walked to the side of the bed and pulled a chair close. He folded his hands in his lap and crossed his ankles.

His father studied him. "Where have you been all this time?"

"Abroad, mostly," Dean answered.

"Abroad? Where?"

"India, for most of the time. Africa, China, wherever the wind took me."

His father frowned. "How have you managed such a feat with nothing?"

"Believe it or not, there was more to me than procuring heirs. I took what little I had and invested it. I have my own fortune now."

The frown turned into a scowl. "Sounds disgustingly mercantile."

Dean shrugged. He wouldn't dare mention how he'd worked on a ship to earn the money he'd invested.

"Have you a wife? Children?"

"No."

"You still loathe the idea of marriage?"

For the briefest of moments, a flash of Lucy entered his mind. "I've never loathed the idea of marriage," Dean replied.

"You certainly did when I suggested—"

"You didn't suggest. You ordered. You ignored that I was already in love—"

"Bah!"

The yell startled Dean into silence. For a bedridden man, his father's voice had not weakened, but his stamina had. That outburst had cost him. He breathed heavily and closed his eyes, bringing a hand to his brow.

"Love means nothing," he said after a moment.

"It meant something to me."

The familiar ache washed over Dean. He'd almost forgotten what it felt like to miss Rosie.

"Even that girl had more sense than you."

Rosalie Abbey, Dean wanted to snarl, but instead, chose not to waste his breath, or her name, on such a stubborn old man.

"I won't be staying long unless you need me to."

"Be off with you. I haven't a need for any wastrels."

Dean exhaled and stood. He walked to the door without looking back and closed it softly behind him. He found Mr. Fisher and Mary speaking softly outside.

"It is so good of you to come, my lord," Mary said. "His lordship speaks of you often."

"Nothing good, I'm sure."

Her smile faltered. "He often forgets what he says, or what time of his life he is in."

Dean didn't know what to say to that. All he knew was that there would be no reconciliation. There would be no forgiveness in either of their hearts. He simply nodded and started to leave the anteroom.

The maid put up a hand to stop him. "Wait."

"Mary, please," Mr. Fisher warned.

"I won't let him go with such ugliness still between them," she said.

Dean stiffened.

Mary pulled an envelope from her pocket and pressed it into his hand. "This will ease your pain."

Dean took the frail and obviously old letter and stuffed it into his pocket to destroy later. Nothing would erase the pain of the past. He wanted to burn all of it: his memories and his feelings for Rosie. He simply longed to forget it all and just go on with his life.

He nodded again and left the anteroom. When he returned to the drawing room, Rigsby and Lord Heath turned expectantly in his direction.

"We will depart tomorrow," Dean announced.

He could feel Lord Heath's disappointment and didn't meet his gaze. Why the man wanted reconciliation, he didn't understand, but it was not to be.

"Well, where shall we go? Rigsby asked. "Home?"

"The women have returned from Bath by now. I can only guess at the trial your mother endured with your sister there," Lord Heath replied.

"I think Lucy's learned her lesson. She's growing up," Rigsby defended.

Lord Heath raised a skeptical brow. "If she is anything like your mother, it will take a babe in her arms to settle her down."

Rigsby cringed. "Don't speak of such things. I don't wish to know anything about babies or the creation of them with my mother or sister."

Lord Heath chuckled. "Squeamish pup."

"Pup?"

Dean swallowed back the urge to smile at their repartee. His father had gotten to him, and seeing the closeness between Rigsby and Lord Heath only made the sting worse. "You shouldn't feel the need to stay. He is very ill. If he worsens overnight, I may decide to stay until the end."

They nodded in sympathy.

"Well, why don't you show us around this monstrosity?" Rigsby suggested.

Dean didn't want to explore the manor. He considered the fire in the hearth, but if he took the letter out now and tossed it in, Rigsby and Lord Heath might ask questions—or worse, try to stop him and salvage the damn thing.

"You want the grand tour? We can start in the hall."

He'd dispose of the letter later, when he was alone.

CHAPTER 20

"Bath will become tedious without you. Are you sure you must go?"

Lucy peered down at the tea she swirled in her cup. She counted the seconds until they would return home and she could stop pretending she was having a wonderful time here. There were bright spots, thanks to Mr. Jeffrey and Thea, but she wanted to be home more than anything, where she could sort herself out in peace. Would her teacup reveal her fortune or provide any indication she might find happiness and love with any other man besides Winchester?

Perhaps she had a future with the man sitting across from her. She looked up at him with a smile. He was handsome, after all, and entertaining and witty... If only she could spare a little room in her heart for him. But she still felt full of Winchester, and there was simply no space for anyone else. Not yet, anyhow.

But time away had shown her she might have to *make* room, because as much as she knew she loved Winchester, she simply wasn't sure she'd ever see him again.

"I thank you for your company, Mr. Jeffrey. It is not I who gives Bath its present charm, but you."

His lips twisted as his gaze warmed, and he accepted her compliment without protest.

"Beware, Lady Lucy. You'll steal my heart with such flattery. How will I go on without you?"

How easy it was to flirt with a man so eager for her attention. Almost *too* easy after battling so long for Winchester's notice. Mr. Jeffrey was certainly more likable and amiable than Winchester. Lucy could spend all day cataloguing their differences, but where would that leave her?

More confused than ever, if her present alternating pattern of contentment and utter misery were any indication. One day she was fine, with nary a thought spared for Winchester, and the next day she could barely stand to see a couple strolling together without feeling an ache so deep it felt like a great chasm was opening in her heart, sucking in all the light and warmth.

But when Mr. Jeffrey was around, which he seemed to be almost daily, along with his cousin, Mr. Farris and aunt, Mrs. Farris, Lucy felt none of those terrible things. His banter was an excellent distraction from her heartache, and with him she felt more like her old self, the half of her that had existed without loving Winchester, who used to toy with her admirers like a kitten with a feather.

"I suspect you'll find another young woman to shower with attention soon enough."

"Never suggest such a thing. There is, and only will ever be, one Lady Lucy. I'll retire my charms and take up monkhood. No other woman will ever be enough for me now."

Lucy giggled, if only to keep up the pretense that she was

as engaged in this flirtation as he was. With relief, she saw that Thea and Mr. Farris were returning from their walk around the manicured garden of their rented townhouse, followed by Lucy's mother and Mrs. Farris.

"We may as well depart, too. I've had my fill of sea air," Mrs. Farris said as she walked up.

Mr. Farris frowned. "The good doctor said one more week to fortify your constitution. We won't leave a day sooner."

Lucy was impressed by Mr. Farris' rare show of strength. He cared for his mother's failing health with diligence. He really was a good chap, and perhaps he would be a good match for Thea? Lucy considered this as she stood and Mr. Jeffrey held out her chair. Turning to follow the group into the house, he took her harm and pulled her aside.

"One moment, Lady Lucy?"

She halted and faced him, half aware he might try to kiss her again, as he had yesterday. Her heart kicked up its pace, but she wasn't ready to do this yet, to forget every lovely, torrid emotion Winchester had stirred in her. Mr. Jeffrey was so much like her in his disposition, and handsome enough to tempt her, with his thick, shining, reddish-gold hair, but there was still something missing.

"Yes?"

"I know I may have shocked you with my ardor yesterday, but if I do come to Yorkshire, might I pay you a call?"

Lucy bit her lip. Would encouraging the affections of another man help her forget Winchester? Would she ever be capable of loving someone else?

She could feel a headache coming on, her own questions tearing her apart. She nodded. That was all she could commit to right now.

He swiftly kissed her cheek and escorted her inside.

Lucy had the uncomfortable sensation she'd regret this moment, but at least having something to regret meant she'd made a choice. She was not a woman to pine and consign herself to spinsterhood over a broken heart. She was a woman of action—careless action at times—but action, nonetheless.

§

Back at home at last, Lucy contemplated the invitation she held in her hand. It was for her brother, but the daring red script on the front called to her. She'd been searching for another quill in the study when she'd spotted it on the desk. It was clearly an invitation. But to what? She set it down again, at war with the urge to open it. She had a multitude of reasons ready to explain why she was here, about why she could be mistaken and open it.

She ambled about the room, tapping the envelope against her hand. Should she do it? Was it worth the trouble? That was the true question. Lately, she'd been feeling out of sorts...restless, even. Ever since that night—her gut clenched as her memory took her back to the dark hall—she hadn't felt right in her skin.

She could still recall the feeling of his hands on her and the way her heart had pounded and her skin had burned. She could close her eyes at night and almost relive the moment her body had come to life, her nerves bursting in unison, like bubbles of light.

Lucy blushed shamefully. She wanted to do it again, and it felt wrong. She felt like an imposter of herself. Here she stood, appearing exactly as she always had, but on the inside, she was different. Now that she'd had a taste of desire and had experienced the clever hands of a rake, she wanted more. The troubling part was she didn't want just *any* rake. She wanted *her* rake. She still wanted Dean.

It didn't help that Thea had had to return home to her family, and now Lucy was alone. She didn't like the idea that she couldn't enjoy her own company, but she just never could stand being all by herself. Who would she share simple observations with? Who would she enjoy a private joke with?

Who would be her voice of reason?

She considered the envelope again. What could this blasted thing be? Her fingernail slipped under the corner and the seal lifted.

"Well, now I *have* to open it. It's practically begging me to."

She tore the rest of the wax seal and unfolded the paper. Scanning the contents, she frowned in puzzlement. It was an invitation to a masquerade? She sighed, her mischievous delight sinking. This little endeavor was not worth the questions that would arise. Thinking swiftly, she refolded the paper, held the waxed edge over the fire just long enough to soften it, and then pressed it closed again. It was not a perfect seal, but it would do if no one inspected it too closely. She left it where she'd found it on the desk and wandered out of the study, defeated by boredom. She entered the library and resolutely chose a book to read. If her reality couldn't entertain her, she was going to lose herself in fiction.

Lucy jerked awake to the sound of laughter. She blinked as she looked around. She was still in the library. The book slid from her chest as she sat up, and then thumped as it landed on the floor. She picked it up and set it down as she stood and walked toward the muffled voices. She pressed her ear to the shared door between the library and her father's study.

First Jonathan, and then her father, spoke. She put her hand on the knob, about to turn it when a third voice stopped her. She froze. Fear, joy, and then sorrow pierced her. He'd returned, as well? She put her hands to her face, swallowing the ache in her throat and fighting the sudden rush of tears. She wanted to slap him and then hug him like a madwoman, content to never let him go. She rested her forehead on the door, hearing the jovial rumble of their talking, the dry banter shared between them.

Then she spun away from the door, rushing past a small table and bumping it with her leg. A tower of books toppled to the floor, creating a racket. Drat! Why did she never put the books away? She dropped to her knees and gathered them, her hands shaking and her mind racing with panic as the door opened.

"Lucy?"

She turned at the sound of her brother's voice. Tears rushed forward, and she couldn't stop them. He froze, and she rushed to him, throwing her arms around him. She sobbed silently.

His arms came around her, and he hugged her tightly. "Lucy?" he said again, with alarm.

Their father joined them. "What on earth is wrong?"

"I missed you both so much!" Lucy sobbed.

She could feel her father patting her on the back, and was grateful for Jonathan's supporting arms, but she could also feel the presence of Winchester just there in the doorway, watching. She wanted to run to him and cling to him, but for now, she would settle for a brother she hadn't really missed but was nonetheless happy to see. He would serve as an adequate decoy for her uncontrollable burst of emotion.

She mopped up her tears and collected herself. She gave her father a hug and smiled.

"Did you only just return?"

"Just. I've seen to your mother already, but she didn't know your whereabouts," her father replied.

Lucy waved to the chaise lounge, where a rumpled blanket still lingered. "I've been here."

"As you can see, we've brought Winchester back with us. We visited his country seat," Jonathan announced.

"Oh?" Lucy turned and pretended to be surprised by his presence in the doorway.

He pushed away from the jam, where he'd been leaning, and bowed in greeting.

"Good day, Lady Lucy."

So, it was Lady Lucy again, she grumbled internally. "Good day, Lord Winchester. How was your journey?" She pulled her gaze from his and encompassed her brother and father in her inquiry.

"Beneficial, I should say. Now that I've done my personal accounting of the lands, I can better advise Mr. Higgins."

"How fortunate for Mr. Higgins," she murmured.

"How was Bath?" Jonathan asked as he picked up one of the books from the floor and paged through it.

"It was…enlightening," Lucy answered. Good God. Bath had been horrible, and Winchester made her so nervous, she couldn't keep her voice even.

"Enlightening?" Jonathan frowned. "When has Bath ever been enlightening?"

"Well..." She hesitated. She was so focused on Winchester that she had lost her train of thought when he moved out of the doorway and into the library, closer to her.

She shook her head slightly, willing herself to calm and return to normal. She briefly peeked his way, testing her ability to react sensibly.

He perused the bookshelves, his back to her.

"Dare I ask your mother what enlightening means regarding Bath?" her father asked.

Lucy smirked to herself. Lady Heath definitely knew whom her daughter might be speaking of.

"That isn't necessary," Lucy said. "I made some new acquaintances, is all. Mr. Farris was there with his mother. Somehow, Mother orchestrated that occurrence."

"Without a doubt," her father said, chuckling.

"And his cousin Mr. Jeffrey joined us on occasion."

Jonathan glanced up from his book. "Mr. Calvin Jeffrey?"

"I believe that is his full name, yes."

"He attended university with Winchester and I."

"Oh?" Lucy turned to both men. "Did you find him likable?"

"He has his charms," Winchester said dryly.

Lucy took a deep breath. His voice still had its way of vibrating through her. "Would you say he is suitable?"

"Suitable?"

"Suitable for what?" Jonathan asked.

"Would you consider him to be a suitable gentleman for an acquaintance with me?" Lucy said to Winchester, a touch of anger taking hold. She didn't know what reaction she was hoping for—jealousy?

"It isn't my place to determine what gentlemen are suitable for your acquaintance, Lady Lucy."

"Perhaps not. I only ask because you know him, and Father does not." Lucy switched her gaze to Jonathan. "What are your thoughts, brother?"

"Are you asking me if he is a suitable husband? He stroked his chin. "Let me think on this."

"Husband?" Winchester asked.

Lucy turned to her father. He regarded them while leaning against the settee.

"Should I expect a visit from this gentleman?" he asked her.

"Heavens, no." Lucy laughed, and then she noticed his peculiar frown as he looked over her head. She spun around to face Jonathan. He froze, and Winchester coughed to cover a laugh.

"What are you doing behind my back?"

"It seems your brother and Winchester *do* find him unsuitable," her father said.

"How so?"

"I really shouldn't say," Jonathan said.

"If you won't tell, then that only makes him more interesting. So, what is it?"

"I'm going to question your mother on this matter." Lord Heath departed.

"He's a rake," Winchester said simply.

Lucy smiled slyly. "That isn't a deterrent for me."

"It bloody well should be," he growled back.

Jonathan scoffed. "He is more in love with himself than he could ever be with a woman."

"He is given to cruelty," Winchester added.

"Is he? How so? I've known men who claim to be vile creatures, and are actually more akin to sheep in wolves' clothing." She watched Winchester's expression as she walked past him and reclaimed the chaise lounge. "I may invite him to stay with us, or perhaps I could ask Mrs. Farris? She may not want to encourage me to find interest in anyone other than her son, though."

Winchester sat across from her in an empty chair. She couldn't read his expression.

"What do you think?" she asked him.

"To be honest, I don't have any strong opinions on the matter," he replied.

But there was something about him. His voice had dropped lower, and his features had hardened.

"Absolutely none?" she needled. "Should I marry him? Or is he more suitable for dalliance?"

"Lucille Eloise, I don't want to hear you utter the word *dalliance*. Ever," Jonathan scolded. "You'll be banished from London for life."

Lucy ignored him. "Your thoughts, Lord Winchester?"

He stared back at her. "I haven't any."

"I assumed you an authority on the subject of dalliance. No?"

"Lucy," Jonathan warned sternly.

"Calm down, brother. I'm only asking questions. Shouldn't I seek answers from those deemed safe?" She focused on Winchester. "I couldn't be any safer here with the two of you than if I were asking a herd of sheep."

He narrowed his eyes at her.

"Mr. Jeffrey would make sport of you and toss you aside," Jonathan muttered angrily.

"Sport? What is sport?" Lucy giggled. She knew exactly what he meant, but loved driving him mad with her indecent questions.

Her brother strode away from her and back into the study. Lucy chased after him. She caught sight of the open invitation on the desk and paused to pick it up.

"What is this?"

Jonathan ripped it from her hand and crumpled it up, tossing it into the fire. "Nothing to do with you."

"It was an invitation to a masquerade," she stated.

He poured himself a drink. "How did you know that?"

"I have eyes, and I read quickly."

"Well, that masquerade is an event not attended by our society."

"Then why do you get an invitation?"

He turned to her. "I'm a man. I get to do all the fun things you can't do without censure."

"Believe me, I'm aware of it." She turned and left him in the study. Winchester stood just on the other side of the door.

"I bet you're happy you don't have a sister like me, my lord."

"I was just about to say something to that effect," Jonathan said from inside the study.

"Did you truly enjoy Bath?" Winchester asked quietly, pausing beside her.

"I did. Mr. Jeffrey helped me see things from a different view. The experience was quite pleasurable," Lucy fibbed.

His jaw tightened. "What things?"

"I wish I had the time to tell you, but I really must get ready for dinner." Lucy moved away, wary of letting herself feel any sort of triumph for garnering whatever little emotion she got from him. He'd already claimed so much of her heart, and she, so little of his. She wasn't going to give more until she got more.

Warm fingers touched hers, and she froze. He moved behind her, and she could feel his breath on the little hairs on her nape.

"Mr. Jeffrey is not good for you."

"Is that so? And you think you know what is good for me?"

Lucy waited for an answer, but when none came, she turned her head and found he was no longer there. Damn him. He'd gone back to her brother in the study.

Slinking closer, she heard the murmur of their conversation. She stood out of view of the doorway and listened.

"Would you like to go?" Jonathan asked.

Silence.

"You look like you could use the distraction, and perhaps a bit of companionship."

"Perhaps," Winchester answered.

Lucy covered her mouth to hide her gasp. She quickly slipped out of the library. The pain of that single word so overwhelming, she couldn't breathe. When she reached her room, she startled Marigold, who was preparing her bath before dinner.

"Good heavens! My heart jumped to my neck!" Marigold laughed in surprise and then focused on Lucy's face. "What is wrong?"

Lucy just shook her head. Her throat was so tight that she couldn't speak.

Marigold poured her a glass of water and brought it to her. "Drink up."

Lucy obeyed, and then she exhaled as she brought the glass down. "I'm so stupid, Marigold."

"Don't say that."

"As much as I want him to love me, he cares nothing about me. I'm merely another woman vying for his affections, and as interchangeable as the next."

"The stupidity is his. If he can't see how special you are, then he isn't worthy of you."

Lucy wished that were true. She set the glass down on her vanity and collapsed on the stool. It was there that she saw the letter. "What is this?"

Marigold unpinned her hair. "A boy brought it for you."

"A boy?"

"Yes. Very mysterious."

Lucy ripped open the letter, hope flaring that it was some secret communication from Winchester. She read it quickly, her hope fading to confusion. Then she frowned.

"Is something wrong?" Marigold asked as she brushed her hair.

"It's from Mr. Jeffery."

"From Bath?"

"Yes. He is visiting his aunt, Mrs. Farris."

"Oh? And he wants to see you?"

Lucy nodded.

"You must have made quite the impression."

Lucy studied her reflection and thought of Bath. In her mind, she pictured the lovely little courtyard where she and

Mr. Jeffrey had sat. He'd whispered things in her ear, and she'd waited to feel anything of the excitement she'd felt with Winchester. It was why she hadn't reacted when Mr. Jeffrey had lifted her chin, bringing his lips to hers and pushing her down on the bench. She had turned away then, but he had still laid upon her and kissed her neck. She should have been frightened, she should have pushed him away with all her strength, but at that moment, she hadn't felt like she was there at all. She had just felt empty.

Mr. Jeffrey wanted trouble as much as Lucy liked to make it. They'd become cohorts in Bath, finding each other at every party and spending the evening searching for ways to make mischief. Poor Mr. Farris had watched them woefully, and Thea… She had lectured Lucy every night about the dangers of encouraging him. He wasn't Winchester, she would say. And Lucy knew it well. That was the whole point. He *wasn't* Winchester. He was interested, and Winchester was not.

She'd let him kiss her neck, and he'd even went so far as to grope her breast. That was when she'd pushed him back. The emptiness inside her had turned to a bitter sting of betrayal. She'd betrayed herself by letting another man touch what she wished Winchester would want.

Now she blinked and considered the note. He wanted to meet her. What should she do?

"Where is the boy, Marigold?"

"He's waiting in the kitchen. Mrs. Hart declared him too thin, and set about fattening him up in a single afternoon."

Lucy reached for her quill and paper. "We must send him away with my response before he's too full to move."

CHAPTER 21

Lucy slowed her horse as her brother and Winchester raced over the hills. She deviated north toward the spire of the chapel and urged Penny into a gallop. She had to be out of sight before either of them thought to look back and find her missing. Hidden by the forest which separated the village from most of the estate, she relaxed and slowed her horse as she crossed onto chapel land and rode along the low stone wall that bordered the cemetery. She spotted Mr. Jeffrey before he saw her. He was walking along a row of headstones.

Lucy dismounted and tied her horse next to his at the gate. As the oldest part of the cemetery, this area rarely had visitors. It's why she'd chosen to meet him here. It was also the least romantic place she could think of. She wasn't in the mood to fight off his advances.

He turned as she drew near and smiled at her.

She returned his smile and admired his way of turning the simplest of gestures into something sultry.

"Good morning, Lady Lucy."

"Good morning, Mr. Jeffrey. What brings you to York?"

"I think you know."

His brandy-colored eyes warmed as he stared at her, and Lucy had to glance away. His reddish-blond hair shone with streaks of gold when the sun shined on it, and despite herself, she found it pleasing.

He held out his hand. "Come walk with me."

She chose to take his arm instead.

They walked along the headstones for a while without saying anything. Lucy let the peace of the cemetery wash over her. She didn't have much time. Soon, Jonathan would come searching for her, and they were not far enough away here to avoid discovery.

"I'd like to see you again soon," Mr. Jeffrey said.

"Oh?"

"There is a masquerade nearby. It isn't something you or I *should* attend, but I've friends who go and proclaim the evening enchanting. I'd like for you to come." He winked at her. "In secret."

"I think I've heard of this masquerade."

There was little else she'd been able to think about since the word *perhaps* had become the most hated word in the English world—at least to her.

"Have you?"

"I saw my brother's invitation."

He nodded. "Yes, but this isn't a party your parents would allow you to attend. I fear it may be too difficult."

"Jonathan will not take me, if that is what you are suggesting."

Mr. Jeffrey slowed and turned her to face him, running his thumb over her lower lip.

Lucy hoped he wouldn't try to kiss her. She wasn't sure

what she was doing, or why she was even encouraging him. Her head and heart were not in accord, and they fought viciously inside her.

"I want to see you, and I know you would enjoy yourself immensely. I know the way you're caged, Lady Lucy. Held by the love of your family, but also restrained from experiencing the things that make life worth living. Don't deny yourself."

She swallowed. Could he see what Winchester did not? She'd grown so tired of this ache in her chest. Was Mr. Jeffrey the remedy for her battered heart?

"Perhaps…" She cringed internally as she uttered the word. "I might be able to get away. I saw the address, and I can ride there."

He grinned and stole a quick kiss. "I knew you could, but I wouldn't have you ride. It's far too dangerous. I will send a carriage to meet you somewhere close, but out of sight."

She thought for a moment. "There is a thicket of trees outside our drive. The carriage can wait there and I can sneak out."

"I so look forward to our adventure, Lady Lucy. In two days, we will see each other again."

He bent again, but she ducked her head and avoided his lips. He kissed her forehead instead.

"I must go now. My brother will be searching for me."

He turned them and they headed back toward their horses. "How will I know you at the ball?"

"Lucy grinned at him. "I will be dressed as an angel."

He leered at her. "And I the devil."

She laughed uncomfortably and then let him lift her into her saddle.

"Until then, Mr. Jeffrey."

"I will be counting the seconds," he said, and then mounted his horse.

They rode off in opposite directions.

Jittery with excitement as she left the cemetery, Lucy turned her horse to cut through the forest. She'd never had clandestine meetings such as this with a man before, and now she was planning to attend a masquerade alone to meet one? Was she losing her mind? Did she even want to go? She didn't know *what* she wanted to do. The things she did want, she couldn't have. She didn't want to feel like the fool she was. She didn't want to care that Winchester was attending this ball, and *perhaps* would find himself a bit of sport. She cringed and her stomach rolled in a nauseating fashion.

"What are you doing, Lucy?"

Winchester's voice jerked her from her restless thoughts. She twisted and found him sitting silent as a statue on his horse. He nudged his horse forward until they faced each other, their legs almost touching.

"What are you doing?" he repeated.

She returned his scowl. "What business is it of yours?"

"Is this how you meant to wait for me?"

She gasped in outrage. How *dare* he throw her words back at her as if he were the one hurting.

"*Perhaps* I've come to realize how futile it is to wait for a man who cares not for me, but again, what business is it of yours? You don't want me."

"And Mr. Jeffrey does?"

Dean could taste his rage on his tongue, but he kept it leashed. From his vantage point in the forest, he had seen exactly what Jeffrey wanted with Lucy.

"He certainly isn't afraid to act like it."

"And when he's had you, what then?" he asked bitterly.

"Why should you care?" she cried.

She was right. He *shouldn't* care, but he did. He seethed and burned with hatred for Calvin Jeffrey. The man didn't deserve to lick the dust from her slippers, but twice, Dean had watched him kiss her—and with enough familiarity that he was sure it wasn't the first time.

"You've been too spoiled, Lucy. You don't realize the hurt you cause your family by acting so recklessly."

"Hurt? Yes, I'm a bit spoiled. They love me and I love them, but I'm not going to find what I want the way they expect me to. My family would happily marry me to Mr. Farris and smile at my wedding. But what of my hurt? Will it not hurt to spend the rest of my life with someone I don't love?"

"You don't know that."

"I do." Her voice broke. "You've shown me that much."

Then she yanked her horse away and rode off into the woods.

Dean cursed aloud and kicked his horse into a gallop to follow her. His stomach was aching with the force of a well-placed punch. So, she wanted to blame him for being a willful, thoughtless hoyden? Well, he had something to say about that.

"Lucy!" he shouted after her, once he'd caught up with her.

She shook her head, her tears ripped from her cheeks by the wind.

"Slow down!"

She threw him a glare and flicked her reins. He hadn't realized her mare was so fast.

He could see Rigsby waving at them from atop the hill and waved back. Lucy raced on, turning west from her brother but still toward the house. Dean chased after her, Rigsby also now in pursuit.

"Lucy!" he shouted after her.

She cut around a copse of trees and was out of his sight for a second.

He rounded the trees, but she'd disappeared.

"Dean!" she shouted.

He pulled on the reins and turned.

She waited just behind the copse of trees.

"Are you insane?" he demanded as he pulled up to her.

"Are you going to tell?" she asked as she panted.

"What?"

"Are you going to tell Jonathan what you saw in the cemetery?"

He leaned forward in his saddle and tried to catch his breath. "I should."

"But you won't." She raised one brow. "We've both things we'd rather not have shared with my family, haven't we, Dean? Or am I only allowed to say your name when you've pinned me against a door?"

He sat up straight and ground his teeth so hard they hurt. "Touché."

"Then we have an understanding?"

"I still don't understand you," he admitted.

"That makes two of us."

She flicked her reins and rode off at a safer speed. Dean followed her, wanting to roar like a beast in frustration. Rigsby caught up to them quickly now that they had slowed significantly.

He pulled up beside them. "What the devil is going on? Where'd you get off to?"

He reached for Lucy's reins, but she jerked them out of his reach.

"I went off on my own for a time, that's all."

"And then decided to tear through the countryside like a madwoman?"

"Yes, precisely."

Dean had to admire her acting skills, but he also wanted to strangle her.

Rigsby turned to him. "Where was she?"

"I found her riding through the woods, near the cemetery."

"The cemetery?" Rigsby huffed out as he still tried to catch his breath. "Meeting someone?"

"I beg your pardon?"

"Farris wrote to me, warning me of Jeffrey's interest. His intentions are far from honorable. You'd do well to stay away from him. If he comes near you, promise me you'll tell Winchester or me."

She gazed directly at Dean. "If I have a need to tell you or Winchester anything, it's to mind your own bloody business."

And with that, she turned her horse toward the house.

The men scowled after her.

"What should we do?" Dean asked.

"Nothing. Lucy sees obstacles as a challenge to conquer. She has to learn for herself."

Dean scoffed. "She'll walk right into his arms."

"If that is what it takes for her to come to her own conclusion, so be it."

"You'd stand by and watch her ruin herself?" Dean asked in dismay.

"Of course not. I will do whatever I can to protect her, but I can't always protect her from herself."

"You could tie her to her bed," Dean muttered, as he pushed his horse into motion.

He disagreed heartily with Rigsby's blasé solution for dealing with the budding disaster that was Lucy and Jeffrey. If it were *his* sister, he'd be knocking on Jeffrey's door right now and pummeling his smug face.

"What about warning your father?"

"We did," Rigsby said in exasperation. "The more we try to stop her, the further we drive her into his arms."

Dean didn't like that answer. From what he saw, she was *already* in his arms. His mood only blackened further as they reached the house and he saw that Lucy had left her horse in the care of the stable hands and escaped them.

He couldn't resign himself to letting the matter go, but nor could he stand there and demand action. He had no right, which bothered him. If he had a sister, he could never just let her make her mistakes, not when said mistake could have such dire consequences. The reason he knew the type of man Jeffrey was, was because many of the same labels applied to him.

He climbed the stairs to his room, sweaty and covered in dust. He peeled off his jacket, waistcoat, and shirt, tossing them onto the floor with disgust. Then he splashed some water on his face. It did little to wash away the dirt, so he rang for a bath.

Once the tub had filled, he sank down into the water and sighed. He hated inaction. He hated that he had no place in this fight. Lucy was headed for self-destruction, and he was supposed to just let her? He could speak to her father again, but he and Rigsby had already outlined all the reasons why Jeffrey was the last person his daughter should be associating with. Lord Heath had reacted curiously, far too complacent in Dean's mind. He'd asked Dean's opinion, which he'd given, and then had acted as if there was nothing else to do.

But Dean had other ideas.

Leaving Jeffrey a bloody pile of pulp was one. Locking Lucy in her room until her old age was another. Preferably with an armed guard—a *female* armed guard.

He sank lower in the water and angrily scrubbed the dirt from his skin. Finally he climbed out of the tub and prepared for dinner, eager to see Lucy. If he could, he would drill into her the stupidity of seeing Jeffrey again. If he couldn't make her family understand, he would just have to convince her himself.

When he entered the drawing room, she wasn't there.

Rigsby stood. "Oh good, we can go into dinner now."

"Are we not waiting for everyone?"

"Lucy's ill. She won't be joining us this evening."

He was skeptical. "Ill?"

"Nothing to worry over," Lady Heath said, smiling at him.

Dean turned to Rigsby for further information, but none was forthcoming. He walked with his friend to the dining room while Lord and Lady Heath continued talking.

"Are you not worried this is some ruse?" Dean asked quietly.

Rigsby blinked at him. "Ruse?"

"To see Jeffrey," Dean added.

Rigsby cocked his head to the side. "You know, that *would*

be brilliant. Claim the female malady, and then sneak off to meet a lover."

Dean bristled all over. "Has anyone checked on her whereabouts?"

"Her maid delivered the message, and my mother confirmed her presence. But it is worth noting, I suppose." Rigsby clapped him on the back. "Why don't *you* go check on her?"

Dean glared at him.

"I'm only teasing. The matter is handled. She's not about to run off to Gretna Green with the man."

Dean pictured that very scenario as he claimed his chair. He tried to eat the delicious fare set before him, but his mind wouldn't obey, and everything tasted like tree bark.

CHAPTER 22

"Are you sure you want to do this?" Marigold asked for the hundredth time.

"No, and yes."

"I think it's very risky to rely on this man. You will be at his mercy."

Lucy sighed. "You've said as much already. And I won't be at his mercy. I will be at a ball attended by my own brother."

"*And* Lord Winchester."

"And him."

Lucy closed her eyes against a wave of uncertainty. She felt naked in her angel costume with the changes that she and Marigold had made. They had worked steadily for two days to complete the alterations, and now, as she studied her reflection, she regretted them.

Marigold draped her white domino over her shoulders, and then her brown wool cloak.

"Good luck," she whispered.

Lucy turned away from the mirror. Marigold followed her

downstairs to the back of the house now silent and dark. Her parents had retired, and Jonathan and Winchester had left hours ago. She didn't want to think about what they could be doing at this moment. She wouldn't reach the masquerade until just before midnight as it was.

She hurried from the house, following the shrubbery wall, and then ducking through it close to the end of the drive. She exhaled with relief when she saw the carriage waiting. The coachman nodded and climbed down to open the door for her.

"Thank you," she whispered.

She sat back and hugged herself against the chill as the carriage started to move. This was by far the worst decision she'd made in her life. With every mile they traveled, she regretted her idea to attend the ball. She even considered asking the driver to take her back and bribe him handsomely for his time, but then she thought of what Winchester could be doing, and who he could be doing it with, and her jealous anger carried her forth.

After what felt like an eternity, the coach turned down a drive. Lucy peeked out the window and could see a large, well-lit manor. Stepping out of the carriage, she saw the other guests all dressed in exquisite costumes and masks, and she smiled with relief.

She entered the front hall and gave her cloak to a footman. The clock in the hall affirmed it was only half past eleven. She descended the stairs to the ballroom, not making eye contact with anyone, but glancing over the crowd for the familiar stature of her brother or Mr. Jeffrey.

There were many devils present. With an inward groan, Lucy remembered that Jonathan's costume was also a devil. She would have to avoid all of them until the unmasking, or

Mr. Jeffrey found her. When she reached the bottom of the stairs, she opened her domino. The guests around her turned to leer at her, and she boldly stared back, fighting a shiver of fear. She'd had Marigold turn her angel dress from one garment to two, like the costume women from Marigold's home country wore to dance in. She'd never bared her stomach in public before, and now she regretted it immensely.

However, knowing she would become a target if she showed any timidity, she threw her shoulders back and walked confidently into the crowd. She needed to act like she belonged here. She accepted a glass of champagne and kept moving to keep anyone from trapping her into conversation, all the while continuing searching for Jeffrey or her brother.

The longer she looked for them, the less she wanted to find either of them. The clock struck midnight, but there was no grand unveiling of the masks. Lucy glanced around frantically. How would she know who was who? There were three devils to her left and two to her right. Should she approach them? She wavered on the idea of moving closer to inspect them. She decided to turn to her right first, since those two devils stood closer together and could be eliminated quicker.

❦

Jeffrey peered around the ballroom with narrowed eyes. Where the devil was she? He'd spoken to every angel in the room—all but one. She wore such a daring and tantalizing costume that there was no possibility that it could be Lady Lucy. He'd seek her out if the woman he was supposed to be meeting had chosen to stay home.

He cursed the raucous shifting crowd and turned to examine the other half of the ballroom.

"Who is it you're searching for?" Mr. Farris asked anxiously beside him.

"The woman I am meant to meet. I arranged to have her driven here, but I suspect she has been frightened away."

"You'll have your pick of women here," Farris murmured.

"I don't want just *any* woman, Farris. I want *this* woman. She's special."

"Then why would she come to a masquerade of debauchery?" Farris asked, recoiling from a man wearing nothing but a mask on his face and groin.

"She craves excitement, just as I do, and she has been woefully bereft of it."

"Who is this enigma?"

"I hesitate to tell you."

Jeffrey surveyed a group of ladies and caught the eye of a gentleman on the other side of the room. He nodded in recognition.

"Who is that gentleman?" Farris asked warily.

He wore not a costume, but only a black mask, black evening attire, and a black domino draped over his broad shoulders with the hood pulled over his head.

He looked like Death himself, Jeffrey mused.

"It is none other than the Earl of Winchester, an old friend from university."

"Winchester? I've had the pleasure. A nice fellow." Farris nodded in recognition and beckoned him over.

"What are you doing?" Jeffrey grumbled.

Farris frowned. "You don't wish to speak with him? He is an amiable fellow."

Jeffrey straightened as Winchester approached. To call them friends was an overstatement. Winchester hated Jeffrey, and Jeffery returned his sentiments.

"Evening, Winchester. I've never seen you here before."

"And you won't again," he answered darkly.

"Are you still visiting with Lord Rigsby at his family seat?"

"I am," Winchester replied with a kinder tone toward Farris. "I've been traveling with him and his father. We've only just returned to Yorkshire."

Mr. Farris smiled in fond remembrance. "Oh, yes. We had the pleasure of seeing Lady Heath, Lady Lucy, and Miss Manton in Bath. A lovely time, it was."

Jeffrey raised a brow. "You're staying in their home?"

"I am."

Jeffrey grinned. "Wonderful."

He would relish the idea of stealing a conquest right out from under him. He could see Winchester's eyes narrow behind his mask.

"If you will excuse me, I must rejoin my friends."

Winchester turned away without another word.

"I will keep hunting for my angel," Jeffrey said with meaning.

Winchester paused and then continued to disappear into the crowd.

Farris frowned in puzzlement at Winchester's retreating form. "What's going on?"

"I think we're after the same woman," Jeffrey said. "And *I'm* going to win."

"Who is this paragon?" Farris asked.

Jeffrey laughed. His cousin was an idiot. "Can't you tell?"

Farris frowned and shrugged.

Jeffrey nudged him in the side with his elbow. "With whom did we spend our time in Bath?"

Farris winced and rubbed his side. Then his eyes widened in dawning horror. "You're meeting Lady Lucy here?" He blanched. "But...I've told you of my feelings for her."

"Relax, Farris. You can have her when I'm done."

Farris stuttered as he followed his cousin to a grouping of chairs.

§

Dean remained where he was, lurking just behind where Jeffrey and Farris had stood. His whole body locked in fury at the sound of Lucy's name. She was here? He scanned the room. It was utter chaos. Clothing had been shed with ambivalence, and couples were groping each other on the settee amid a circle of onlookers. He searched in vain for Rigsby, but he wasn't anywhere in sight.

An angel, Jeffrey had said. Did that mean Lucy had dressed as an angel? The one saving grace was that the odious man had not yet found her, but he was only one danger among hundreds of drunken, lecherous men, and Lucy was presumably alone.

He had the urge to throttle her when he found her, and somehow, someway, instill some goddamn sense in her head. He scrutinized the room again, but there were too many angels, now in various stages of undress. There *had* been one angel who stood out among the others, though. He searched for her now with renewed vigor.

The crowd parted before him as if he truly was the specter of death, and no one dared to meet his eye. He climbed the stairs to a balcony overlooking the ballroom for a better view. He searched the crowd, praying she wasn't foolish enough to leave the negligible safety of the ballroom.

And then he saw her.

A man was attempting to pull her onto the dance floor, but she was resisting. Dean moved without thinking, sprinting down the stairs. When the crowd grew too thick at the bottom to pass, he simply jumped over the railing, his domino billowing out behind him. A woman screamed, others turned and applauded, but he didn't hesitate as he landed on his feet and barreled into the crowd.

He swooped down on them, the man cowering as Dean loomed over him.

He let go of Lucy's hand immediately. "So sorry."

Dean caught her as she stumbled back against him.

She turned and faced him, her skin turning pale.

"I'm—I'm sorry. Please forgive me, sir."

She righted herself and tried to move away.

He slipped both arms around her and pulled her tight against him. The feel of her bare skin momentarily stunned him. He bent close to her ear. "How could you be so reckless, Lucy?"

He had intended to be stern and frighten her, but his voice had come out dark and velvety. He felt her shiver under his hands, and then her hands settled on his shoulders under the domino. He breathed in the familiar scent of her, his rage and fear quickly turning to need. *No.* He couldn't succumb. Her safety came first.

"Dean?" she said shakily.

He nodded once.

Her eyes grew misty and then hardened. "What are you doing?"

"I'm saving you."

"I don't need you to save me."

"The hell you don't." He slid his hands up her back.

Her mouth dropped open, and her gaze moved to his lips.

The urge to kiss her swelled inside him. As much as she wished to hate him at this moment, he could tell that she still wanted him. The knowledge tortured him. He took her arm and towed her through the crowd.

"Where are you taking me?"

To a bedroom, his heart whispered.

"To find your brother, and get you out of here."

She planted her feet and tried to yank her arm from his grasp. "No!"

"Jesus Christ, Lucy. Do you think this is a game? We need to get you out of here."

"Jonathan will tell my father. Nothing I could say would stop him."

"As he should. You are out of control. You won't stop until you've ruined your whole family."

"Please. I'll leave right now and go home."

"I can't leave you alone," he growled. *"Where the bloody hell is your brother?"*

As he scanned the crowd, she twisted her wrist and slipped out of his hold.

Dean cursed and went after her, but he lost her in the crowd of dancers as another set formed. He could see her across the way, but she was too far from his reach.

❦

Lucy gulped down breaths of air as she fought the urge to cry. She cut through the crowd, coming upon a group of chairs and a sofa. Then she met the gaze of a devil who was sitting there and panicked. He stood slowly. She had to press herself against the crowd behind her in hopes they would part and swallow her into their midst. The man beside him stood as well, costumed like a fox. She recognized him instantly.

"Mr. Farris?"

He nodded. He did not seem pleased to see her.

The devil removed his mask and Lucy sighed in relief. "Mr. Jeffrey."

He bowed low and replaced his mask. "I've found you at last, my angel."

She moved forward, and he tugged her onto the sofa beside him, putting his arm around her lower back and caressing the bare skin of her midriff. She stiffened. His touch made her feel as if she was stepping into a lake and sinking into the slimy mud.

She loathed herself for coming here and wearing this ridiculous costume. She wanted nothing more than to leave but feared she was in far too deep now. Perhaps if she begged Jonathan, if she swore on her own grave that she was going to change, he would not tell their parents what she'd done. As much as she hated to admit it, Winchester was right. She *was* a fool, and she was courting disaster without care or thought. She'd run from the one person who only wanted to see her safely home.

"Are you enjoying yourself? Didn't I tell you how diverting this masquerade would be? If only *ton* parties held as much entertainment."

Lucy disagreed. "I'm not so sure, Mr. Jeffrey. I think I

should go."

Mr. Farris leapt up and presented his hand. "I'd be happy to escort you."

She could have cried for joy. "Tha—"

"No. I went to great expense to bring you here tonight. You must stay." Mr. Jeffrey held her in place. "Fetch her more champagne, Farris, and then be off with you."

Mr. Farris regarded Lucy apologetically.

Lucy looked to him beseechingly, but he turned and left them. He had deserted her.

"I'm happy to repay you for the cost of the carriage."

Jeffrey turned his head and nuzzled her neck. "I was hoping you'd say something like that."

She cringed and leaned away. "I meant with money."

He chuckled. "I would never accept money from you. I've no need of money, but I have great need of *you*."

Lucy pulled her hand from his. "This was a mistake. I shouldn't be here."

He spread his fingers over the bare skin of her stomach. "But I've got you now, and I'm not about to let you go."

"My brother is here. He will have a different opinion on the matter."

He narrowed his eyes. "No doubt so will the gossip mongers. How devastating it would be if word of your presence here reached their ears."

"Who would spread such unfounded lies?"

Then she gasped with a mixture of joy and relief as she saw another man suddenly beside them.

"Winchester," Jeffrey growled.

"Jeffrey. Unhand the lady so that I may escort her home."

"You?" Jeffrey sneered. "You only want her for yourself.

Find your own bit of fluff, old boy."

"I am not a bit of fluff!" Lucy insisted, insulted. "Unhand me at once."

Jeffrey glared at her but did so.

She stood and took Lord Winchester's offered arm.

"It's a pity how those pesky rumors begin. How much damage they can do," Jeffrey murmured.

"As much damage as a bullet through the heart," Winchester said, turning to Lucy. "Wouldn't you say so?"

"Hmm, yes. Bullets hurt no matter where you put them."

"Just ask Lord Harris."

Winchester smirked at Jeffrey and ignored Lucy's sharp look of surprise. Then he turned them away, shouldering a path into the crowd.

"How do you know about Lord Harris?"

"Your brother told me about the duel he fought for you. Let's leave before he or I have to shoot Jeffrey on your behalf, shall we?"

"Where is my brother?" Lucy asked as she clung tightly to his arm.

"I haven't any idea. He'll find his own way home."

She nodded. She didn't care what happened now as long as she was leaving this awful masquerade. She caught sight of a man wearing nothing but a mask on his face. The same mask covered his groin. She averted her eyes and leaned into Dean.

He put his arm around her and held her close. After gathering her cloak, they waited in the torch light of the drive for a hack.

Lucy didn't say anything. She shivered, but she wasn't cold. Her stomach turned restlessly from emptiness and her jumbled emotions. She wanted nothing more than to be home and in her own bed. She stared at Dean's profile, his arm still tightly around her.

She bit her lip. Perhaps where she stood right now was better than her bed. But she kicked herself for allowing these feelings to consume her. What would it take to get him out of her heart and mind?

He handed her into the carriage and sat across from her, though she wished she still had his warmth beside her. She supposed, now that she was safe from the masquerade, he wouldn't feel the need to keep her protectively under his arm.

The carriage crunched down the drive, the pool of light from the torches illuminating the front of the manor before darkness enveloped them. He didn't speak, and she didn't have anything sensible to say. Nothing that came to her mind sounded like an intelligent defense for her antics tonight. She realized it was over, this life she took for granted, the bubble of innocence she moved in.

It was all over.

She knew things now. What it was to feel desire and want. How her body could feel at the hands of a man. The endless pain of rejection by that man. She was not of the *demi monde*. She was not a merry widow of independent means. It wasn't in her ability to become the woman he wanted. And why should she? She didn't want to be those things any more than he wanted to be a husband.

That was clear now.

Sadness enveloped her as she accepted that truth in the darkness across from him. For the rest of her life, she would wish differently, but it was time that she accepted what was. He would never be hers.

But that didn't mean she couldn't be his.

CHAPTER 23

The hackney stopped at the end of the drive, across from where she'd started this disastrous evening. They'd been traveling for an hour, and he hadn't said a word to her. She hadn't said anything to him, either, but now her thoughts wanted to burst forth, and she feared his moody silence. He handed her down and they both paused and considered the shadowed drive to the house, as if neither of them wanted to breach the barrier that would lead to the inevitable consequences of the evening.

"We can go this way."

Lucy led him to the break in the shrubbery she had ducked through before. Without a word, he followed her, and they walked along the shadows to the rear of the house.

"How many times have you done this?"

"None. This was my first and last time."

She could feel his gaze on her as they walked. They were about to enter the main garden, where they would be in view of the house. She paused and removed her mask.

"What are you going to say to my brother?"

"I've thought about that on the way back, and I've decided

not to say anything. I will let you decide if and when to tell your family. I presume you have your own reason for what you did tonight. I can't begin to try to explain it for you."

Lucy blushed shamefully. She nodded and turned to walk forward.

"Wait." He grabbed her hand, his tone furious. "Why don't you try explaining it to me first?"

"Here?"

"Have you a better place in mind?"

She shook her head.

"Have you always been a walking disaster?"

She poked his chest. "I am *not* a disaster. Yes, I've done some stupid things, tonight taking the cake. But in the past, I've only dared to dance around the edge of propriety, because…"

"Because why?"

"Because I'm bored."

He scoffed and laughed at her. "You're *bored*?"

She put her hands on her hips. "Yes. And let me tell you why. I can sing, I can dance, I speak French, my needlework is passable, and can you guess what else?"

He looked like he was enjoying himself now. "What?"

"My curtsy is perfect."

He applauded her.

"Exactly. Your mocking applause sums up the importance of all those things. I'm supposed to do all that so I can enter society and select a husband with the same enthusiasm with which I choose a new bonnet."

He folded his arm and grinned at her.

"I've seen love," she said in a soft voice.

He sobered.

"I see what my parents have. I've seen my friends succumb to it one by one, and it tears them apart and puts them back together as shiny new people with something that means so much more than all my paltry talents. I want the same, but from the start, I knew that not just any man would do. So yes, I'm bored. Sometimes I wish I had been born a man so I could do the things that inspire me to be better than who I am. I don't want to be told how to live. I just want to live."

"Sometimes even men don't get to do exactly as they wish. Not without consequences."

"Such as?"

"It's too late to drag up my past tonight."

Lucy perked up. Was he finally going to reveal more of himself? She hesitated to go back to the house now. Once they reached it, he would leave her, and she would never get another chance like this.

"I'm afraid to go back there," she admitted.

"Whatever happens, your family will love you through it."

The press of his hand on her lower back urged her forward, but she couldn't do it. If she took one step forward, it would be one step farther from him, and this moment where his attention was completely hers.

She swallowed. "What of Mr. Jeffrey? Do you think he will tell?"

Dean's anger shimmered around him like vapors of heat. "Not if he values his life."

She turned to him, pressing her hands to his chest.

He kept his hand on her back, and it almost felt like he was embracing her again.

"I haven't thanked you yet."

"For what?"

"For rescuing me. For being my voice of reason."

He snorted, but he didn't take his arm from her, and he didn't immediately back away, either.

"That might be the first time I've ever been anyone's voice of reason."

"You're good at it. I didn't want to listen, but I should have. You were right about everything, especially Mr. Jeffrey."

He tensed. She could feel it under her hands and see it in the way his lips tightened. She waited, watching the subtle changes in his face. He still held her, though, and it gave her such hope.

"Why did you want him?" He asked it so quietly that she wasn't sure if she had imagined it.

"I didn't."

"Then why would you do something like this? Why risk everything to see him?"

There was so much she could say. Most of it, she knew, he didn't want to hear. But how could she hide her feelings any longer? After all they'd been through? He had to know how she felt, and that she understood.

"I just wanted to feel something—anything—other than the ache you left me with."

She watched him swallow.

"What is it you want of me, Lucy?"

He said it with such graveness, as if she were asking the world of him.

She rested her cheek on his chest. "I just want you to love me."

She almost moaned when he rested his head on hers. Sheer relief flooded her. He hadn't pushed her away. It was enough to make her weep with joy.

"Stop it. Do not speak with such desperation. I am not worthy of it. I am not worthy of *you*."

She smiled as she wiped a tear away. "You say that, but the only one who believes it is you."

"I can't give you what you want." He sounded pained.

"I know," she said. "I'm not asking you to marry me."

"Then what is it you want from me?"

"Whatever you will give me. We've come this far. Can't we go a little further?"

He stared down at her silently, his eyes shadowed and his lips a hard line. Then he took her hand and led her back to the house. "Where is your room?"

Lucy led him to her room, her heart fluttering in anticipation the whole way. She opened her door and saw Marigold there, asleep in the chair by the fire.

"Wait here. My maid is in there sleeping."

He nodded and slipped into a shadowed alcove.

Lucy shook Marigold awake. "I'm back."

"Are you alright?"

"Yes. Go to bed," Lucy urged.

Marigold slipped out into the hall and down the servant stairs.

Dean emerged from the shadows and closed the door softly behind him, locking it.

Lucy stood waiting in the middle of the room.

He approached her slowly. "Is this what you want?"

She nodded.

He undid the ties of her cloak and domino, tossing them over the chair. Her nerves stretched as he studied her. He didn't appear pleased, only angry. It dampened her excitement significantly.

"Try not to act so resigned to seducing me," she quipped.

He gave a soft bark of laughter. "What would you have me do?"

"Anything," she replied.

He stepped back from her, removing his domino, followed by his jacket and waistcoat. Then he pulled his shirt from his trousers.

Lucy watched in dismay.

"What's the matter?" he asked as he undid his shirt cuffs. He strolled forward and tipped up her chin, forcing her to meet his gaze. "Isn't this what you wanted?" He pulled the shoulder of her dress over her arm, brushing the exposed skin with his knuckles. "Passion, pleasure, the taste of the forbidden. A temporary easement of your boredom."

He cupped her breasts. Lucy pushed his hand away.

He moved around her and climbed onto the bed, lounging against the pillows, his arms folded behind his head. "I'd like you to undress for me."

She turned to face him with disgust.

"What's the matter? Am I too dull for you?"

"Stop it."

He moved to sit on the edge of her bed. "This is what happens in affairs, Lucy. Come here."

She hesitated, but she couldn't resist moving closer to him. Part of her knew he was baiting her, and the other part just wanted whatever he would give.

Nothing he offered was going to be enough. Ever.

She flinched when he raised his hands to her stomach. Her skin was so sensitive there, so unused to being touched by hands other than her own.

He laughed softly. "You're skittish. I won't hurt you."

"You already have."

"I warned you, didn't I?"

"You did."

"Affairs are about sex, Lucy. Carnal needs met by mutual accord. Is that what you want?"

She shook her head.

He ran his hands down the sides of her hips. "This isn't love, only desire."

"How do you know so much about love?" she asked as his hands caressed her body. She shouldn't be letting him touch her this way. He was only doing it to prove his point, but his touch had always felt so right, and watching his face while he did it... His expression said more than his words.

Then he stopped, his hands resting on her hips.

Lucy took a guess. "You've been in love."

Bleakness covered his features. "I have."

"Please tell me."

She pulled him up and directed him to the chair before the fire. She pushed him into it and claimed his lap before he could stop her.

He glared at her with reproach while she draped a blanket over them.

"Comfortable?"

She smiled impishly. "Very. Now tell me everything, or I shall torture you until you do."

છે.

Dean grimaced. What could he do? They were in so deep already. He exhaled and rested his head against the back of the chair. He closed his eyes when she rested her head on his chest, the soft touch of her breath caressing his neck. It felt so good to hold her like this. *Too* good, *too* comfortable.

He hadn't told anyone this story. He didn't even like to remember it himself, but he supposed it was past time to tell her. More than anyone, she deserved to know the truth.

He swallowed. With the words came the emotions, and he found it hard to begin.

"A long time ago, I believed in all-consuming love. The earth couldn't have shaken my love, but then it did that very thing. My father determined that I was to marry the oldest daughter of our neighbor, Lenora Abbey, for land entailed in her dowry. But I was in love with her younger sister, Rosie. We argued for hours, days even. Upon his honor, he'd given his word and it was done. I still refused. No one could *make* me marry Lenora."

Dean stopped. His father's yelling echoed in his head, but all he could see was Rosie's face, the streaks of her tears.

"Lenora killed herself because of me. She was sensitive, Rosie had said, prone to melancholy, and my rejection of her pushed her too far. It was my fault."

Lucy gasped. "I'm so sorry."

"I loved Rosie desperately, but after her sister took her own life…she despised me. She couldn't believe I could be so callous."

Lucy sat up and cupped his cheek. "It wasn't your fault."

"Wasn't it? I refused her, and she took her own life. To punish me, my father banished me from my home. Rosie never spoke to me again, and the only communication I received from my father was a letter to tell me of Rosie's marriage. That was ten years ago."

"He banished you?"

"Only until he became too ill to manage the estate, and his solicitor sent for me. My father despises me, Rosie's family despises me... Eventually, I end up hurting everyone who cares for me."

Lucy held his face. "That isn't true."

"I've *already* hurt you."

"Yes, but I asked for it."

He laughed softly. "I never wanted to hurt you."

"I know. You warned me, and I didn't listen. But none of that matters. Lenora died by her own hand, not yours. As for Rosie, she's a fool to blame you for such a thing. If she really loved you, she wouldn't have let you marry her sister. She would have fought for you."

Dean laughed again. "She wasn't as obstinate as you."

Lucy raised a brow. "And look where that got her? Not married to you."

He chuckled as she undid the buttons at his neck, slipping her hand inside and over his heart.

"Here beats the heart of a man who is far kinder and honorable than he wants to believe. I see it, my family sees it, but you still refuse to see it."

"It isn't just my past that keeps me separated from your world, Lucy. It's the choice I've made. I chose this life, and it is not a life you would want to live."

She kissed the hollow at his throat. "I want anything that involves you."

He tensed and shifted beneath her.

She kissed the crease under his jaw next.

"Lucy..." he warned.

"Dean..." She said his name against his skin and then

pulled away. "I may not have your love like Rosie did, but I will take whatever you will give me."

He closed his eyes, her words staking him through the heart.

She sobbed. "I'm so sorry."

They snapped open again. "What?"

She climbed out of his lap. "I'm sorry I'm making you stay here. Go if you wish it."

"But I don't want to go."

"You don't have to stay on account of my feelings. I've done so much to you... You had your reasons. They were different from mine, but in a way, we are the same. Neither of us wanted a life not of our choosing, and here I am, forcing you to stay with me even if only for the rest of this night. I'm sorry."

Lucy covered her face and Dean shuddered. Then he stood and gathered her close to him, feeling her sobs like wounds to his heart.

After all this time and regret, she might be his worst victim. All she ever wanted from him was love, and he'd refused to give it. He'd denied her, and he'd denied himself. He was a fool. She'd been on his mind since the moment he'd arrived, and he'd told himself it meant nothing, that craving her the way he did—her smell, her laughter, the softness of her skin—was something he could brush aside. But he couldn't let her go. She meant everything to him.

CHAPTER 24

"Don't say another word."

He bent and lifted her, carrying her to the bed and setting her down. Then he pulled his shirt over his head, enjoying her reaction. He dug his fingers into her hair and began pulling out pins.

His decision washed over him slowly, realization and relief filling him. What he was doing felt right. She had been right all along. He'd fought valiantly, but succumbing was so much easier.

She studied him, her eyes twinkling with unshed tears as he divested her of her costume. She didn't try to stop him, only stared at him in wonder.

He laid her back on the bed and joined her there, his trousers still on. He swallowed the urge to laugh. She wanted to say something, he could see it in her expression, but she remained quiet. He bent and set his lips to hers, briefly remembering their first kiss—that horrible kiss. It was her first attempt to seduce him, and she'd been trying again ever since.

"I'm remembering our first kiss."

She smiled at him, a brilliant, happy smile. "I tried so hard."

"But you did not succeed," he teased.

"You shall have to teach me."

"I thought I had."

He bent his head again and claimed her mouth. She tasted like heaven. He would never have enough of tasting her and smelling her. With each breath, he filled his lungs with her.

He pulled back again and lay beside her, taking his time studying her, letting his gaze consume her the way he'd wanted to for so long. After all they'd been through, now he would finally have her. He could slake his craving, quieting the demons inside him, and simply feast.

His need to claim her was so strong, he shook.

꧁

Lucy watched him in awe. Then he closed his eyes and he shuddered, startling her.

"I need to touch you."

She nodded, needing his touch as much as he wanted to give it. She pressed his hand to her breast and couldn't control her erratic breathing as his hand gently skated over her skin, his touch soft and tender.

Dean cupped her breast, molded her, and cherished her breasts and skin until he'd covered every inch of her chest with his lips and fingers.

She shivered with anticipation, her skin alive and burning with need.

His gentle touch moved between her legs and she parted them, already aching for the taste of pleasure she knew they could find together.

He slowly explored her, knowingly touching just the right place at the right time with the perfect amount of pressure, masterful at keeping her on the edge of the stars, but never letting her go any further.

Lucy panted with frustration by the time one finger entered her, her body clasping him in her hot core.

"Please," she begged.

"I'm not done worshiping you," he whispered against her skin.

He took her nipple into his mouth, the tingling suction pushing her further into the abyss. She squeezed her eyes closed, moving her hips against his hand, striving for her own release. Her body tensed, simmering with pleasure.

He took his hand away. "No."

"Damn you."

Dean chuckled. "This time, I will feel you climax with me inside you."

Lucy tossed her head back against the pillows. "Please!"

She watched him undress, tossing his trousers to the floor. She peeked at his swollen manhood. It jutted out from a nest of brown curls and brushed her leg, silky and hot against her thigh. She immediately reached to touch him.

He grasped her wrist. "Wait."

"I don't want to wait. I've waited forever."

"Then you can wait a little bit longer."

"For what?"

"For the rest of our lives, Lucy. We will never have this moment again. Let me make it perfect for you."

His powerful words filtered through her haze of desire and her mind fractured, her heart filling with piercing joy. It was an explosion of pure bliss, like the sparks of color in a firework. The rest of her life would never be long enough. She wanted forever with him. She'd argue with God himself and demand it if she had to.

"Yes!" she cried.

He moved farther down her body, setting his lips on the sensitive skin of her midriff. Her skin tingled and pulsed with his touch, flashes of heat moving through her like licks of fire. She wanted to move and shift, but his hand on her hip held her still as he kissed a trail to her navel. His tongue danced around the edge and dipped inside.

Then his mouth moved lower, Lucy's nerves coiling tightly as he kissed a path to the apex of her thighs. She couldn't look, her bravery abandoning her as he nuzzled her curls, parting her folds with his fingers and tongue. His mouth vibrated against her as he hummed low in his throat. He flicked his tongue against a part of her so sensitive that the slightest touch sent bright white shards of pure delight through her body like thunderbolts.

Her cheeks burned. Her legs were restless as he parted them with his shoulders and settled over her sex. Then two fingers filled her, sinking deep inside her as his tongue swirled around her bundle of nerves. A scream crawled up her throat and her body went rigid, the pleasure so acute and intense she had to fight the urge to cry out.

She moaned, guttural and deep, hips rising from the bed, nerves clamoring for that sweet pinnacle.

But he moved away, cutting off the flow of sensation.

She reached for him. *"No!"*

He leaned over her, one hand sliding under her hips to lift her as he positioned his erection at her entrance.

"Yes."

She'd never wanted anything more. Her knees clamped around his hips and her arms snaked around his neck as he slowly invaded her, her passage stretching and burning. He retreated and then relentlessly drove further, his spine and muscles flexing under her hands, claiming her.

Lucy trembled, the stinging invasion of his shaft filling her until she couldn't breathe. But as he settled against her, skin to skin, the pain ebbed. Then he moved again, his thrusts short and sweet. The pinching friction turned to deep pleasure, building rapidly until she writhed beneath him, nails scoring his back. Pleasure consumed her, her body and soul singing with rapture.

He kept his pace as she floated among the stars, biting back her cries of ecstasy as she held onto him.

"Oh God, Lucy... You are heaven."

He moaned, thrusting harder and faster until he groaned, shuddering with his own release, hugging her so tightly she didn't know where she ended and he began.

Finally, they were one.

He kissed her forehead and cheeks, her eyes, and then her lips.

Lucy blinked away tears as she clung to him, savoring the press of their sweaty bodies, the scent of their lovemaking, and the taste of his skin mixed with hers.

There were no words for what she felt, no words to describe the array of emotions inside her. She didn't need any.

He rolled to his side, hugging her back to him. Then he nuzzled and kissed the back of her neck. "Are you all right?"

I'll never be the same again, she thought. She was his now, and he was hers.

"I'm perfect."

She felt his smile against her skin.

CHAPTER 25

Jonathan held his head as he stumbled into the front hall long after the crow had called for the morning. He searched, but there was not a servant in sight. He cursed and climbed the stairs to his father's study, where just a finger of the good whiskey there would alleviate his misery. It was there he found the servants, all clustered around the closed door.

"What the devil is going on?" he croaked, his throat painfully dry.

The servants all scattered, and that was when he got a bad feeling. He walked to the door and leaned close.

"If that is what you wish."

He heard Winchester's voice and threw the door open.

"What's wrong?"

"Good God, boy. Have you heard of knocking? This is a private meeting."

Jonathan glanced back and forth between his father and Winchester.

"What is going on?" he demanded.

"If you must know, Winchester has made an offer for your sister," his father replied.

Jonathan's mouth went slack. He snapped it shut. "Are you mad?"

"Mad?" Winchester repeated. Then he snorted and started laughing. "Are you still drunk?"

Jonathan clutched his head, the room still spinning. "Does this involve Jeffrey? He said something to me about Lucy..." He shook his head. The evening before came at him in jumbled fragments.

"Jeffrey won't be a concern anymore," Winchester said.

Jonathan closed his eyes and leaned against a table. "No. Don't do this to protect her. Whatever she's done now, she deserves the consequences."

"Jonathan," his father scolded. "What are you blathering about?"

"I'll tell her myself."

Jonathan turned and stomped his way to his sister's room. He pounded on the door.

"Lucy! Wake up, you cretin! I'll have your head for this."

He turned the knob and the door swung open. He almost lost his balance but caught himself. He saw his sister hastily tying her robe.

"What are you doing in here?" she screeched at him.

He winced and covered his ears, glaring at her. For the first time in his life, he could say he truly despised her. For too long she'd done exactly as she pleased, with little to no repercussions.

"What have you done?" he asked darkly.

She straightened and shifted nervously. "What do you mean?"

He strode into the room and kicked the door closed—or tried to. He stumbled and fell but quickly regained his feet and pushed the door closed.

She folded her arms and glared at him. "Are you drunk?"

"*I'm* asking the questions, minx. Now…" He blinked. "Where are we?"

"We're in my room. Get out and take yourself to bed."

"I will not—" Something caught his eye. A black mask poked out from under the skirt of her bed. "What is that?"

He lurched forward. She darted out of his way as he grabbed for it, staring at it in horror…

The bed, sheet, and coverlet twisted and wrinkled. He scanned the room, but there was no other damning evidence.

"I *told* you to leave him alone," he ground out. "But you must bend everyone to your will like puppets."

"I love him!" she cried.

"Well, I'm glad *you've* got your feelings all sorted out, but did he tell you he loved you?"

She didn't answer. The stricken expression on her face was enough.

"What have you *done*, Lucy?" he bellowed, throwing the mask at her feet. "Now I must make him my enemy. I must call him out and hate him, and I don't want to. I've already shot one man for you."

"No!" she cried. "This is my fault, not his."

"Damn right it is. You couldn't leave well enough alone."

Her door burst open again, their father barreling through. "What the devil is going on in here?"

"Lucy has gone and ruined everything," Jonathan blathered on. "She has sed—"

Lord Heath grabbed his son by the neck of his cravat and yanked him from the room.

§

Lucy hid the mask under her robe as she peered into the hall. The astonished faces of the staff, her mother, and Dean stared back at her. He was trying very hard to mask his laughter behind his fist. She held his gaze and couldn't help smiling.

It was then her mother entered her room and closed the door. She tapped her foot and pinned Lucy with a serious glare. "Is there anything I should know?"

"Nothing pertinent, no."

"Are you going to marry him?"

Lucy frowned. "Who?"

Lady Heath stalked forward, away from the door, where surely ears lurked. She grabbed her daughter's arms. "Lord Winchester! He has asked for your hand."

"He has?" Lucy could have jumped with joy, but her mother held her firmly to the ground.

"You must get dressed and give him your answer with haste, before he decides the lot of us are not worth the trouble."

Lucy was ready to burst with happiness. "You like him then?"

"Of course, but what's more important are *your* feelings. I know in the past I've pushed gentlemen your way that were not to your liking. I don't want you to feel pressured to settle for someone likable, when love is worth waiting for."

Lucy grinned. "Then I'm done waiting, because I love him more than I can adequately express."

Her mother hugged her tightly. "Hurry and dress."

❧

Dean knocked on Rigsby's door. His valet answered.

"Is he decent?"

"He's in an ice bath, my lord."

"Perfect."

Dean pushed his way into the room. Rigsby sat chest-deep in the ice bath, a towel draped over his face. Dean lifted the towel and smiled down at his friend's red-lidded glare.

"How are you feeling?"

"Like I'm living in a bad dream."

"How so?"

Rigsby leaned forward in the tub and splashed water on his face. He shook the excess from his hair and sighed gustily. He met Dean's gaze warily. "Please say you're not falling on your sword for my sister."

"I'm not."

"But Jeffrey... You've been up in arms since she mentioned seeing him. I know he said something last night, but for the life of me, I cannot remember what it was."

"It's not important now."

"It is, dammit. Why are you marrying my sister?"

"Maybe because I want to."

Rigsby scoffed. "You? Marriage? Those two things have been as opposite as the sun and the moon."

Dean chuckled. "I know, but things change."

"Since when? Since your masquerade mask happened to end up in her room?"

Dean cocked a brow. "So *that's* where I left it."

244

"I'd be bloody furious if I didn't believe that *she* had something to do with this."

Dean choked on his laughter. "You think I'm the victim here? That she lured me into a trap, compromised me, and now I must pay the ultimate price?"

"Am I supposed to believe you seduced her?" Rigsby scoffed.

"Is that hard to believe?"

"When it comes to my sister, yes. Lucy is as fierce as a tigress, she's as bullheaded as a—bull! You're mad to want to marry her, let alone be coerced into it. I knew she fancied you, but I'd hoped your distinct distaste for her sort would be enough to keep the both of you safely apart."

"You thought wrong."

Dean thought of Lucy the first day he'd arrived. The moment their gazes had caught across the lawn. An invisible bolt of lightning had struck him. He'd fought it, but now that he was no longer dodging it, he could see the elusive something that had pulled them together, the wildness inside them that bound them together.

"I'm trying to be angry at you, but I can't. I pity you."

Dean laughed. "Don't pity me."

"One by one, they fall," Rigsby muttered.

"I beg your pardon?"

"Alberhill, Draven, Bainbridge, and now you. Who's left?"

Dean smirked. "Just you."

Rigsby glared at him and then splashed him with some ice water. "Get out. I don't know if this marriage insanity is catching."

"It is. Shall we summon Miss Manton back? You seemed rather taken with her in breeches."

Dean ducked as a chunk of ice flew over his head. He laughed as he left Rigsby to his melancholy bath. He still had a proposal to make.

He strode inside the front hall, waiting for Lucy in the drawing room as her mother had instructed. Just as he entered, Lord Heath stopped him in the hall.

"This arrived for you," he said, his voice somber as he handed Dean the missive.

Dean looked down at the paper edged in black.

It was at that moment that Lucy came tripping down the stairs. She'd already seen the paper in his hand. She put a hand to her mouth.

He tried to slip it into his coat. "It's nothing."

She came to his side. "It isn't nothing. Someone has died."

Lord Heath startled him then by gently pulling his hand back out of his coat, still clutching the letter. "Open it, son."

Dean nodded and they followed him into the drawing room. Lucy sat beside him on the sofa as he tore the seal and read the scant few lines he'd already guessed. His father had died at last.

Dean and the principal steward, Mr. Fisher, had prepared for this event for months now, and very little needed to be done except have the funeral. Dean would attend, if only for the sake of Mr. and Mrs. Hales' good opinion of him. He closed his eyes and waited for the grief, but none came. When he opened them, Lord Heath had gone, and only Lucy remained.

She covered his hand and squeezed. "I'm sorry."

"There is no need to be sorry."

"But I am. I can't imagine what it must feel like."

"It feels like nothing," he said curtly.

She pulled her hand away and remained silent.

"I'm sorry. I don't want to punish you for his transgressions."

"I understand."

"Do you? Your father is everything a father should be—loving, forgiving, and affectionate. All my life I was—" He swallowed. "I was a tool. He thought of me only as extension of himself, trying to mold me *into* himself. I did everything I could to not become him, and now I am glad to be rid of him. I don't even want to be the Marquess of Lawrence, because the name will always make me think of him. I know I *have* to, though I will insist those closest to me still call me Winchester."

Lucy nodded. "Of course."

Dean swallowed back his anger. The past would finally be put to rest now. This was his new beginning, his chance at lasting happiness. Nothing would stop him this time, not even his father's death. The man had stood directly in his path to love, but not anymore. Perhaps he should feel guilty his father had died without any family present, but family hadn't meant much to him, and Dean was certain that Mary, his maid, had been there at the end. One person to cry over his father was all he'd deserved. Dean's only regret would be losing his Winchester title, a solid, comfortable name he'd had for all his life. Now he would become the Marquess of Lawrence.

Lucy stood. "Do you want to be alone?"

"No." He cursed himself. He was being an arse. "Don't go." He stood, crumpling the paper and tossing it into the hearth. He offered his arm. "Let's walk outside."

She bit her lip and nodded.

He led her outside, and they strolled silently along the gravel walks. After a while, he managed to bury his anger toward his father and focus on what this morning *should* be about.

He pulled her out of view of the house, seeking privacy in the rippling tendrils of a weeping willow. "Lucy…"

She smiled timidly.

"Have you ever been proposed to?"

"Just once, if you remember Lord Whippet and the fountain, but I don't consider it a true proposal."

"He dropped to one knee. "Then this is a first for both of us."

Her eyes grew misty as she smiled down at him. "Forgive me if I bungle this."

He chuckled. "Likewise."

They both laughed, and the tension eased. Dean's heart throbbed as he absorbed her beauty. She'd made it clear what she'd wanted from him from the beginning: his love and his affection. They were things he'd thought no one would ever want again. Now she would have all of it.

Love.

The word had once made him bitter and angry, but now it bloomed inside him like a sunrise, full of color and hope.

"Lucy, will you be my wife?" he asked, his throat thick.

A single tear fell and caught in the corner of her smile. "Yes."

He stood and caught it with his thumb, dipping his head to taste her sweetness.

She threw her arms around him and he lifted her, spinning her around until he was giddy and disoriented. When he set her down, they still clung to each other.

"Thank you," he said.

"For what?"

"For not giving up."

"I tried to, but I couldn't. Every time I looked at you or spoke to you, no matter how many times you told me not to, I fell in love with you a little more."

"I may live to regret saying this, but thank God for your stubbornness."

She giggled and he claimed that giggle in another kiss, pinning her to the trunk of the willow.

"I love you," he said, the words so heavy in his heart but light when spoken.

"I love you, too, Dean, since the moment I saw you... After you shaved off your beard."

He chuckled. "You didn't like my beard?"

She kissed his jaw. "I prefer to see your whole face."

He gathered up her skirts.

"Dean!" she gasped.

"Shhh. You said you wanted to experience new things, didn't you?"

"I did." She exhaled shakily, as his fingers stroked her core.

"Let me show you the advantages of marrying a man like me."

CHAPTER 26

The eve of December third, a freak snowstorm covered the land in snow. Lucy squealed with delight when she saw this the next morning, the day of her wedding, but her mother required smelling salts.

Lucy had refused a large wedding, choosing instead to have only family and her closest friends attend a simple service in their village church. There was no pink tulle, despite her mother's fervent wishes. Heather, Anabelle, Hazel, and Thea all attended, but Rose and Charlotte could not. She worried over their whereabouts when neither responded to their invitations.

For the past week, she'd got to spend her days lounging with her friends, sharing amusing stories of their first days as married women. Hazel's experience was not so amusing.

"I'm so sorry, dear. I wish you would have confided in me. I would have tossed the old bat out myself," Lucy said.

Hazel laughed. "It sorted itself out wonderfully."

Anabelle hugged her sister. "In the future, try to remember you don't have to suffer alone. We are here for you."

"I know."

Heather smiled tearfully. "I'm so happy to see you all. We've changed so much since we met at the Vale house party. So much has happened!"

"Yes, but I still wish Rose and Charlotte could have been here, as well. Has anyone heard from them?"

"I've received letters from Charlotte, but not Rose," Heather replied. "But Charlotte does mention Rose, and that she's taking care of her sick father. I suspect postage is too expensive."

"Well then, we will have to visit her, won't we?" Anabelle said.

Everyone nodded in agreement, and the somber tension evaporated.

Lucy couldn't have asked for a better beginning for her new life. She was marrying the man of her dreams, and most of her friends would be there to see it.

The best gift of all was the groom himself. Dean had purchased a small manor for the two of them, only an hour's ride away. She could still see her family whenever she wished.

After a small wedding breakfast with the guests, it was almost time for Lucy and Dean to leave, so she retired to her room to change. She glanced back down the hall to find a small army of women following her.

"What is this?"

"We've come to give our goodbyes," Heather said.

"And I, of course, must speak to you privately," her mother said with a blush.

Lucy sighed. "Come along."

She led them to her room, giving Marigold an apologetic smile as they filed in, claiming every available surface to sit.

"We've moved the party into my room," Lucy quipped.

"So it seems. I shall leave you. Your trunks are packed and I've set out your blue carriage dress."

"Thank you, Marigold. I have plenty of help to change. Go ready yourself for the journey."

"Yes, ma'am."

Lucy met all the expectant stares of her friends and her mother, and emotion washed over her. She hadn't cried once today, but now her tears rushed forth. She had too many blessings to count, and she had these beautiful women to thank.

She stepped forward and hugged her mother first.

"My dear," Lady Heath said, squeezing her tightly and whispering in her ear, "I really must speak with you. It is a delicate tradition."

"No, you don't," Lucy whispered back.

Her mother pulled back and frowned at her. "But I must. How will you know…?"

"I don't ever want to hear you discuss the intimacies that occur between man and woman. As far as I'm concerned, a stork delivered me with the morning post."

Lady heath rolled her eyes, and Lucy had the distinct feeling she was looking at her future self. She laughed. "Don't worry, Mother. I've many married friends now." She winked. "I'll figure it out."

All the women laughed except her mother, who shook her head at her daughter in exasperation.

She turned Lucy away from her and helped her out of her wedding gown while the others chatted. It was then Lucy noticed Thea's red-rimmed eyes and sorrowful air.

"Dear, what is the matter?"

She tried to smile. "Nothing."

Everyone surrounded Thea. Hazel took her hand. "It's obviously not nothing."

"We're all here for you, darling. Whatever it is, we can help," Anabelle added.

Thea laughed as tears spilled over. "That isn't really true, is it? You've all gotten married and begun new lives, and I'm still waiting for...for... I don't even know what I'm waiting for!"

Lucy put her arm around her. "You're waiting for a man worthy of you to come along."

Thea shook her head and sobbed. "There isn't such a man. Tomorrow, I will leave and—and be forced to wed my cousin."

There was a collective gasp.

Lucy stood in front of Thea and clasped her shoulders. "What do you mean?"

"I'm not supposed to be here. I ran away from my family and took the post coach just to get here. When I return, I shall be married to Richard."

Lady Heath moaned. "My heavens!"

"No," Lucy said. "I will not allow it."

Thea shrugged out of Lucy's hold. "I don't have a choice, and neither do you."

"You will stay here. Mother, tell her!" Lucy cried.

Lady Heath nodded, but she didn't look hopeful.

Thea gave Lady Heath a watery smile. "Thank you, but I couldn't burden you like that. My family will come for me."

"Then you shall come with me," Lucy said. "They don't know where I will be living from now on."

Thea wept harder. "I can't impose on your new marriage."

"I won't let you return to your family and be married to your toad of a cousin."

"She can come with us back to Scotland," Heather suggested.

Anabelle and Hazel moved closer. "Or with either of us."

"When you turn twenty-one, you will be free of your family's control," Hazel said. "We will hide you until then."

Thea covered her face with her hands and cried. They all gathered around her, a little coven of comfort.

Lucy wiped fresh tears from her cheeks as she sat back against the squabs, across from her husband. A blanket of snow covered the ground and chilled the air. She lifted the blanket over her lap and patted the seat.

He chuckled as he moved to sit beside her, wrapping his arm around her.

She rested her head against his shoulder and sighed.

"I hope that is a sigh of contentment."

"I'm far more than content."

"Oh?"

She turned her head to him, and he kissed her lips, making her sigh again.

"I have something I should tell you."

He raised a brow. "Should I be afraid?"

"No. But you may be cross with me for not speaking with you first." She sat up straighter. "I tend to do things like that."

"I've noticed," he said with meaning. "So, what is this something?"

"Thea will be coming to stay with us tomorrow."

His brow furrowed. "Is something wrong?"

"She's run away from her family. They're trying to force her to marry her cousin."

Dean scowled. "Force her?"

"She wasn't even allowed to come to the wedding, but she snuck away and took a mail coach. Please understand. I know it sounds ludicrous, but in two weeks, she will be twenty-one and they cannot force her then. We only need to shelter her for a little while."

He scoffed. "And then what? She returns to them?"

Lucy panicked. She didn't want this to be their first fight. "She only agreed to stay because we will be honeymooning in Brighton. After that, she can go to visit Anabelle, Hazel, or even Heather. She won't be a burden."

"Of course, she won't. She needn't leave when we return. She can stay forever if she wishes."

"You mean it?"

"Did you think I would turn her out?"

"No, but I was afraid…"

"She is family. I know more than anyone how it feels to have your hand forced. We will shelter her as long as she needs it."

Lucy jumped into his lap and peppered his face with kisses.

"You are the most perfect husband any woman could ask for."

He chuckled, wrapping his arms around her so she couldn't leave his lap. "Are there any more surprises I should be made aware of?"

"Just one, but I promise you will love it."

CHAPTER 27

From her bedroom window, Lucy viewed the garden of her
new home. It was sorely in need of attention, but at present, it
still awed her. The full moon shone brightly on a landscape of
frost. It sparkled in the light, glittering, like every leaf had
been covered in diamonds.

Her heart was so full, it hurt. Was it possible to be so happy
that it was painful? She laughed to herself. Her nerves a bit
shaken, she turned away from the window, toying with the tie
of her robe.

"Are you ready?" she whispered.

Marigold sat behind a screen with her drum. "Yes, ma'am."

"Do you think he will like it?"

Marigold giggled. "I cannot imagine a man who would
not."

Lucy agreed, but she was still nervous. She'd only danced
like this in front of Marigold and Thea, when Marigold was
teaching them the ancient style of dancing. She had never
imagined she would now do it for her husband. It had been her

guilty secret, her distraction during her absence from the season. If her mother had known what they'd been up to…

Lucy grinned. She'd probably be living in a nunnery right now.

She heard him knock softly on the door.

"Come in," she said, her voice shaky.

He walked in, noticed the candles that adorned every surface, and his eyes blazed with heat as his gaze touched her. He closed the door and began to remove his coat.

"Wait." Lucy bid. She directed his attention to the screen. "We're not alone."

He hesitated. "I don't understand."

"Take a seat." She waved to the chair in the middle of the room. He glanced at it as if seeing it for the first time. He slowly sat, raising one brow at her. "What is this?"

"Your surprise. Just watch." Lucy took a deep breath. "I'm ready, Marigold."

Marigold tapped out an exotic and primal rhythm on the drum. Lucy closed her eyes as she pulled on the ties of her robe, letting the rhythm wash over her, feeling the beats inside her body. She loved this music, how it reverberated inside her, willing her body to move as though it was she who made the music.

She swayed slowly at first, feeling the way her hips moved, feeling the pounding of the drum as her pulse. She pulled open the halves of her robe, shimmying her shoulders so it fell to the floor at her feet. Then she stepped away from it. She'd tied a sash around her hips, over the red nightgown. The sash dipped and swayed with her hips, enunciating her movements. She opened her eyes and willed herself to look at him.

He leaned back in the chair, his hands gripping the arms, his knuckles white.

Lucy grew bolder in her movements, her confidence soaring as he watched her. Her chest and stomach undulated as she moved closer to him, until she stood directly before him, her hips popping to the beat, her rolls fluid with the music. She snaked even closer, dipping and rolling her hips, daring him with her gaze to reach out and touch her.

He did, his hands grabbing her hips as she swayed.

She laughed huskily, teasing him.

"Enough." He shot to his feet and pulled her hips to his.

She could feel his state of arousal.

"I'm not done yet."

"Make her leave."

The drum stopped and Marigold departed without another word.

Lucy bit her lip. The heat of his body washed over her.

"Did you like it?"

"Do you have to ask?"

He pressed his forehead to hers, then swooped down and caught her lips. He lifted her off her feet, carrying her to the edge of the bed. He set her down again, laying her back with her hips on the edge. Then he ran his hands up her legs, pushing her nightgown to her hips. He paused to undo the knot on the scarf, slowly pulling it out from under her. He slid her nightgown down to her waist and spread her thighs apart. "Don't move."

She couldn't, even if she wanted to. His burning gaze held her immobile as he stood back and slowly undressed.

By the time his hands reached his trousers, she trembled with anticipation, exposed to his wandering inspection. Her own body was growing wet and ready for him, and her nerves were stretched with longing.

He undid the buttons slowly, inching his pants down over his hips, focusing on her core. He licked his lips and Lucy shivered.

He inched the trousers lower, and she greedily waited for his manhood to spring free. She wanted to touch him this time, to explore him as thoroughly as he had her. Lying still and observing was not in her nature. She pushed herself to her elbows.

"I didn't tell you to move."

"Since when do I listen?"

She reached for him, pulling him free and admiring the treasure she had found. She sat up to better explore him and he didn't stop her. He dropped his head back and sighed. She smiled in satisfaction and touched him gently. "Tell me what to do."

He put his hands around hers and showed her how to squeeze and stroke him.

"Like this?"

He closed his eyes. "Yes," he moaned.

Lucy turned her attention back to her quest and explored, feeling the silky, smooth skin, so hot and soft. She traced a vein that ran down the side. She cupped his jewels, both curious and aroused by the feel of him, and the sounds her touch elicited from him.

"I want to know more," she said hungrily.

He groaned. "I can't handle more."

"Please, Dean."

"Lucy." He bent over her, forcing her back to the bed. "I need you. I've missed you. I've longed for you these past weeks. Don't make me wait. We've all the time in the world now for me to show you anything you want later."

His words thrilled her, the emotion behind them more than the actual words. He said them with such power, such need.

She caught his mouth as he drew near. "I love you, Dean. Take me."

He seared her with his kiss, but then drew away.

"I love you, too. I know I've said it before, but I can't say it enough now."

Lucy stilled. She knew this was not easy for him, not after Rosie. "I know. I can feel it when you touch me."

"You can?"

She smiled. "You've said it many times without saying it. From the very beginning, your actions spoke louder than your words. Your lips would say no, but your eyes would say yes."

"Now my lips, my eyes, my heart, and my head say the same thing. I love you."

She took a deep breath, her heart swelling with joy and love. She arched up and kissed him. Enough words had been said. She wanted to *feel* his love. She wanted to taste it on his skin. She kissed him hungrily, or perhaps he kissed her.

Then he thrust inside her, holding her open as he filled her completely. He moved his hands to her shoulders and pulled her nightgown, freeing her breasts and breaking the kiss to pay homage to them.

Lucy tossed her head back, riding the wave of his thrusts, losing herself in the tide of her pleasure and her love for him.

"Stay with me. We have all night. We have forever."

She couldn't stop it. Her climax rushed over her, drowning her in sweet rapture.

Dean woke, feeling the chill of the early morning now that the fire had burned low. He pulled the covers over her shoulders, drinking in her beauty, staring in wonder at the sole reason for his happiness.

Then he stood and stretched, seeing the sun breaking through and the pink clouds through the window.

Peaceful.

That was exactly how he felt now. He'd found his peace after all this time. He'd spent years searching for a home for his soul, the place where the past could no longer touch him. He'd searched for it in the most distant and exotic places, the antithesis to his life in England.

But all he'd needed was Lucy.

He surveyed the room, pleased with the home he'd bought for them. It was like Aunt Harriet's, and he knew Lucy would love it as much as he did. It was a home for a family, a home for laughter and love.

Chuckling silently at the mess their lovemaking had created, Dean gathered his scattered clothing. He bent to pick up his jacket and waistcoat, tossing them on the chair, and an envelope fell out. He frowned as he picked it up.

He turned it over and saw that it was addressed to his father in a feminine script. He remembered now.

He put on his trousers and crouched on his haunches to put another log on the fire and warm the room, considering what to do with the old letter his father's maid had given him months ago. He'd intended to burn it that night, but then he'd gotten drunk with Rigsby and Lord Heath and forgotten. Should he burn it still? The past was the past, and this time, it would stay that way. Nothing but the future mattered now.

But the woman had had a reason for giving it to him. He remembered the beseeching expression on her face. At the time, he'd been too angry to consider its importance, but now... He took a deep breath, at last his anger was gone. Would it stay that way? There was only one way to find out.

He tore the seal and opened it with trepidation, afraid of the feelings that would come back when he faced anything to do with his past.

My Lord,

I have longed to write this letter to you. Our families have been torn asunder, but I feel the blame for Lenora's death was wrongly cast upon your son.

All her life she was of a melancholy nature. She felt too deeply, and it left her weak of heart. It was not Lord Winchester's rejection that took her life, it was her own heart. She'd given up some time ago. My daughter was taken from me by her own hand, not your son's.

I shall never forgive myself for pushing her into a marriage she did not want. She knew of her sister's affections for him, as did I. If anyone is to blame, it is my husband and myself. We didn't listen to our daughter or our conscience.

Sincerely,

Margarete Abbey

Dean crumpled the letter and closed his eyes. It wasn't his fault. Lenora's mother had not blamed him for her death.

He'd already closed his father's house, wanting nothing to do with the past, and had moved Mr. and Mrs. Hale to the cottage, where their work would be less tiring. But if he was being honest with himself, it was also because he was afraid to see the Abbeys, to be continually haunted by terrible memories —and his father.

He'd let his heir decide what to do with that drafty pile of stone.

Dean waited for the sensation of relief to come, but Lucy startled him, appearing at his side.

She took the letter and read it silently.

He realized suddenly that *she* was the reason he didn't feel relief. He didn't need it any longer. She'd absolved him, cleansed him, and given him the ability to love again.

She smiled at him now. "I told you so."

A bark of laughter escaped him.

"I'm usually correct in most matters, if not all."

He smiled, his soul lighter, younger somehow. Then he stood and pulled his wife to her feet. "Have I told you I love you yet today?"

"Not yet."

He touched his nose to hers. "I love you."

"I love you." Grinning, she focused on his mouth, running her tongue over his bottom lip. "It's too early to be out of bed."

He swept her into his arms, the letter forgotten on the floor. "You are correct, as usual."

THANK YOU

Thank you for reading *Anything But Innocent*! Please take a moment to leave a review of this book. I sincerely hope you enjoyed Lucy and Dean's love story.

Turn the page to read an excerpt of the next book in the Desperate and Daring series, *An Unconventional Innocent*!

❧

Support Dayna Quince by buying direct! Subscribe to her newsletter to receive a special discount code for 50% off any ebook and 25% off paperbacks from her Red Rose Press Shop on her website www.daynaquince.com

EXCERPT

AN UNCONVENTIONAL INNOCENT

Dorothea raced through the frozen orchard, her lungs burning, her breath pluming out before her like a dragon's and fogging her glasses. Her heart pumped, and her fingers tingled from the cold inside her thin gloves. Her legs simply screamed for her to slow.

She wouldn't, though, not when running felt so good. She wheeled her arms as her boot found a bit of ice on the ground, and squealed as she caught her balance. She couldn't help laughing at herself as she slowed at the last row of trees and stepped over the low stone wall marking the end of the property and orchard.

"Drat," she huffed.

Mr. Hale was gone, and her letter to Rose would not go out today.

Hands on her hips, pulse pounding wildly, she huffed again in annoyance and turned to walk back to the cottage.

Then she froze, the sight of a lone man on the road startling her. She was tempted to slip back into the orchard before being seen, but something stopped her.

He swayed on his feet while hugging himself.

"Oh, dear," she whispered.

Lucy and Winchester had only left yesterday, but Thea had already taken to talking to herself in their absence. Who was this man? And what was he doing walking in this dreadful cold without a coat?

She chided herself. *She* didn't have a proper coat, either, having forgotten it in her haste to catch Mr. Hale.

She shouldn't intervene. He could be a drifter or a drunk, and Lord knew what he would do if she intercepted him. She waited in indecision.

He was walking slowly—limping really—and he didn't appear to have noticed her.

She wrapped her arms around herself and shivered. "Sir?"

He swayed again as he raised one hand in...salute?

She had a sinking feeling in her stomach. "Are you in need of aid?"

He hobbled quicker, a muffled reply erupting from him, and then he stumbled and fell to the ground.

Thea cried out as she ran toward him. "Help!" she screamed, though she didn't think anyone could hear this far from the cottage.

"Sir?"

She helped him roll to his side. He shook violently, his teeth chattering. His lips were blue, and his cheeks red and veined from the cold.

"My God, you're nearly frozen."

His blue eyes focused on her. "Win—tttt—test—ter."

"I'm sorry?"

She knelt on the ground, cradling his head in her lap. She had nothing to cover him with, nothing to provide warmth. She cursed herself for having left the house without a coat. Nothing in her letter had been so important that it couldn't wait. Her hands shook as she pulled him by his lapels to bring him closer to her.

"There is a cottage just up the lane. You can get warm there, and we can summon the doctor."

"Win—win."

Thea shook her head. "Whatever it is, it can wait until you've warmed up a bit. Can you stand?"

He nodded. She came to her feet and helped him to his, but it was not easy. He was much taller than her, and his movements were slow and disordered. He wheeled his arms as he came to his feet and steadied himself. Then he did an odd hop, and Thea surmised that one of his legs must be injured.

She ducked under his left arm and put hers around his back. "Please, let me help you."

He winced and settled his arm over her shoulders.

"Are you injured?"

He nodded jerkily.

"Come on, then."

They started off slow, and the more he leaned on her, the more Thea realized how grave his condition really was. Had she not seen him, he might well have died alone out here on the lane.

"Only a bit further now."

She had tried to sound cheerful, but her own teeth had begun to chatter.

Finally they reached the post that indicated the beginning of the drive to the cottage.

"You see? We're halfway there."

She fisted her hands to keep her fingers warm and noticed

the side of her that pressed against him stayed warm. He felt rather nice and muscular. She bit her lip. She didn't have to worry about a telltale blush when her cheeks were already stinging and red from the cold.

"W—wait."

He stopped them suddenly, just inside the drive, the shelter of the shrubbery shielding them from the biting wind.

"L—le—eave me. Get— help."

Thea frowned. "I couldn't do that. I can't leave you here alone. It's only a little further."

He leaned into the shrubbery and his eyelids drooped. "I—can't—move."

He's too cold, and he needs help immediately.

She peered down the drive, the cottage so close and yet so far, the curve in the drive keeping it just out of sight. Then she moved closer to him, seeking the warmth derived from their shared body heat while she frantically thought of what to do next.

Inspiration struck. If he was making her warm, she would do the same for him. She pressed her whole front to his, and looped her arms around him, rubbing his back vigorously.

"Lean into me and put your arms around me," she urged him. "If I can warm you up a little, then we can get you warm enough to make it to the cottage."

He slumped into her, burying his face in her neck. His skin was alarmingly cold, but the warm gust of his breath on her neck was reassuring.

She shivered again, but this time, not from the cold. She'd never held a man like this before. She'd never been pressed so tightly against someone.

There was a long list of things she'd never done.

Thea pressed her lips together. She should be ashamed to admit that she was enjoying this moment.

"There." She made herself pull away from him. "It's just around the bend. Can you make it?"

He nodded once and fell into her again, as if he didn't want to let her go.

She wiggled to his side and struggled to get him moving again. He hung on her heavily, only one of his legs moving efficiently, the other mostly dragging. They came in view of the cottage and were halfway across the circular turnabout when the door opened, and the footman, Jacob, came out to assist them, followed by Mrs. Hale.

The older woman waved a towel in the air. "Good heavens!"

"I found him on the lane," Thea said. "He's injured."

Thea huffed as Jacob took the man from the other side and assisted him into the cottage. She was reluctantly relinquishing her foundling, when, unexpectedly, he grabbed her hand. He leaned heavily on Jacob, but his grasp on her hand was firm.

She held his hand as she followed them into the cottage and up the stairs to one of the guest rooms.

"Put him on the bed, Jacob," Mrs. Hale instructed.

The man was laid on the bed, still conscious, as far as Thea could tell, but he held his eyes closed and grimaced at every movement.

"Fetch the tub and plenty of buckets of hot water, if you please, Jacob."

"What shall I do?" Thea asked with worry.

"Rub his hands, Miss Manton. We'll try to warm what we can before the bath is ready."

Thea rubbed one of his hands vigorously, and Mrs. Hale did the same with the other.

His fingers were cold as ice, and his skin had a bluish tint.

"How long do you think he was out there?"

"I can't rightly say. A long time, it seems. No coat to boot." Mrs. Hale smiled at her. "You saved his life."

Thea chewed her lip. "I don't know about that."

"The ground is frozen, and snow is imminent. He very well could have died out there," Mrs. Hale went on. Then she rubbed his jaw briskly with her hands to warm his cheeks. "The poor soul. I bet he's mighty handsome with some color in his skin."

"Mrs. Hale!" Thea said in a scandalized whisper.

Mrs. Hale chuckled and winked. "He appears to be a gentleman, Miss Manton."

Thea didn't know what that wink meant. She wasn't versed in the language of winks. She glanced down to see his blue lips smiling and his eyes blinking open. He tried to speak, but his teeth only chattered.

Mrs. Hale nodded toward Thea. "You've arrived at Winchester cottage, sir, by the grace of the fair Miss Manton."

Thea stuttered in embarrassment. "I—Mrs. Hale," she ground out in warning. "Will you desist?"

The other woman chuckled as Jacob and the matronly maid, Mrs. Croft, returned. "You will have to leave now, Miss Manton. What would your mother say if I were to let you undress a man?"

Thea wanted to stay, but she couldn't for the sake of propriety, and because she couldn't endure any more of the woman's teasing.

She moved away, stopped short by the grip of his hand on

hers. She'd forgotten she still held his hand. "I have to go now, sir. You will be well taken care of, I promise."

His blink was slow and weary as he focused on her. "M— my angel."

A warm flush filled her. "I will check in when I can."

She squeezed his hand one more time and let go. She bit her cheek as she left the room, fighting back a smile. Then she closed the door behind her and went to her room.

She didn't want to be smitten with a stranger, but she was.

Marigold joined her in her room, curious about the whole situation as she helped Thea undress.

Thea told her how she'd found him and helped him to the cottage.

"Did he say anything?"

My angel.

Thea marshalled her thoughts. "He said 'win,' many times."

Marigold wrapped a warm shawl around Thea. "Win?"

"His first words were 'win test ter.' Oh! Winchester?" Thea gasped. "He must know Lord Winchester!"

"Why was he out walking in this cold?" Marigold wondered.

"Perhaps he wasn't, initially. Perhaps his carriage crashed. His driver could be injured and awaiting help!"

At this, Thea bolted from her room and into his, across the hall.

Mrs. Croft tried to block her entrance. "Miss Manton! What on earth? You cannot be in here with an undressed man."

"This is far more important than my sensibilities. I must ask him where he came from. He could have an injured coachman waiting for help that is not presently coming."

She pushed past Mrs. Croft and paused.

He was there in the tub, chest-deep in water and naked as the day he was born. His head was thrown back, and his eyes were closed.

"He is barely conscious. You will not be able to get anything from him," Mrs. Hale said as she draped a blanket over the top of the tub, covering his lower half.

Thea knelt beside the tub. "But I must try."

"Sir?"

He didn't respond.

"Exposure to the cold for as long as he endured takes a toll on the body. He will wish to sleep for some time."

Thea nodded in understanding. "Please, sir. Is there someone waiting for help that you had to leave behind? Do we need to search for them?"

He didn't respond. He seemed better, but extremely tired, just as Mrs. Hale had said.

Thea put her hand to his cheek. "Sir?"

He roused a little.

She caressed his cheek, feeling the stubble of his beard under her fingertips.

He turned his face into her hand and nuzzled it, and Thea sucked in a breath. Then he kissed her palm. She prayed no one had seen that brief kiss but her. It seared her palm, the heat radiating up her arm to her body.

"Sir," she whispered. "Please."

His eyes slowly opened, and his head turned to hers. He licked his lips. "Water," he said gruffly.

Thea turned to Mrs. Hale. "Water!"

Once she held the glass, she gingerly held it to his lips.

He took a sip, and then a large gulp.

"Careful now," Thea said.

He blinked at her, his stare languid and dreamy.

Thea wasn't sure how aware he was.

"I found you on the road. Did an accident befall you? Shall I send someone to recover the horses and driver?"

"No," he answered drowsily. Then he licked his lips, as if his mouth was still parched.

Thea offered more water. "You were alone?"

"Yes." He rested his head against the back of the tub. "I'm so cold."

She stared at him until Mrs. Hale roused her from her spot.

"We must add more hot water. You should go now. What would your mother say?"

Mrs. Hale shooed her from the room, and Thea left reluctantly.

"Please come get me when he is dressed and in bed. I wish to sit with him while he recovers."

The older woman sighed. "I shouldn't allow such a thing."

Thea raised one brow. "I wasn't asking, Mrs. Hale."

Want more? Download *An Unconventional Innocent now!*

ALSO BY DAYNA QUINCE

The Fated for Love Series: Four Books

Mine, All Mine

Sweet Torture

Storm on the Horizon

To Love, Honor, and Obey

Desperate and Daring Series: Nine Books

Desperate For A Duke

Belle of the Ball

Just One Kiss

Anything But Innocent

An Unconventional Innocent

Mad About You

A Rogue Of Her Own

Hero Of Her Heart

An Undesirable Duke

Dare To Love A Scot

The Northumberland Nine Series: Nine books

One Wild Dawn

Two Wicked Nights

Three Times the Rake

Four Times the Temptation

The Five Second Rule for Kissing

The Secrets of the Sixth Night

Seven Lovely Sins

Eight Rules of Engagement

The Nine Lives of Lord Knightly

Standalone Novellas and Anthologies

Once Upon A Christmas Wedding:

Marrying Miss Bright

Have Yourself A Merry Little Scandal:

At The Mistletoe Masquerade

Star Frost Lovers Series:

The Ruin of Miss Phoebe O'Roarke

Rise of the Duke

A Rogue So Wicked

ABOUT THE AUTHOR

Dayna J. Quince was only fourteen when she developed a serious addiction to romance novels. What began as an innocent desire to read became an all-out obsession. She gave book reports on romance novels, got in trouble for reading during lectures, and would rather spend her time reading than attending high school parties. After all, high school boys could not compete with the likes of Stephanie Laurens' Devil Cynster. After getting her first job, her addiction only got worse. She now had her own money to spend and a car to get to Barnes and Noble as frequently as she wanted. She managed to maintain a somewhat normal life, marrying her high school boyfriend who was aware he was competing with fictional men for her attention. Dayna soon began writing her own romance novels, inspired by her love for all things romance. Dayna and her husband live in Southern California with their two children and three fur babies. Dayna is happiest at home where she can be with her family and write to her heart's content.

42058380R00166